The

Huntsman's

Tale

MORE BY THIS AUTHOR

Historical Fiction

The Testament of Mariam

This Rough Ocean

The Chronicles of Christoval Alvarez

The Secret World of Christoval Alvarez
The Enterprise of England
The Portuguese Affair
Bartholomew Fair
Suffer the Little Children
Voyage to Muscovy
The Play's the Thing
That Time May Cease

Oxford Medieval Mysteries

The Bookseller's Tale
The Novice's Tale

The Fenland Series

Flood
Betrayal

Contemporary Fiction

The Anniversary
The Travellers
A Running Tide

The Huntsman's Tale

Ann Swinfen

Shakenoak Press

Cover design by JD Smith www.jdsmith-design.co.uk

For

My nephews & nieces:
David, Susan, Steven,
Alison, Nadine, & Nicholas

Chapter One

Oxford, Late Summer 1353

The carter leaned in over the drop-counter of the shop, waving a folded paper in his hand. The man was familiar, for I had known him since boyhood. His regular route took him in circular fashion around the villages and small towns of northwest Oxfordshire: Witney, Burford, North Leigh, Woodstock, Long Hanborough, and all the small settlements on the fringes of Wychwood Forest. About every three or four weeks he came into Oxford.

'Geoffrey Carter!' I said. 'What brings you here?'

I hoped I did not sound anxious, for a letter from my old home might bring bad news. My mother had been ill in the spring and we had received no recent word of how she did.

'Letter from your mother, Master Elyot,' he said, leaning further in and handing it to me.

Reassured, I looked down at it. My mother was not greatly lettered, but she could read and write well enough, and had kept the books on the farm while my father lived. Her writing was a little more shaky than in the past, but if she could write to me, she must be in good health.

'Come you in-by, Geoffrey,' I said, 'and take a sup with us. I was about to close the shop for dinner.'

'Aye, I will that,' he said.

He disappeared from view, but I could hear him hitching his horse to the ring in the wall of my shop, followed by the rustle of a nosebag. He passed my scriveners Walter and Roger in the doorway as he came in and they left for their dinner at a tavern in the High Street. I laid the letter down beside the book whose cover I had been polishing and shuttered the shop window.

'Will you not read it?' he said, nodding toward the letter.

'Come through to the house first,' I said. 'Margaret will be pleased to see you.'

We found Margaret in the kitchen, just dishing up a vegetable potage, for it was Friday, not a day for meat. Alysoun and Rafe were already seated at the table, but jumped down when they saw the carter.

'Master Carter!' Alysoun cried. 'Have you brought me something?'

'Alysoun,' Margaret said, chiding, 'that is no way to greet a guest. Back to your places, both of you. Good day to you, Geoffrey.'

'And to you, Mistress Makepeace.' He doffed his knitted cap, leaving his hair standing up in spikes, like an untidy hedgehog. 'I hope I find you well.'

'In good health, I thank you. Sit you down. 'Tis but bread and a vegetable potage, I fear. And I can see that you are yourself in good health.'

Indeed the man's blooming – if weatherbeaten – countenance bore witness to that good health, although I knew that in winter time or prolonged rainy seasons his was a hard life.

The children were seated again, but were watching Geoffrey keenly. He sat down opposite them, with a deceptively bland look on his face, while he felt about the many pockets of his rough coat. Then he drew out a small bag and looked at it in astonishment, as if he had no idea how it had come there. He placed in on the table beside his dish as I spoke the Lord's blessing over the meal.

'Whatever can that be?' he said, after the Amen. He gazed at the bag in wonder.

'Well,' I said dryly, 'I observe that it is stained red. I

hope you have not been poaching conies, Geoffrey.'

'Ah, now there is a thought.' He shook his head and pushed the bag across the table to Alysoun. 'Perhaps you should open it, my maid.'

Alysoun looked uncertainly from Geoffrey to me, and back again, while Rafe stuck his thumb in his mouth, a habit which neither I nor Margaret had been able to cure. Clearly deciding that the bag was too small for a dead rabbit, Alysoun loosened the drawstring and peeped inside.

'Strawberries!'

'Aye.' Geoffrey grinned at her. 'Came across a patch of wild 'uns this side of Cassington. I thought I might meet someone who could make use on 'em.'

Margaret picked up the bag and laid it beside her plate.

'That was kind of you, Geoffrey. I have some good thick cream from Mary Coomber's dairy. We shall have them after the potage. But why are you here? Is all well back at home?'

'All's well, mostly,' he said, taking the thick slice of bread she passed him. 'I've brought a letter for The Master.' It was an on-going jest of his, that my university education had made me a Master of Arts, though I suspected he really thought my cousin ranked higher, as master of his own farm.

'A letter?' Margaret asked.

'From our mother.' I took my penknife from the pouch at my belt, and lifted the unmarked wax seal from the folded paper. I scanned the few lines quickly.

'Aye, as Geoffrey says, all's well. She regrets we were obliged by her illness to put off our visit earlier, but she is quite hearty now, and hopes we may come before the busy time in the shop at the start of the Michaelmas term.'

Folding the letter and placing it beside my bowl, I took up my spoon. Margaret had flavoured the potage well with garlic and thyme, and the vegetables were fresh from our own garden this morning.

'What say you, Meg? Shall we pay our visit to the

farm?'

I saw that both children had stopped eating, and were watching their aunt keenly, having the wisdom not to interrupt.

'Geoffrey said that all is *mostly* well,' Margaret said. 'What do you mean by that?'

'No more nor less than the usual, mistress. The hay is in, though it took near a fortnight longer than usual. And the harvest looks to be good, but Master Edmond fears he may lose much of it.'

'But why?' Margaret frowned. 'The weather seems set fair.'

''Tis not the weather that worries 'un, 'tis the want of hands.'

Geoffrey paused to wipe round the inside of his bowl with the heel of his bread.

'Ever since the Death, labour has been wanting, and it grows worse year by year. Near half the village perished, as you know, and of those that lived, some who were villeins to the manor have upped and left, mebbe to get their freedom here or in Banbury, like. Those who live by day labour go where they are paid the most. And with a new lord at the manor, that is *not* Master Edmond.'

'So the manor has been sold, then?' I said.

Geoffrey screwed up his face. 'Aye, some fellow from London. A merchant, or some such, not a true lord. He's not liked.'

I was prepared to take that with a grain of salt. There is no greater prejudice than that of the true countryman against strangers, especially Londoners. And for the place of a much loved lord to be usurped by such a stranger was an affront to the entire community. The de Veres had been lords of the local manor back beyond memory, probably since the Normans came.

'And he pays well, this new man?'

'Aye.' Geoffrey smiled grimly. 'Twice what your cousin can pay, and what's a poor man to do? There is little enough work for the day labourers. Harvest is the one time o' the year when they may earn enough to put a little aside for the bad times. Most o' them will go to work for this new fellow. A few will stand out against him and work for Master Edmond, but 'twon't be enough to get all the harvest in, he's thinking, even if the weather does hold.'

I was not surprised Geoffrey was so well versed in my cousin's affairs. Talk flies round a village. A man need only keep his eyes and ears open.

'This man who has bought the de Vere manor,' I said, 'what is he called?'

'Gilbert Mordon,' Geoffrey said, as though the name had a bad taste in his mouth.

'You dislike him yourself?'

He made a snorting noise. 'Speaks to me as if I was some serf of his, or a piece of dirt under his boot. Tries to order me about.'

I nodded, with a sympathetic smile. Geoffrey Carter might not be a wealthy man, nor did he own land, but he made a comfortable living with his independent business of carting, and owed fealty to no one. His house was one of the most pleasant in the village, Leighton-under-Wychwood, near which our family farm lay, though he possessed no more than a modest toft and croft. His wife was the respected village midwife, and his children went warmly clothed and well shod in leather. Any man who tried to treat him as a serf was either woefully ignorant or a fool.

Margaret brought a jug of cream to the table and began to dish out the strawberries, keenly watched by the children to see that all had fair shares.

'And what is his business, this Master Mordon?' she said. 'He must have considerable means if he has purchased that manor, for it holds rights of warren and even some rights to hunt in the royal forest. Pass the strawberries to your father and Master Carter, Alysoun.'

'He is a pepperer, so they say.' Geoffrey spoke with some contempt. 'How can a man become lord of a manor by selling pepper?'

'That generally means he buys and sells all manner of spices,' Margaret said, taking her seat again. 'Not only pepper. You would have to possess a fair amount of coin even to make a start in such a business. You do not need me to tell you that spices from Africa or Arabia are costly indeed. They must be brought hundreds of miles from far off countries. Though I've heard that some businesses have been bought up cheap in London since the Pestilence.'

'Does he mean to live on the manor?' I asked. 'Or stay on in London?'

'From what I have heard, he has left his business to be run by his journeyman and now plans to lord it over us all in Leighton-under-Wychwood. He has come down this two-three weeks ago with his wife and a parcel of his London friends, to live at the manor house. The last four months there's been all manner of "improvements" afoot there, though no one is sure what that means.'

I smiled down into my dish of strawberries. I could imagine the frustrated gossip and speculation travelling through the village as builders and plasterers and painters came and went. Since the whole de Vere family had perished in the Death, the manor and its demesne lands had been under the supervision of a steward acting for the heir, who lived in Leicestershire and had no interest in retaining the manor.

'You have not given me your answer, Meg,' I said. 'Shall we go to visit Mother and Cousin Edmond? I can lend my help with the harvest. It will be one more pair of hands.'

'He will be glad of you,' Geoffrey said.

'Aye, we must go,' Margaret said, 'for Mother has not seen us since last summer, and she will hardly know the children.'

'We did not go at Christmastide,' Alysoun pointed out, 'because of the snow.'

'That is settled then,' I said. I turned to Geoffrey. 'I generally close the shop for a time in the summer, since most of my business is done when the students are here in

Oxford. It will take me a few days to finish work I have in hand. Do you go back home after this?'

'I've an errand in Woodstock first, then home after that.'

'You should be there before us. Do you tell my cousin that we are coming. It may be that I can bring one or two others with me to help with the harvest. We shall see.'

'He will be glad of any pair of willing hands,' Geoffrey said. 'I will tell him, surely.'

I looked across the table at Jordain and smiled persuasively. 'It will do you nothing but good,' I said. It was the following day, and I was in search of more labourers.

'I cannot leave the lads.' Jordain glanced across the room in Hart Hall which served for both eating and studying. The two students who had failed their disputations at the end of Trinity Term had been obliged to remain in Oxford for the summer, preparing to try again at the start of Michaelmas Term. Although their heads were bent over their texts of Boethius's *De Topiciis Differentiis*, it was perfectly clear that they were listening intently.

'Bring them with you,' I said. 'It will cause them no harm to have a rest from their studies for a fortnight. Three weeks at most. They will work all the better afterwards for some fresh air and exercise.'

One of the students, Giles Wetherby, slid his eyes toward me. His expression was hopeful.

I raised my voice, as if I had not known that they were listening.

'Can you wield a scythe, Giles?'

'Indeed I can, Master Elyot,' he said eagerly. 'If I were at home now, I should be helping with the harvest.'

'And so can I.' Guy Trevick half rose from his stool in his eagerness.

Their claims did not surprise me. Though both came of the landed gentry, they were not so nobly born that they would have regarded harvest work as beneath them. When the yield of the harvest stands between life and death for every soul on a manor, it is the duty of all those who are fit to lend their labour, even women and children. Certainly had these boys gone home for the summer, they would have been working in their fathers' own fields during the next few weeks.

'But how would we get there?' Jordain asked. 'It must be all of fifteen miles.'

I could see that he was weakening.

'I shall be hiring a horse and cart from the Mitre,' I said, 'as well as the horse Rufus. I shall ride, while Margaret drives the cart with the children. You may ride in the cart, unless you wish to hire horses yourselves.'

I knew that Jordain would hardly have the cost of a horse in hand, but the students might.

The argument went back and forth, but I could see that I would prevail. The victory was determined when Guy urged that they might bring their books to continue their studies in the evening, after the day's work was done. I thought it wiser not to point out that they would be far too tired to study after the exhausting hours of unaccustomed physical labour in the fields.

'You will close the shop, then?' Jordain said, as he walked with me to the door. Behind us I sensed that the two students were exchanging grins of pleasure.

'Aye. It will be well for Walter to have a time for rest. His back has been troubling him for some weeks now and it grows worse when he crouches over his work. His sight is failing for close work. I have offered to purchase a set of spectacles for him, but he is suspicious of them. That is a battle I have yet to win. Roger will visit his mother over to Otmoor, but if he finds her in better case, he will borrow a horse from a friend and ride over to join us.'

'So with you and Margaret, as well as the three of us, you will add five and perhaps six to Edmond's harvesters.'

'Aye. I might have one other in mind. I cannot have this upstart Londoner forcing Edmond to lose the bulk of his harvest.'

It was early evening by the time I left Hart Hall, but I

thought I had time to walk out past the East Gate before Margaret would expect me home for supper. I was aware that this was one of the evenings Philip Olney usually visited his woman and their son in the cottage just this side of the East Bridge. I knew little of Philip's earlier life and was not sure whether he would know how to handle a scythe, but even he, surely, could learn how to stook corn. Beatrice Metford, I knew, was country born, and was likely to have helped with the harvest when she was a girl. As for their crippled son, Stephen, he would surely benefit from a little time in the country. During this hot summer weather Oxford was not the healthiest of places for a delicate child.

The town authorities did their best to keep the streets clean, but here in the town, as in the country, labour was short. The Camditch, which encircled part of the town, and in older days had served as a sort of moat when it needed defending, was now little better than an open sewer, used by many to dump every manner of rubbish. To clear it would be a major task, and in summer it bred any number of diseases.

Our family farm was a rambling structure, with extra rooms tacked on in those generations when there were many children, so I was confident Edmond could accommodate any labourers I could recruit for him. Unlike some earlier generations, my parents had only three children who survived infancy – myself and Meg, and our elder brother, John, who had perished in the Pestilence like our father. After their deaths I had been unwilling to return there from my life in Oxford, so my cousin Edmond had taken over the farm.

In truth he was my father's cousin, not mine, son of my grandfather's younger brother. Some fifteen years my senior, he had a growing family and would be doing well but for this lack of labour. We had held the land for two hundred years, and both my father and grandfather had gained permission to extend it by clearing uncultivated land as assarts. Even in my boyhood we were still uprooting old tree stumps, for the new land had been carved out of the edge of Wychwood.

The farm lay about a quarter of a mile outside the village of Leighton-under-Wychwood, our near neighbour being the de Veres' manor of King's Leighton, usually known simply as Leighton Manor. I suppose, from its name, it had once lain in royal hands, but had been bestowed as a favour upon some ancestor of Sir Yves de Vere, the last lord.

It was still warm as I made my way along the High and out of the East Gate, for the weather continued to hold fair, with the promise of a good harvest. Just outside the gate, on the left hand, before the Hospital of St John, stood a row of small cottages, each with a small toft in front. Behind, a croft the width of the building would stretch back, providing room to grow vegetables, with perhaps an apple tree and a pigsty. Beatrice Metford's cottage, the third in the row, looked, as usual, much fresher and prettier than its neighbours, and the owner herself was on her knees in the front toft, weeding her beds of herbs. As I opened the gate, she rose to her feet, brushing the dusty soil from her skirts.

'Master Elyot!' She smiled shyly as she dropped me a curtsy. 'How kind of you to visit us. Will you join us for supper?'

'Nay, mistress,' I said, 'I thank you, but I am expected at home. Is Philip not here?'

'He is with Stephen out the back,' she said, 'picking beans for salting. I will fetch him for you.'

'Do not trouble. I would not interrupt your weeding.'

She laughed. 'I hardly need the excuse, for I do not love weeding, but I am done for this evening. Come away in.'

I followed her into the cottage, which was small but immaculate, save for the normal detritus of family life. Stephen's hornbook and Latin primer lay on the table beside the pile of mending every woman does battle with. A savoury smell rose from a three-legged iron pot standing in the hearth beside the fire. Beatrice gave it a quick stir before she led me through to a tiny kitchen, where a door stood open on to the garden at the back.

'Master Elyot is here to see you, Philip,' she called, and stood aside for me to make my way down a brick path laid along the centre of the garden.

It went back further than I expected. Philip and Stephen were at the far end, both engaged in picking beans and dropping them into a basket at their feet. Stephen was propped on his crutches, but appeared to be managing the task without difficulty. The whole area was laid out meticulously, as I expected, with beds for lettuce, carrots, leeks, garlic, and onions as well as beans and peas. In another bed, seedlings of winter cabbage and kale had already been planted out, while under two apple trees half a dozen hens were scratching about. There was no pig.

'An excellent garden, Philip,' I said, by way of greeting. 'I did not know you were a gardener.'

He smiled hesitantly. I think he was still not quite sure when I was teasing him. 'It is mostly Beatrice's work,' he said. 'And Stephen's. But I help when I can.'

'And a *brick* path,' I said. 'As if this were some noble's demesne.'

At that he laughed. 'Old broken bricks, you will observe. I was able to acquire them when a small outbuilding at the college was pulled down.'

'Acquire?'

'They were dumped over the outside wall, as too broken to be of use. I borrowed a wheelbarrow and trundled them out here.'

That must have been courageous of him, I thought, for if one of the other Fellows had seen him, he might have been betrayed. Perhaps that was when Allard Basset had first discovered his secret family.

'Come, Stephen,' he said, 'that is enough beans for now. It will take your mother all evening to pod them and salt them, even if we help.'

He stooped to pick up the basket, but Stephen was before him.

'I can carry it, Papa.'

With surprising dexterity he managed to carry the basket as well as wield his crutches, setting out ahead of us up the path to the cottage.

'I see,' I said quietly. 'The brick path is much easier for him to negotiate than earth or gravel would be.'

'Aye.'

He said no more as we followed Stephen in through the kitchen to the main room of the cottage. Like Beatrice, Philip urged me to sup with them, but again I said I must go home, and explained why I had come.

'My cousin will be so short-handed for the harvest that he would be glad of your help, if you would think of coming,' I said. 'Many of the Fellows will be away from college during the summer. Why should you not come? I'd be grateful.'

'The summer is one time when I am free of university duties and have time to be with Beatrice and Stephen,' he said.

'But could they not come as well?' I glanced across at Beatrice. She had her back to us and was sampling the contents of the iron pot, but I could see that she, like Jordain's students, was listening. Unlike them, she joined us.

'I should be glad to lend a hand,' she said. 'I can use a sickle, and I can stook the corn. Thresh and winnow as well, if need be.' She smiled at Philip. 'It would be so good for Stephen to see a little of the world outside this cottage.'

'It would need careful managing,' Philip said slowly. 'Lest word get back to Merton.'

'Jordain already knows about Beatrice,' I said. 'Otherwise, there will only be his two students from the university with us. They are both decent lads. I am sure we may persuade them to keep your secret.'

Philip turned to Beatrice. 'I know it would do Stephen good, and you see little enough of the world yourself, tied here by . . . by everything. But it will be hard work.'

She laughed. 'No harder than I did every year on my father's farm, as you well know. Let us go! I am sure Mistress Farber, two doors away, will feed the hens.'

'Very well.' He turned to me, and suddenly gave a broad smile. 'I daresay time away from my books will be good for me as well.'

As he walked with me to the gate, I asked tentatively whether he knew how to use a scythe.

'Of course.' There was a touch of scorn in his voice. 'On my father's manor I always helped with the harvest, even after I came to Oxford.'

He paused, his hand on the gate. 'Beatrice's father was one of our tenants. I met her one summer, after I was already a Fellow. Helping with the harvest. She was just a young girl then, and I had my feet set on the academic ladder.' He shook his head. 'Who knows how different things might have been, had she been nearer my age and we had met before . . .'

'At least on my cousin's farm you can spend a few weeks without pretence. I am glad you are coming, Philip.'

He gave me a nod, and turned back to the cottage.

I did not head at once toward the East Gate into town, but walked the short way to the East Bridge and stood there, looking upriver, where the Cherwell flowed down from Holywell Mill, past the town meadow and the perimeter wall of St John's Hospital. This evening the westering sun lay golden on the water, where a half-grown family of ducklings followed their mother in and out of the patches of rush and weed that grew along the bank which sloped down from the hospital wall. The air was full of the scent of fast flowing water and the lush greenery of the water plants. These were probably the self-same ducklings I had seen on that unhappy evening when I had found the body of William Farringdon floating here, but my thoughts were turned further back, to an evening when Elizabeth and I had paused on this very spot.

We had met by chance. Elizabeth had been sent by

her father, the bookseller Humphrey Hadley, to fetch goose feathers for quills from Thomas Yardley's farm on the other side of the river. I had been rabbitting with Jordain and two other students, who had gone ahead with our spoils, to persuade the cook at Tackley's Inn, where we lodged, to cook them for our supper, but I had stopped to watch the river, as I often did. I must have been about sixteen, and although I had known Elizabeth from seeing her in her father's shop ever since I had come to Oxford two years earlier, I had never been alone with her before.

We greeted each other, somewhat shyly, and I expected her to pass on over the bridge, but instead she set down the sack of feathers she was carrying and leaned on the parapet beside me.

'I often wonder what the river sees, as it flows away toward London,' she said. 'Imagine what it could tell us if it could talk.'

'All manner of tales,' I said, too abashed to look at her, and gazing instead at a family of ducks, perhaps the very ancestors of these swimming here now, nine years later. Students were expected to live a celibate life, ignoring the very existence of women, but it was a rule barely acknowledged. I had not ventured into the town's whorehouses, but I was not so innocent that I did not know of their existence. I was not tempted by them, but the presence of this girl beside me filled me with a mixture of excitement and fear.

A strand of her red-gold hair, loose in the breeze, brushed against my face, and I trembled.

'Should you like to see London, Nicholas?' she asked.

'Aye, 'tis said to be a wonderful place, with ships travelling afar, and the Tower, and royal palaces, and merchants selling everything under the sun.'

'And more people than you can count.'

'But I love Oxford,' I said loyally.

'I love Oxford too,' she said, 'but I should like to see London, just once.'

Well, she had never seen London. The Pestilence had taken her, just after Rafe was born, as it had robbed so many, young and old, of their due span of years.

I sighed, turned my back on the river, and walked home.

I had learned more about Philip Olney in this evening's brief meeting than in all the years before that I had known him. I could understand why his life had taken the course it had, although it was not my course.

At supper I told Margaret that Jordain and Philip would also been coming with us to Leighton-under-Wychwood.

'We agreed that Beatrice and Stephen will travel in the cart with you, but Philip will hire a horse.'

'The cart will be somewhat overloaded,' she said, 'even if Jordain's students ride. There will be Jordain, Mistress Metford and myself, and three children, as well as any luggage we may take, even if it is no more than a change of clothing.'

'It will not be as heavy a load as the Farringdons' furniture which Jordain and I brought back from Long Wittenham,' I said. 'We need not make haste. The horse and cart we can hire from the Mitre will do very well.'

'Shall we manage the journey in a day?' she said. 'Stopping at an inn for the night would be an expense.'

'Oh, Aunt Margaret!' Alysoun had been listening, and her face glowed. 'Can we stay at an inn? I have never slept at an inn.'

'You would not care for it, my pet,' I assured her. 'Poor food and bugs in the beds.'

Margaret shuddered, but Alysoun looked not a mite dismayed.

'I think we may manage it in a day,' I said to Margaret. 'If we make an early start. Perhaps Beatrice and Stephen might come to us the night before.'

Margaret opened her mouth as if to object, then closed it again. I knew that it would be difficult for her, deciding how to treat Mistress Medford. My sister was warm hearted and tolerant, but the presence of a scholar's mistress was something she had never had to deal with before.

'How old is the boy?' Alysoun asked, before Margaret could respond to my suggestion.

'The same age as you,' I said, 'but he was ill when he was small and one of his legs is weak. He must walk with crutches.'

'Poor boy.' She looked thoughtful. 'So he can't run and play?'

'He certainly cannot run, but I am sure there are many games he can play with you, when he need not run. Games like chess or tables.'

These were both games she was newly learning herself, so it would be good if she had an opponent of a like age.

'I think he does not know many children,' I said, 'so you must remember that.'

'I will be very *kind* to him,' she said earnestly.

'There is no need to be especially kind,' I said hastily, for fear of what that might mean. 'Just treat him like Jonathan Baker, except that he cannot walk so easily.'

'May not Jonathan come with us to the farm, Papa?'

We had already had this discussion. 'Nay, my pet. His father needs his help in the bakery.'

Young as he was, Jonathan could undertake simple tasks in the bakery, or serve the shop's customers when his father was occupied.

After the children had gone to bed, Margaret and I sat down together, she to her mending, I to stitching the binding of a book which had worked loose.

'This Beatrice Medford,' Margaret said, tentatively.

'You will like her, I promise you. And she is a respectable woman.'

She raised her eyebrows at that.

'To all intents and purposes, she is Philip Olney's common law wife, and has been these seven or eight years.

He may not own to it or he would lose his fellowship, and how could he provide for them then?'

She looked troubled.

'The Church would not approve.'

'There are a good many similar arrangements amongst men of the Church,' I said dryly. 'Even amongst popes. Are they committing a mortal sin? Probably. But is it our place to judge? As for Beatrice spending a single night here, I think no harm can come of it. It will give you the chance to get to know her, and for the children to meet before the journey.'

'Very well.' She said it with reluctance. 'I suppose it will make an early start the easier.'

The next day was Sunday. Before we attended Mass at St-Peter-in-the-East, I sent a note to Philip at the cottage, inviting the three of them to sup and spend that night with us, so that we might make an early start on Monday. As we were turning up Hammer Hall Lane to the church, a lad caught my arm and handed me a scrap of paper, on which Philip had hastily scrawled: 'We thank you. We will come around six o' the clock.'

After Mass, when we reached home, I said, 'I will go to the Mitre now to hire Rufus and the horse and cart for tomorrow.'

'It will be an expense to keep them the whole while we are there.' Margaret frowned. 'Should you not find some means of sending them back to Oxford? One of the stable lads could come with us, drive the cart home, with Rufus hitched behind.'

'Nay, it will be useful to have them with us. The cart can help with carrying the harvest, and if I have Rufus I shall be of more use to Edmond.'

She smiled. 'You are looking for reasons to ride about on that horse, as if you were a gentleman.'

I laughed. 'Rufus is no gentleman's horse, though he is a useful beast.' I paused. 'After I have been to the Mitre, I may go to St Mildred Street.'

'You haven't told her that we are going away?'

'Nay.' I shook my head. 'Why should it matter?'

'You know very well why.' But she said no more.

At the Mitre I was, fortunately, able to hire both Rufus and a horse and cart that I had used before. There would be no alarming ferry this time for the cart horse to endure, as Edric Crowmer's horse had faced some weeks before. This beast was big, slow, but well muscled, so I was certain he would make light of the load, though his ambling pace would be an irritant to Jordain's students. It seemed that Guy had his own horse stabled in Oxford, and Giles had hired a lively beast from the Cross Inn. If they became too impatient, I would send them on ahead.

My business concluded at the Mitre, I stood hesitating outside, on the corner between the High and St Mildred Street. When I had brought Emma Thorgold to Oxford in her boy's clothes, we had been at ease with each other, totally caught up in the escape from her stepfather and his vicious dogs. Then Margaret had clothed her in a fine gown and my eyes had been opened. Emma was a lady, an heiress to a considerable estate, far beyond an Oxford shopkeeper in rank. I had been avoiding her ever since, for I could not resolve the confusing conflict in my heart. It was my wife Elizabeth I still loved, though she was lost to me forever. Yet Emma had also touched something in me.

This was foolishness, lurking on the corner like a lovesick boy. It was no more than simple politeness to tell Mistress Farringdon and her girls that we would be away for two or three weeks. I did not know whether Emma was still with them, or whether she had already left for her grandfather's manor.

I made my way slowly up St Mildred Street. They would be home from Mass long since, for their parish church, St Mildred's, was but a few houses away, My tentative knock on the door of the small cottage, leased to Mistress Farringdon by Merton College, was answered at once, as the door was thrown open by her daughter Juliana.

'Mama, it is Nicholas!' she cried. 'Come in, Nicholas. We have not seen you for *weeks*!'

Mistress Farringdon came up behind her and put her hands on Juliana's shoulders.

'My dear, it is Master Elyot to you. And it has not been weeks.'

'Nicholas will do very well.' I smiled at them.

'Will you dine with us?' she said, curtseying and urging me into the main room of the small cottage. Every woman in Oxford seemed bent on feeding me.

'Nay,' I said. 'I cannot stay. I came only to give you a message.'

I glanced about. The little girl Maysant was playing with some carved wooden animals on the floor, but there was no sign of Emma.

'My family and I are leaving tomorrow to help with the harvest on my cousin's farm, near Leighton-under-Wychwood. We shall be away for two weeks, or perhaps three. Margaret will come this afternoon with some food we cannot take with us, in the hope you may make use of it. Jordain goes with us as well. I came to ask if you need aught, or if I may do aught for you before we leave.'

'As always you are so kind, Nicholas,' Mistress Farringdon said, 'but we shall do very well. I have my work at Mistress Coomber's dairy, while Juliana is learning to keep house and minding Maysant for me.'

I turned to her daughter. 'I have not forgotten that I promised you more books to read, Juliana. I have a collection of French tales of Robin and Marian which you may borrow. I will give it to Margaret to bring with the food.'

No one had made any mention of Emma, so I thought she must indeed have left for her grandfather's manor.

'May God be with you, then,' I said, 'until we return. Should you need to reach me, Geoffrey Carter will always carry a letter for you.'

I turned away to take my leave, but as I did so I heard a light step on the stairs leading up from the kitchen to the bedchambers. Emma had not left, after all.

Chapter Two

She stood for a moment in the open doorway, an indistinct silhouette, a shadow against the bright sunlight flooding in from the east-facing garden, through the open door behind her. Then she stepped forward and became real and tangible, holding out her hands to me, her face radiant.

'Nicholas! Why have you stayed away from us?'

She did not wait for an answer but came closer, taking both my hands in hers. I could not, without insult, snatch them away, but I felt a tremor like fear pass through me, and felt sure she must have known that my hands trembled.

I had seen her swathed and bundled in her mourning-black death-black novice's habit, only the white wimple and novice's veil relieving that grim hue, while nothing of her showed but her face in its tight frame, and her slender hands, ink stained. I had seen her moving as free as a boy in cotte and hose, sitting astride Rufus within the circle of my arms. And – shocked into my right senses – I had seen her slowly descending the stairs of my home in a fine gown which had once been Margaret's best, looking what she was in truth, a gentlewoman.

Now I saw her changed yet again. She wore what must surely be one of Maud Farringdon's simple brown homespun gowns, meant for daily work about the kitchen. After Mass, she must have gone to her bedchamber to change out of her Sunday wear. The gown was too large for her, so she had belted it in with a girdle of dark brown cord, but unlike her religious habit, it was not designed to conceal her figure, and the neckline was cut low, revealing an under tunic of fine white linen.

Like all unmarried girls, she had left her hair uncovered. In the time since she had left Godstow Abbey, her shorn hair had begun to grow again and now clustered close to her head in soft fair curls, which reminded me of her boyish disguise. Having discarded the fine gown, she was less intimidating, but nevertheless I gently withdrew my hands.

'My lady,' I said, 'I had thought you would have left for Sir Anthony's manor by this.'

A slight spasm passed over her face, though whether at my withdrawing of my hands from hers, or my chosen mode of address, I could not be sure.

'Nay, *Master Elyot*,' she said crisply. 'My grandfather has not yet sent my escort. When he does, of course I shall go to pay my respects to him.'

'And you will then take up your position as his heir,' I said, stating, not questioning, 'and remain on the manor.'

'That is not yet decided,' she said, having stepped back a pace.

I noticed that Juliana was watching us closely, while Mistress Farringdon looked troubled. 'Emma has some thought of remaining in Oxford,' she said. 'And we would be most happy for her to live with us, but she owes a duty to Sir Anthony.'

'Should I stay in Oxford,' Emma said, speaking to Mistress Farringdon, but keeping her eyes fixed on my face, 'I will not be a burden to you. I shall find some way to earn my keep.'

There was a shade of defiance in her voice.

'It must be difficult, I know,' I said slowly, 'after all that has happened, to go back to the manor, but I believe you were happy there as a child.'

She inclined her head. 'I was. But I am no longer a child. Perhaps my grandfather will not take kindly to me.'

'I liked him, and I am sure you will also. He cares very much for you.'

I said it spontaneously, without thinking that by urging her to leave I was adding to the pain which I tried to suppress at the thought of her gone.

'I remember him with fondness,' she said, 'with love. Though I saw little of him after my mother married Falkes Malaliver.'

'Then you must come to know him better,' I said, fully aware now that I was driving a knife into my own heart. Nay, what was I thinking of? I had decided that Emma Thorgold was not for me. Let her leave Oxford and be done with it!

'Did I hear you say that you leave Oxford tomorrow?' she said.

I nodded. The cottage was so small that it was no wonder, had she been at the top of the stairs, if she had heard everything that I said to Mistress Farringdon and Juliana.

'Then perhaps I shall go to Long Wittenham while you are gone. That will be best. I shall send to my grandfather tomorrow, to say I am ready to come.'

She reached out and touched my arm.

'Afterwards, Nicholas, we shall see.'

Somehow I made my way home, more confused than ever about my feelings for Emma Thorgold. Perhaps these next weeks, separated by many miles, we might both come to our senses. For now, I must turn my mind to conveying my family and friends to Leighton-under-Wychwood and helping Edmond gather all of his harvest safely in. It was almost Lammastide. Time we were on our way.

Precisely as the bells of St-Peter-in-the-East rang out for Vespers at six o' the clock, there was a soft rapping on the door of the shop. Although the shutters were closed for Sunday, I was at work, writing up my accounts and parcelling up two books which Walter would deliver the next day after we left. He would then lock up house and shop, leaving the key with Mary Coomber, who had promised to feed the hens and to use any of the garden produce that would otherwise go to waste.

'Mistress Medford,' I said, as I opened the door. 'Come away in. And Stephen.'

I looked beyond her, but the street was empty.

'Philip is not with you?'

'We thought it best that we should not walk through the town together,' she said, colouring. 'He will come soon, directly from Merton.'

I showed them into the shop, relieving her of a modest bundle, while the boy kept a firm hold on his own. I could see that he was fierce in his independence.

She looked about her curiously – at the two scriveners' desks, with their pots of coloured inks and piles of parchment, at the shelf of secondhand books just inside the window, and the shelves along the walls stacked with *peciae*, the short sections from the standard student texts, available for hire.

'I have never been inside here,' she said, 'though I have often walked past on the way to market. Look, Stephen – so many books!'

Stephen had already edged toward the shelf of books by the window and was eying them eagerly, but made no move to touch them.

'Do you like books, Stephen?' I asked.

He nodded, but did not speak.

'Then we shall take something with us for you to read while we are away,' I promised. 'But for now, come through to the house and meet my family.'

Margaret and Beatrice were formally polite with each other, and I could see that Beatrice was not what my sister had expected, fresh and pretty in her neat gown and white apron, but very quiet and modest in her bearing, even deferential to Margaret. On the other hand Alysoun came bouncing forward to greet Stephen, and had soon dragged him off to a corner of the kitchen, where Rafe was playing with the puppy Rowan. The children, I thought, would manage this better than the women.

I had no time to observe them further, for there was a louder knock on the outer door. I went through to let Philip in.

'They are here already,' I said to his query. 'It was a long walk for Stephen.'

'He manages very well,' Philip said, 'as long as he is not hurried.'

He set down his own bundle and a satchel on my desk, and untied from a strap of the bundle a leather flask.

'I have brought this from Merton's cellar, to toast the success of our mission to rescue the harvest.'

I smiled at him. Now that I knew him better, Philip continued to surprise me. It was clear that he regarded our visit to the farm as a release from the constraints of his difficult life in Oxford. I hoped it might prove so.

At first our meal together was somewhat restrained, but under the influence of Philip's flask – which proved to contain not ale but excellent French wine – we all began to relax. We even allowed the children a taste of the wine, well diluted. Though Rafe made a face and would not drink his, Alysoun and Stephen both asked for more, which was refused by both Margaret and Beatrice. I think there was a little bravado between the children, as to who could drink the most. By the time we had finished, Margaret and Beatrice cleared all away together as though they were becoming friends, while Philip carried Stephen up to the children's room, where he would share Rafe's truckle bed. Philip would have the truckle bed in my room, and Beatrice would share with Margaret.

We were all, perhaps, a little awkward with each other, with so much unknown and unspoken between us, but, in order that we might make an early start the next morning, we retired soon after supper.

Lying awake in bed I could no longer push aside the thought of Emma travelling south to her grandfather's home, while we travelled in the opposite direction to the farm. It should have made my feelings duller. But it did not.

It was before dawn the next day when Philip and I reached the Mitre. Jordain was before us, leading the hired horse and cart out into the High. The heavy-built cart horse, with his feet as broad as plates, was placidly chewing an apple, the juice dribbling down over his chest. The ostler slapped him cheerfully on the shoulder.

'He's a good lad, is Strider,' the man said. 'Let him go his own pace, and he'll pull you forty miles a day.'

This was a gross exaggeration, as I knew well, but I also knew the beast was strong and willing.

The stable lads had already saddled Rufus for me, and a mare called Star for Philip. With Jordain driving the cart, we rode back to the shop. Although I glanced aside, up St Mildred Street, there was no sign of life about the Farringdons' house.

While we were loading the cart with our assorted bundles, three excited children and a skittish dog, Walter arrived to take charge of the shop. I handed over the keys and the two books to be delivered.

'See that you take some rest while we are gone,' I said. 'I can see that your back still troubles you.' For he was moving awkwardly.

'Ah, 'tis but age, Master Nicholas,' he said. 'We must all come to it.'

'That is foolishness,' I said briskly. 'You are not of an age to be decrepit for years yet. It is crouching with your nose nearly in the ink that has done it. When we return, we shall try what spectacles may do, whatever you say.'

He shook his head stubbornly, but I can be just as stubborn, when I set my mind to it.

Margaret wedged a large basket of food between the bundles of clothes, so that we might take dinner on our way, without the need to stop at some wayside tavern, which she did not trust. The previous afternoon she had needed Alysoun's help to carry baskets of supplies to the Farringdons, for we all feared that Maud Farringdon's earnings at the dairy were scarcely enough to feed her household of four.

At the last moment before we set off, I remembered my promise to Stephen and fetched two books of stories that Alysoun enjoyed and stowed them in my satchel. Jordain and Margaret would drive the cart, turnabout, while Philip and I rode alongside. Jordain's two students were to meet us at the North Gate.

The early summer dawn was casting a glow over the golden stone of the town gate as we reached it, to find Guy and Giles with their impatient horses, eager to be away from their studies. Once through the town wall and into the broad sweep of St Giles, our party spread out, the four horsemen and a cart making up an uneven company. It would be difficult for us to stay together.

'Let the two of you ride on ahead,' I said to Giles, 'and give your horses some exercise. Wait for us where the road to Witney branches off to the west from the Woodstock Road. Do you know it?'

'Aye,' he said. 'Not far past the turning to Wolvercote and Godstow. There is a crossroads. The turn to the left leads to Witney and Burford, the one to the right runs east and meets the road to Banbury.'

'That is the place.' I nodded. 'Master Olney and I must stay with the cart and must go at its pace, but if you let your horses have their heads now, mayhap they will take more kindly to a slower pace afterwards.'

The two students grinned happily and set off up St Giles at a fast canter, throwing up a cloud of dust which blew back on us. Margaret coughed and frowned, wiping the dust from her face with her sleeve, and Jordain apologised.

'They were discourteous,' he said. 'I am sorry, Margaret.'

She shrugged. 'No more thoughtless than any lads at that age. Shall I take the reins?'

'Nay, I will drive yet a while. I know that you have been up all hours preparing food. Do you and Mistress

Medford rest for now.'

Indeed, it was somewhat trying for Philip and me to hold back our own mounts to the plodding pace of the cart horse, but there was nothing else for it, if we were to stay together. Since the Pestilence there were many masterless men roaming the country, and although most of our route would be on well travelled roads, a cart carrying women and children, with but one man, clad in a modest scholar's gown, would seem easy prey, should they be caught unawares on a quiet stretch of the road.

Our progress through the day continued in much the same way as we had started out, the students riding ahead for a time, then waiting for us to overtake them. Around midday, near Witney, we found a stretch of grass beside the road, partially shaded by trees, and called a halt. The riding horses were hobbled and allowed to graze, while Strider was unhitched and given a nosebag with a feed of oats, since he was by far the hardest working of all.

'This is a fine feast you have brought for us, Mistress Makepeace,' Philip said, as the two women laid out cold pies and pasties, a basket of cheeses, loaves baked that morning, and another basket of lettuce and radishes.

Margaret smiled at him, but shook her head. 'Little enough. I have kept some back for our supper.' She glanced aside at the children and students, who had already fallen upon the food. 'Best make haste, or it will all vanish before our eyes.'

It was pleasant under the shade of the trees, for it had become increasingly hot beneath the unremitting glare of the summer sun, but we could not linger long if we were to reach Leighton-under-Wychwood before nightfall. During the afternoon Philip and I took the opportunity to exercise our own horses from time to time, one of us taking the place of one of the students, for the horses were fretting at the maddeningly slow pace of the cart.

The sun was declining in the west, sending its rays blindingly into our eyes, when we turned north before reaching Burford, on to the narrower road which would take us to Leighton-under-Wychwood. By now we were all tired, and the three children were asleep, curled up amongst the bundles in the cart. Both Margaret and Beatrice were pale with fatigue, and Jordain (who had taken over most of the driving) rubbed his shoulders from time to time as though they ached.

Just after turning on to the by-road, we halted for a brief supper, but perched, all of us, in the cart, too tired to do more than satisfy our hunger with a few mouthfuls, too tired even to speak. Alysoun and Stephen woke briefly, but Rafe slept on.

'Not far now,' I said, by way of encouragement. Jordain had visited the family farm in the past, when we were boys newly at Oxford, but to the students, and to Philip and Beatrice, it must have seemed as though the journey would never end. The cart horse, too, was tiring. It had been a long day and a heavy load for him.

Our brief snatch of food over, Philip, Guy, Giles, and I remounted and we headed on. Even the boys had lost the energy of the morning and were content to ride at our slow pace.

The sun had dropped behind the trees of Wychwood, which had begun to gather about us, and a sliver of moon was rising in the east, as we came to the village.

'Barely a quarter of a mile now,' I said.

Something must have woken Alysoun, for she sat up, rubbing her eyes.

'I can see the church,' she said, before yawning so much I could see the gleam of her teeth. 'Wake up, Stephen!' She poked him. 'We are here.'

'A little further,' I said apologetically to the boy, whose face was drawn and pale in the dimming light. 'Through the village, along the lane, and then we are there.'

'That leads to the de Veres' manor,' Alysoun said, pointing to the branch off the lane beyond the church. The way to the manor had become overgrown and neglected since the death of the de Vere family, but I saw that it was newly cleared.

'Only there aren't any de Veres any more,' Alysoun added.

She was too young to remember them, but they were not forgotten in the village.

'Look!' Margaret cried, pointing ahead. 'Edmond has hung out lanterns for us.'

The fitful gleam ahead of us was a welcome sight and I think even Strider sensed that his hard day's labour was nearly done, for he pricked his ears forward and moved a little faster. Someone must have been listening out for us. Even on the summer-dried earth of the lane, the horses' hooves and the rattle of the cart's wheels heralded our arrival. The door of the farm was thrown open, casting a broad path of light across the yard as we clattered in. Edmond's wife Susanna surged forward, crying out a welcome, followed by Edmond, silent as usual in the face of Susanna's exuberance, but grinning broadly.

We were all stiff from the journey, whether we had ridden or travelled in the cart, but the horses must be seen to first. Amidst the flurry of introductions, Edmond and his two half grown sons, James and Thomas, helped us remove their gear and lead them into the stable, where, by the light of a candle lamp, we carried in buckets of water. The mangers had already been filled with hay. I caught up a handful and buried my nose in it.

'This season's fresh cutting,' I said, appreciatively. 'Sweet as honey.'

'Aye,' Edmond said. 'We managed the haysel by working past dusk every night, at the risk of slicing off our toes with the scythes, but I have lost more of my labourers since then, tempted away by the man Mordon and his London money. Even Jos Gidney and his two sons.'

I shook my head in disbelief. The Gidney family had worked for ours generation upon generation.

Edmond ran his fingers through his hair, which had streaks of grey in it which had not been there last year.

'I would pay them more if I could, but I cannot. Prices at market are poor this year. Good weather means a good harvest, but low prices for what we sell.'

'Well, I have brought you workers who do not need paying,' I said, 'at least your own barns will be full and your household well fed.'

The others were already heading toward the house as Edmond bolted the stable door and took my arm.

'I am grateful to you, Nicholas,' he said quietly as we crossed the yard. 'When Geoffrey Carter brought us word that you were bringing friends to help with the harvest, Susanna sat and wept. You know Susanna. She will not weep if she burns her hand on the fire or wrenches her back lifting a heavy load. She has as stout a heart as any man. But she wept. That is how hard it has been since this new man bought the manor.'

'There is more to this than paying the labourers higher wages,' I said, looking at him shrewdly.

'Aye, there is, but we will talk of it later. See, the women have unloaded your cart, and Susanna has a hot supper waiting for you.'

It was a fine farmhouse supper of roast pork with braised apples and onions, with a frumenty well flavoured with the juices from the meat, and followed by a dried apple and raisin pie, lavishly covered with thick cream. Even the children woke up enough to enjoy it, although their eyes were drooping toward the end. When they had been carried off to bed, sharing chambers with Edmond's younger children, we were not long in following them, for farmers keep early hours. Susanna ushered her large body of guests to various corners of the rambling farmhouse, but I paid them little heed, taking myself off to the slant-roofed room up under the eaves, which had been mine since early boyhood.

I woke early the following morning, for I had left the shutters on the single window standing open, so that the first light of the rising sun fell across my face, already warm and promising a good day. The previous night Edmond had told us that he had, that very day, begun the first cutting of his wheat field. Today we would resume work there.

As I swung my legs out of bed, I groaned. I rarely spend a whole day in the saddle, and somehow the slow pace had proved especially trying to those infrequently used muscles which make themselves known after disuse. Still, I thought with a wry smile, wielding a scythe all day today would find out a whole new set of neglected muscles to complete the picture.

I looked out of the window over the back of the farm, where the dairy and hen houses stood. The large wheat field stretched out just beyond, the field to the right of it given over to barley this year. Further to the right, but out of sight from here, a smaller field, one of my grandfather's assarts, was probably planted with oats, while the other assart, also out of sight, but to the left, would hold peas and beans. It had been the field of oats last year. The family vegetable garden was at the front of the house, near the barns and stable.

Down in the farm kitchen I found Susanna, Margaret, and Beatrice all hard at work, for Susanna, like my sister, baked her bread every morning. Edmond's eldest daughter, Hilda, was helping, but looked as though she would rather be elsewhere.

'Are the children awake?' I asked generally.

Beatrice glanced at me as she slid a freshly baked loaf off the bread paddle on to the table. There was a smudge of flour on her cheek.

'They have gone to let out the hens and collect the eggs.'

'And the others?'

'Master Edmond has taken Philip to look at the wheat.'

The outside door opened, and my mother stepped inside, carrying a basket of vegetables. With a start, I thought, *She has grown so small.*

'Mother,' I said, putting my arms around her, basket and all. 'It is good to see you, after so long. You are quite well again?' She had lost weight, and her hands looked frail, but her eyes were as bright as ever.

'Aye, do not fuss, Nicholas. I am quite well. I have seen the children already, out by the henhouse. Margaret, take this.'

Margaret kissed her and took the basket from her.

'You need not have given us your vegetables, Mother Bridget,' Susanna said. 'We have plenty.'

'Aye, well, I have more than I can use in the cottage garden. And who is this?'

I introduced Beatrice and explained our arrival to help with the harvest.

'Edmond has told me,' she said briskly, taking an apron from the basket and tying it about her waist. 'What shall I do to help, Susanna?'

'Where are the others?' I asked Margaret, as my mother joined Susanna in shaping the risen dough into loaves.

'Jordain and his students are still abed,' she said severely. 'I hope they may not think they are on holiday. In university term time they would be at lectures by this.'

'I will rouse them,' I said, but as I reached the bottom of the stairs I heard the sound of their footsteps, so instead I went outside and joined Edmond and Philip at the wheat field.

'It is a fine crop,' I said, surveying the gold heads stirring in the slight breeze. The stalks were nearly up to my shoulder. 'A good crop of straw as well.'

'Aye,' Edmond said. 'We'll keep the best of it for thatching the dairy and one of the barns, 'tis time they were done afresh. With the barley and oat straw, there will be plenty for bedding.' He rubbed his hands cheerfully together. 'Let us break our fast, if the women will allow us into the kitchen, then we may make a start. The few labourers who still work for me will be here soon.'

The kitchen was rich with the scent of baking, and all the women flushed and rosy with their efforts.

'Do you aim to set up a bakery?' I asked Margaret. 'I see you have all been exercising your skills.'

A side table below the wide window was set out with loaves braided and slashed, fashioned into pyramids and spirals, sprinkled with poppy or fennel seeds. On the main table, where we had eaten the previous night, a heap of ordinary round loaves lay waiting for us.

'Have you forgot the day, Nicholas?' Susanna said. ''Tis Lammas on Thursday. These are the loaves baked from yesterday's first cut of the harvest. And since the first of the wheat is already cut and ground, we will hold the Lammas feast this evening.'

'Of course!' I said. 'I had indeed forgot. We have timed our arrival perfectly, then.'

A thought struck me.

'And our mill is working well? Water enough in the stream?' In a hot summer like this, sometimes the stream ran a little low to turn the wheel.

Leighton Manor owned the mill at which all the villagers were obliged to take their corn to be ground, but our family, owning our own land, had a small mill driven by a leat from the same brook that drove the manor mill. We ground our flour there. After the de Veres' heir had appointed a steward to manage the manor, its mill had fallen into disrepair and Edmond had allowed the villagers to use our mill, charging a smaller portion of the flour than the manor used to charge.

Edmond and Susanna exchanged a look.

'Master Mordon,' he said grimly, 'had the manor mill repaired in good time for this year's harvest and demanded his right of multure. The villagers began cutting that field on the south slope last week, and when he heard some were bringing their corn to me, he had his servants dig a channel to divert the leat away from our mill. Now we cannot even grind our own corn, but must take it to him, where he is charging twice what Yves de Vere did.'

'But–' I gaped at him, shocked. 'To cut off the stream that drives your mill? That is surely illegal?'

'Aye, almost certainly, but by the time I have taken him to court, how many weeks – nay, months – will be lost? At the moment we have ground only the small amount we have cut new, for the Lammas loaves, but we will be forced to grind more when our stores of last year's flour run out.'

'And the villagers will suffer,' Susanna said. 'Those who have little land need every ounce of their flour to survive the coming year. They cannot spare more for the manor. And he ensures that he wrings every hour of service out of the villeins, working on his land. They will be fortunate if they are able to cut what little corn they grow themselves.'

We sat down to break our fast in somewhat sober mood after this, although the children – who had no interest in mills – chattered happily. Before we left for the fields, another thought occurred to me.

'What court can you take the man to, Edmond? For surely he will himself have the right to hold the manor court.'

'Indeed. I suppose I must await the next visit to Burford by the king's justices in eyre.' His face was grim, but he shrugged impatiently. 'Come, let's to work.'

No more than half a dozen labourers had gathered in the yard when we came out of the house, where once there would have been a score. And all of them were older men whom I had known since I was a boy, too loyal and too stubborn to be wooed away by the man Mordon's bribe of higher wages. They all carried their own scythes, fitted and balanced each man to his own needs. Edmond's sons carried a further collection of scythes out of one of the barns, and we gathered round to choose those which best suited us.

'I sharpened all, day before yesterday,' James said, 'but there's whetstones on the shelf, left of the door.'

Like the others, I pocketed a small whetstone to take with me into the field, to save coming back when the blade began to dull. There was a large grinding wheel in the barn, driven by a pedal, which would do a better job at the end of the day, but the small stone would serve while we worked.

Thomas showed Stephen, Alysoun, and Rafe how to plait straws to make a binding for the sheaves of corn.

'You must make the plait as long as the distance from the sole of a man's foot to the knee,' he said.

'But how can I measure that?' Alysoun objected.

'Well, then, from the sole of your foot to your waist,' he said.

Rafe grew bored and wandered off, but the other two were soon able to make the plaits well enough to serve.

'Hilda and I will take our sickles round the edges of the field,' Susanna said, 'if you, Margaret, together with Mistress Medford, will stook, with the children's help. I think even Alysoun helped with the stooking a little last year.'

She looked dubiously at Beatrice. 'Can Stephen . . . ?'

Beatrice smiled at her. 'We shall not be walking fast. He will certainly be able to help with binding, if not with building the stooks. And please, I am Beatrice.'

Rowan, who had been running about the farmyard exploring its feast of new scents, ran between Edmond's feet, nearly tripping him. He caught her up and tucked her under his arm.

'We cannot risk this puppy with us. Either she will be sliced in two, or she will cause an accident. She must stay here.'

Alysoun looked rebellious as he started toward the house, but I shook my head at her.

'Not in the kitchen, Edmond!' Susanna warned. 'The Lammas loaves!'

'Aye, you have the right of it. She must stay in the barn.'

Rowan was soon incarcerated, and as we set off for the wheat field her mournful howls followed us.

At the edge of the field, Edmond tipped out the contents of a sack he carried, and a collection of rough gloves tumbled to the ground.

'Help yourselves,' he told us. Like all good masters,

he had a care for his labourers' hands.

In the months since last summer's harvest I had not laid hold of a scythe, save for a brief time helping to clear the overgrown garden behind the Farringdons' cottage in St Mildred Street, but it is a skill that once learned is never forgotten. There was no need for discussion as we spread out in a line across the near edge of the wheat field, Edmond, James, Thomas, Jordain, Philip, and I, together with the students Giles and Guy, and the handful of labourers. As we began to swing our scythes in the slow, easy way that a man may keep up all day long, I saw that Philip and the two lads had spoken truly. They all knew what they were about. Jordain, like me, came from country stock, though his family were poor tenants, and held their land partly through customary service on their lord's demesne, so he too had wielded a scythe from the time he was tall enough. Probably, again like me, at the age of about ten.

As the men moved slowly up the field, not hurrying, Susanna and her daughter used their smaller sickles to cut the corn too close to the hedgerows for a scythe to be used. Behind us, moving more slowly, Margaret and Beatrice were gathering armfuls of the cut corn into bundles and securing the sheaves with the braids made by the children, before standing the sheaves, pair by pair, into stooks of six each. There they could dry in the sun before being carted to the farmyard for threshing and winnowing. Alysoun struggled to help. Binding the sheaves was too much for her small arms, although Stephen, who was a little larger, and whose use of crutches had strengthened his arms, could just manage. She and Stephen together were able to lift a sheaf into place in the stook.

The promised fine weather continued to hold, with a sun almost too hot for the work. Soon all the men were stripped to their shirts, and the two students even shed those, but I had no wish to burn my back to the colour of a roasted crab apple. I had even donned an old straw hat of my father's. The brim was unravelling, but it gave some protection from the sun. The scent of the cut stalks is sweet, but not everything about harvest is pleasant. Biting flies rose up from the disturbed corn and feasted on us. Twice I saw an adder slither away in front of me, and I was glad that I wore shoes, unlike several of the labourers. Rabbits, too, fled before us, deeper and deeper into the wheat, before some burst out, making a frantic dash for the field edge. James brought down two of them with his slingshot, so there would be rabbit pie for tonight's Lammas feast.

'Does this Mordon fellow lay claim to all the conies in the neighbourhood?' I asked Edmond, after James had retrieved the second one. 'He might claim they all come from his warren, and are his by right.'

Edmond shrugged. 'No doubt he might try, but there are plenty of them living wild hereabouts – aye, and eating our vegetables – so no one will be telling him about any we catch. Though I did hear he tried to fine Bertred Godsmith, who took a coney in his own croft, but there was a near riot in the village. That time he backed off. Another time, he might not.'

After a while, it became clear that our numbers were unbalanced. We needed more women for the stooking, so halfway through the morning, as we took a break for a drink of ale, two of the labourers walked down to the village to fetch their wives to help. After that, the women began to catch up, but there was still a good deal of cut corn lying when Edmond called a halt, and we all lent a hand to the stooking in the afternoon, until all that was cut had been set to dry.

'About a third of the field, I think,' I said, as we walked back to the farm behind the women, who had hurried ahead to begin the cooking.

'Aye, near enough.' Edmond slung his scythe over his shoulder and scratched at his insect bites. 'Two more days should finish the wheat. About the same, three days for the barley. Maybe two days for the oats. Another two or three for the beans and peas. We should manage it in two weeks or a little more, if the weather holds. It would have taken twice, three times as long without the help of you and your friends. We could not have done it. Half the harvest lost or spoiled, surely.'

'It does us no harm to set our books aside for a time,' Philip said, coming up behind us. 'It is too easy to forget, living a pampered life in an Oxford college, how much hard labour and sweat goes into providing us townsfolk with food. I know I shall be stiff tomorrow, but it has done me good – despite the flies you breed here. As large as bumblebees!'

The women had all disappeared into the kitchen, and the children had set Rowan free, so that she was rushing about like a mad thing. The three farm dogs, well trained and quiet, lay with their chins on their crossed paws watching her in some amazement. We gathered, all of the men, about the well in the yard, and poured buckets of water over each other, which was some relief after the sticky heat of the day and eased the insect bites somewhat. Guy and Giles donned their shirts again, wincing a little as cloth touched sun-burned skin. Then we carried trestles and boards out of one of the barns, and set up the tables for the Lammas feast.

The labourers, who had gone down to the village, returned with their families and before long we were all gathered, seated on stools around three tables. At the centre of each table several of the elaborate loaves held pride of place, for as the custom is, the first cut wheat of the harvest provides the flour for the Lammas loaves, a thanksgiving to God for providing, of His bounty, bread for mankind, the staff of life.

We had been joined by the village priest, Sire Raymond.

I murmured aside to Susanna, 'Is Sire Raymond not required to attend the Lammastide feast at the manor?'

She shook her head. 'Nay, Master Mordon has brought his own household priest from London. I think he looks down on our country priest.'

And there he was mistaken, I thought, for it was Sire

Raymond who had taught me as a boy, well enough that I was able to hold my own when I went as a student to Oxford. He was growing old and somewhat frail now, but he called down a blessing on the Lammas loaves, on the harvest, and on the present company, in a voice as sweet as ever, which always seemed to me to sing God's words, even when he spoke them.

The women must have been cooking long before I had risen in the morning, or mayhap Susanna and her daughter had already prepared much before we arrived, for the tables groaned under the weight of every kind of savoury and sweet pie, mounds of richly golden butter moulded into floral shapes, early apples stuffed with dried plums and baked with honey, jugs of thick cream, great rounds of yellow cheese, and smoked hams. Edmond passed from table to table, slicing the Lammas loaves and ensuring that everyone had a piece, even the youngest baby from the village, a stout lad just learning to sit up, who tore his bread apart with great interest and dropped most of it to be quickly scooped up by the dogs.

We had settled well into our meal, finding ourselves with hearty appetites after the day's work in the field, when there was a late arrival.

Into the circle of light cast by the candle lanterns James and Thomas had hung from hooks in the wall of the barn, stepped a man of my own age, a woman on his arm, and a boy of about fourteen following.

'So you are able to join us, Alan!' Edmond rose from his seat and drew the newcomers to the table.

As the light fell on them, I saw that it was Alan Wodville, a boyhood companion of mine, with his wife and the orphaned nephew he had taken in, when the lad's parents died in the Pestilence.

Alan nodded to me. 'By rights, we've no part in your harvesting, Edmond, though we thank you for inviting us.'

'You have always come in the past,' Edmond said. 'By reason of cousinage, you are part of the family.'

Alan was indeed a distant cousin on Susanna's side. I

shifted along the bench to make room for him, while Susanna drew his wife Beth down beside her, and the boy Rob squeezed between James and Thomas.

Edmond served them with Lammas bread and Hilda went round the table, filling everyone's cups from a large jug of ale.

'I had feared you would be summoned to the table of the new lord of the manor,' Edmond said. 'Does he not hold the Lammas feast for all of his people?'

Alan drank deeply of his ale, and shrugged. 'I think he feasts only his fine friends from London. He would see no need to treat those who work for him. He has only London manners. He may own the manor, but he knows nothing of his duties.'

I could hear in his voice more than the dislike everyone showed for the new man. There was anger there too. I turned to Edmond.

'But why should you think Alan would feast at the manor? Is his position confirmed?'

'Ah,' Edmond said, 'you will not know. Alan has indeed taken up his father's old position there. He is the manor huntsman, now that the manor has a lord again.'

Alan shook his head.

'I am turned away,' he said grimly. 'I am no longer his lordship's huntsman.'

Chapter Three

Everyone stopped speaking and stared at Alan. Studying the well known lines of his face, I realised that he had grown even more like his father, who had been huntsman to the de Veres, and his grandfather before him. The whole family, back beyond memory. They were quiet men, speaking little, moving through the woods as soft as any wild creature, skilled in all the arcane knowledge of the hunt, such as lords demand. Though to be sure, everyone in the village also hunted, legally and illegally, but they had little care for the rituals of the lordly hunts. Alan had been brought up in the certainty that he too would be the de Veres' huntsman one day, and had been learning the skills almost before he could walk. By the age of fourteen he was already assistant huntsman to his father on the de Vere manor.

When we were boys, Alan and I had often gone poaching with my elder brother John, deep into Wychwood. There had been hares on the open stretches of rough ground, and twice we had taken a deer, but never a boar, for they were growing rare. Out of respect for the de Vere family, we had avoided those parts of the forest where they hunted, instead going deep into the king's domain. The fearful punishments if we had been caught added spice to the adventures. It was always Alan who was first to spot the tracks or fewmets of our quarry. We had stayed good friends until we had gone our separate ways – I to be a scholar, he to be a huntsman – though we had seen little of each other since.

The future which had been so clearly laid out before Alan had all come to naught with the deaths of the entire de Vere family. His father had died soon after, of some disease of the lungs, and Alan had been left with nothing but a cottage and barely land enough to sustain himself, his wife, his sister, and the boy. The heir to the manor had employed him for a few duties, but it could hardly have paid much. Somehow he had scraped through, even working sometimes as a labourer for Edmond, though he must have found that humiliating. It was not surprising that someone should have suggested to the new owner of Leighton Manor that he should employ Alan as his huntsman. If Mordon intended – as it seemed – to live the life of lord of the manor, a manor with rights of the chase in Wychwood, then he would need a skilled huntsman who knew every yard of the ground, and every creature dwelling in the wood.

So it seemed that Alan had been given the post of huntsman once more. Yet now, barely weeks after this Master Mordon had arrived, he was cast off. What could have happened?

Edmond's thoughts must have echoed mine, for he demanded, 'What is this? No longer his huntsman? The man has been in residence but a few weeks, and has not even been hunting as yet! How can this be? Do his London friends dare to think they know our forest?'

His tone was scornful, and he leaned forward enquiringly. Alan shook his head.

'Not now. I've no wish to cast a blight on your feast. We will speak of it later.'

He refused to say more, and the temporary shadow cast by this news was soon dispersed as the ale went round and the lavish food was consumed. Later, when the children had been sent off to bed and the women were clearing away the broken meats of the feast, I looked about for Alan, hoping to speak to him quietly about his disturbing news.

Edmond saw me searching. 'He has gone back to the village with the others. I cannot make it out. This Master Mordon is a fool if he thinks he can hunt in Wychwood without a huntsman of Alan's skill.'

I would try to find an opportunity to speak to Alan before many days were out. From all I had heard, the advent of this new man to the manor did not augur well for the village and its people, or indeed for Edmond, after the interference with our mill stream. Perhaps it was nothing but the ignorance of a London merchant about the customs of the countryside and he would mend his ways when he knew us better. Yet somehow all that I had already learned of the fellow did not promise much chance of that. On the other hand, he might tire of country life and yearn for the excitements of London once more. Perhaps he would return there, never to trouble Leighton-under-Wychwood again. It would be easier to judge when I saw him for myself, should that happen during my short time here at the farm.

The next morning I awoke even stiffer than before, as I had expected, but this was but normal, after the first day's harvest work following months as a sedentary Oxford bookseller. Edmond and his sons would not be suffering, for their daily physical labour would keep their muscles in fine trim, while mine had grown soft, so I held myself back from complaint over breakfast, though I noticed that Jordain and Philip also winced from time to time. In their youthful pride, the two students also said nothing, though I noticed that they moved a little more carefully than usual.

The day progressed much as the previous one. The labourers from the village brought their women with them from the outset, and the work went well, so that by the end of the second day less than a third of the wheat field remained to be cut. There was no Lammas feast in the evening and we went to bed with the sun, in the country fashion.

Edmond was out early the following morning, and came in looking pleased.

'The first day's cut is already dry enough to bring

into the barn,' he said, as he helped himself to nearly half a loaf and a large chunk of Susanna's cheese. 'I think I will set some of us to hauling it in, while the rest finish cutting the field.'

'Aye,' I said. 'With less than a third of the way to go, we should manage it. Then will you move us to the barley, or do you want to make a start on dressing the wheat?'

'Oh, the threshing and winnowing may wait yet a while,' he said, washing down his bread and cheese with a deep draught of ale. 'We shall cut the barley first. Best to get all the corn safely in, while the weather lasts.'

I nodded. 'We have been fortunate so far. This exceptional hot sun cannot go on forever.'

While it did, however, work in the fields was exhausting in such heat. The children, who had found it exciting at first, were more reluctant to spend the entire day under the broiling sun in the insect infested field, and by that afternoon had slipped back to the farm again to play with Rowan and pursue some games of their own. Thomas hitched up the farm cart and Jordain brought ours into service, so with Giles and Guy helping they hauled the first day's cut wheat back to the barn, where the sheaves were stacked up ready for threshing when time allowed. Four men short at the scything, we proceeded more slowly, but managed to cut the last of the wheat as dusk was drawing in. The last clump of stems had been left standing in the centre of the field, which would be ritually cut by custom the next day.

As we were eating our supper that evening, later than usual, since we had stayed in the field till the task was done, Alan's nephew, the boy Rob, knocked on the door.

'My uncle says, do you need another pair of hands at your harvesting?' The boy spoke his message with reluctance, and a certain glint of angry pride in his eyes. 'I can also come, if you wish it so.'

Even if Alan had learned to swallow his resentment at being obliged to work as a day labourer, the boy clearly had not. Alan had been training him up in his own huntsman's skills, and he must have hoped for a better future than working as a farm labourer.

'Aye, I should be glad of him,' Edmond said easily, 'glad of you both. For despite these friends coming from Oxford, there can never be too many at harvest time. You will be welcome to start tomorrow, along with the rest of us. Tell Alan so. And your aunt too, if she can be spared.'

The boy nodded briefly. If he was at all mollified at being bracketed with 'friends from Oxford', he showed no sign of it, but bowed stiffly and left with his head held high.

Susanna sighed and shook her head. 'Poor lad, he has not taken this change of fortune kindly.'

'Perhaps tomorrow we may discover what lies behind this mysterious dismissal,' I said. 'I will try to contrive an opportunity to speak to Alan apart.'

'Aye, do that,' Edmond said. 'You were always good friends. I do not like the way matters are going at the manor.'

Before heading to the barley next morning, we had one last task in the wheat field. The final clump of uncut wheat still stood proud in the centre of the field, while all the rest stood dotted about in stooks, drying in the sun. The air was filled with the warm scent of ripened grain and the sweetness of the cut straw.

Sire Raymond had walked up to the farm and joined us as we gathered around the last of the wheat. It is said that the spirit of the wheat lodges in the last uncut sheaf, and to ensure good fortune and a bountiful harvest next year, the priest blessed the standing corn, before taking a sickle and cutting a large spray of fat ears of corn together with about two feet of straw, which he handed to my mother, the oldest woman present.

While we watched, she began to weave the straws swiftly together. She might be aging, but her fingers were still as nimble as ever, and I had watched her do this each year since I was younger than Rafe, who was now watching intently, peeping out from behind Margaret's skirts.

First my mother made a wreath like a small crown,

weaving into it strands of rosemary, lavender, and thyme, which she handed to Edmond, and then began the more complex task, creating the figure which some call a 'dolly', though in fact it is a representation of a hare. When I used to do my lessons with Sire Raymond, he told me what he understood to be the origin of the straw figure, for he had always been interested in old customs.

'In the olden days,' he said, 'when men had not heard of our Blessed Lord and worshipped all manner of pagan gods, they believed that there was a goddess called Eostre, who watched over the fertility of the land.' He shook his head, smiling gently at such folly. 'It is from her name that our word Easter comes, for the early fathers who brought the Faith to England thought it wise to humour the people by letting them keep some of their customs, such as celebrating the first appearance of the new growth of the crops in Spring.'

'But what has that to do with the straw hare?' I said.

'Folk believed that Eostre often took the form of a hare, so by weaving her image out of the last cut straw, honour was done her, and if the straw hare was kept safe, to watch over the farm for a twelve month, the crops would prosper in the coming year.'

I remembered this conversation now, as my mother handed the straw hare to Sire Raymond to be blessed. As always, he smiled benignly as he did so, happy to respect ancient customs, even if they carried a whiff of pagan magic.

'Now', Edmond said, 'Alysoun shall be our harvest maid this year, in thanks for all who have come to help with the harvest.' He placed the wreath on Alysoun's head, and she blushed with pleasure.

Then the last sheaf was cut, and some of the heads of grain beaten into the earth where it had stood, to ensure the fertility of next year's crop. Alysoun was raised up on the linked arms of her cousins James and Thomas, before being paraded about the field and back to the farm, where Susanna hung the straw hare carefully from a hook over the kitchen door, after taking down last year's hare. It too would be buried in the field.

Before we returned to our work, we all drank to the success of the crop, and ate one of the small saffron cakes my mother had brought from her cottage. Saffron is a precious herb, and the cakes are always very small, but golden and sweetened with honey.

We could not spend long back at the farm, so as soon as Sire Raymond left to return to the village church, we went back to the fields. Today we would make a start on the barley field, while more of the wheat that had dried enough in the sun would be carted to the barn. When I looked over the barley, however, I thought Edmond had been too optimistic to think it might be cut in two days. This was relatively fresh land, only assarted about twenty or so years before, and regularly manured every winter since then, by stock grazing on the stubble and new grass. The result was a rich soil, not tired with years of tillage, bringing forth a very dense and healthy crop of barley which would require some labour to cut. Only two days remained before Sunday, when we would be obliged to leave the work. I thought we should not finish before the evening of Monday, but I did not express my thoughts aloud.

We had barely made a start when Alan, his wife Beth, and the boy Rob appeared and joined us, after a brief greeting. Beth seemed perfectly content with the work, but like most village wives she probably was accustomed to helping with the harvest, even if her husband ranked above the other villagers, on account of his position as the manor huntsman. Alan looked grim and the boy rebellious, but they set to work along with the rest of us, and both could swing a scythe as well as any.

Although the sun continued to shine undiminished, I could feel a change in the air. If anything, the heat was even more oppressive, and the air was heavy as a wet cloth, so the sweat which sprang up as we worked seemed to drench us worse than before, never drying off our skin in the heat. Away in the east, there were the first traces of cloud to be seen for several weeks, distant still, but curdling thick and grey along the horizon, promising a thunder storm before too many days had passed. I knew there were villages where the people continued with the harvest even on Sundays, but although Sire Raymond was tolerant in many things, he would not permit farm labour on a Sunday, save for the necessary daily care of the stock. A man might tend a sick ewe, his wife could milk the cows, but no one might dig a ditch, mend a hedge – or cut the harvest grain.

I cannot say that anyone has much enjoyment from cutting barley. Added to the heat and the maddening attention of the insects – worse than ever – barley is a vicious crop, spiky and painful to handle. It was worse for the women, gathering the sheaves and building the stooks, than it was for us, swinging our scythes, although even we could not avoid some contact with the sharp barbs. Still, the barley must be gathered in, for without it there would be no ale in the coming year. Wheat for bread and barley for ale. The oats, which still awaited us, would provided porridge for us and extra nourishment for the horses when hay alone meant poor fodder in the depths of winter.

Despite my best efforts, I was not able to speak to Alan privately, either that day or the next. I began to think he was avoiding me, though I could think of no reason why he should do so. As I expected, when we made our way back to the farm in the near dark of Saturday evening, about a third of the barley field remained uncut. And the worrying sense of a change in the weather weighed heavily upon us.

Our large household walked down together for Mass at the village church of St Mary the Virgin the next morning. It was a modest church compared to our Oxford parish church of St Peter-in-the-East, consisting as it did of no more than a nave without side aisles, and very short transepts to north and south. There was a stumpy tower at the west end, which held the single bell, though it was a bell with a very sweet voice. Leighton Manor possessed its own small chapel, used on weekdays, but the de Vere family had always attended Mass at the village church on Sundays, along with the villagers. Some early Lord de Vere had installed a window of stained glass at the east end of the chancel, behind the altar, which depicted the Virgin holding the infant Christ Child up to admire a blossoming tree of uncertain variety. The flowers were almost as large as the Baby's head. The remaining windows of the church were plain glass, quite thick and irregular.

Against the right wall of the nave a fine stone tomb held the carved life-size figures of a Lord de Vere, his shield marked with the Crusader's cross, with his lady lying beside him. Perhaps this was the same man who had presented the window to the church. Before the altar, a new and shining brass plate, set into the flagstones of the floor, was engraved with the image of Sir Yves de Vere, last of his line, who – with his wife and children – was buried beneath it. I disliked walking over it on occasions when I took communion here, for it seemed like an act of cruel disrespect for a man I had known and liked.

Yves de Vere, being a practical and humane man, had not presented the church with a window, but with the new fashion of wooden benches called 'pews', so that the congregation might sit instead of standing throughout the service. There had always been a narrow stone ledge set into the wall of the nave near the west door, where the elderly and infirm might rest weary bones, but the idea that those who were hale and hearty might sit down during service was a new one, at the time when Lord de Vere arranged for the pews to be carved by the village carpenter and installed some six years earlier. I was familiar with pews from those Oxford churches which had begun the practice, but here some of the older villagers had muttered their disapproval, saying that only by standing and kneeling throughout the service could one show proper respect and piety in God's house, not by sitting relaxed and idle. However, I noticed now that none of these die-hard traditionalists any longer stood resolutely at the back of the nave, behind the pews, but took their seats along with the rest of us.

Although the church was humble, it was the first place of worship I had known, and Sire Raymond's voice, speaking the familiar Latin words of the Mass, was the voice I had first heard intoning those beautiful phrases as a child, long before I understood them. The familiarity enfolded me now, warm and comforting.

Alan's nephew Rob was serving as altar boy, although I could not see Alan himself. That is one disadvantage of pews – it is much more difficult to look about you when you are fixed, sitting in one place, than it is if you stand. Alan was somewhat short, wiry and compact, easily hidden in a crowd. However, he was certain to be here somewhere in the congregation, and I would find him after the service. As far as I could tell, there were no strangers here, so Master Mordon and his London friends must be hearing Mass in the private chapel at the manor.

The Mass concluded, Rob preceded Sire Raymond down the nave, swinging a brass censor on a chain and casting the scented smoke of incense over the congregation. That too was familiar. Not the expensive and exotic perfume of the incense used in town churches, but some village concoction of homely herbs, gathering in the meadows and gardens of Leighton-under-Wychwood and presented reverently by some of the village wives to the priest.

Since we were seated near the front of the congregation – our family being the highest ranking in the parish after the lord – I was delayed in leaving the church. Out in the lane I saw Alan with his wife and nephew already beyond hailing distance.

I turned to Edmond.

'I think I will call on Alan at home,' I said. 'Easier to speak with him there than in the midst of the harvest. If I am delayed, do not let Susanna wait dinner for me.'

Edmond nodded. 'Aye, see what you may learn. You have always known Alan better than I.'

'When we were younger, that is true enough. But now? However, I think we should try to discover what lies behind this so sudden dismissal.'

He made a face. 'Alan is not the first. This fellow Mordon has cast off almost all the old household servants from the manor. And there has been other trouble.'

I raise my eyebrows in query. The man had wasted no time in stirring up such trouble.

'You recall Matt Grantham?' Edmond said. 'He inherited that small property – over next to the manor demesne land – from an uncle by marriage on his mother's side of the family.'

'Aye, I know him. Big burly fellow. Somewhat short of temper.'

'That is the man. It seems this uncle's father used to hold some land – not this same land – by villein service. Now it seems Master Mordon is making a claim that Matt and all his family are villeins, owing customary service to the manor.'

I frowned. 'That cannot be, surely?'

'Indeed not, but Mordon and his London lawyer say they will take Matt to court and bind him to villeinage. The whole village is hot with anger at it, and none more than Matt himself. He has been making all kinds of threats in the alehouse when he is cup-shotten.'

'Best if he keeps a cool head,' I said. 'It will soon be shown that he and all his forebears have been freemen. But Matt has never been one to keep a cool head.'

'He has not. His friends are trying to talk sense into him. 'Tis to be hoped they may prevail.'

As I walked down the village street after Alan, I pondered this latest revelation about the new lord of the manor. Leighton-under-Wychwood had always been a quiet place, with harmony between church, manor, and village. And mostly a happy place, until the Pestilence came. Even when the harvest was poor and times were hard, the villagers had been able to look to the manor for help. Although the de Veres had not been one of the great families, possessed of riches, they had always been willing to share what they had with the needy. Later, with the family gone and the manor falling into neglect, the de Veres had been mourned, but a general opinion had prevailed – perhaps more hopeful than wise – that a new lord would once again prove a shield against those hard times. Yet now, on every side, the new man seemed bent on destroying all that had held firm for generations. He had rejected our priest, treated his huntsman, servants, and villagers with arrogance and hostility, and damaged the only other substantial family, ours, by the obstruction of our mill.

Alan's cottage stood about halfway along the village street in the opposite direction from our farm. It had the usual amount of land before and behind, much the same as Beatrice's home in Oxford, enough to grow the family's vegetables, some fruit trees, some hens, and a sty for a pig to be slaughtered at Michaelmas. Unlike the rest of the villagers, however, Alan's family held no farmland, since they had always served as the manor huntsmen, an occupation which took up all their time, having overall responsibility for the manor's hunting dogs and their gear, those of the horses used in the hunt, and all the equipment – bows, hunting spears, crossbows, nets, traps – I could hardly name half of it. In addition, they must undertake the training of the kennel boys, the hunt assistants, and any grooms who took part. A noble hunt has the most precise of customs and rituals, and woe betide any huntsman who fails to observe them.

Could this be the cause of the rift between Alan and the new lord? Surely not! Alan was probably more learned in all of a huntsman's duties and the arcane practices of the hunt than ever this merchant fellow could be, however well versed he was in the buying and selling of spices. Perhaps it was the other way about, some dispute arising from the townsman's ignorance.

Alan was standing before his cottage, morosely regarding a row of lettuces which had been savaged by rabbits.

'Good day to you, Alan,' I said.

He nodded a reply. 'Those b'yer lady conies,' he said, 'since there's been no hunting, they have been multiplying –' he gave a sharp bark of laughter, '– like rabbits!'

I smiled. 'I am glad to see you have not lost your sense of humour. And I am sure some have been hunted for the pot, though perhaps not legally.'

He gave me a somewhat twisted smile. 'Come through,' he said. 'I saw you following me. Beth has taken a jug of ale out to the back. There's some shade there. What I would give for the cool air of the woods!'

I followed him through the house, smiling a greeting to Beth, and out into the longer strip of land that lay behind the house, where there was a rough table under an apple tree, and a couple of stools. There was a distinct whiff of pig on the small breeze.

'Looks to be a good crop,' I said, nodding to the apple tree as we sat down.

He grunted.

When he had poured us each a cup of ale, he rested his elbows on the table and his chin on his fists. 'Good to see you back, even if 'tis only for the harvest.'

'Aye. Two-three weeks. But I do not find all well here in Leighton.'

He grunted again and took a pull of his ale. I could see that he would say nothing unless I asked him outright.

'Let us not weave a dance around this, Alan,' I said. 'What has happened? Why has this new man showed himself such a fool, dismissing the best huntsman in Wychwood?'

'And,' he said, bitterly, '*and* he still demands that I arrange the hunt he plans for next week. "Do not think you can escape that duty," he says, bastard that he is. "You have been paid for this month, so you will oversee the hunt for my guests, or I'll have the law on you." Bastard.'

'What law?'

'Did I ask him? Means to have his miserable shillings back, I suppose.'

'But *why*, Alan. There must be a reason.'

'Aye, there is a reason.'

I waited. If I read the signs aright, he was going to tell me.

He drained his cup, poured more ale, and ran his fingers through his hair. He kept it cut severely short.

'We had already had some disagreements. With the help of that same lawyer fellow, he has gone through all the forest laws, back to Adam in the Garden, I'm thinking, never taking heed of those that have been eased with time.'

'Like?'

'Like nowadays commuting the punishment to the payment of a fine, instead of what happened in the past – crippling a man's dogs, or cutting off his hand. Mordon favours the old ways, he says. Puts the fear of hellfire and damnation into the poachers. He says. So I say: The king himself has brought in more humane treatment of poachers in the royal forests, like Wychwood. I know my forest law. My father drummed it into me, with a sharp knuckle to my head if I mistook it.'

'And this man would cut off a poacher's hand, rather than settle for a fine?'

'Aye. Or both hands. Bloodthirsty bastard.'

'You said that you had already had these disagreements about the forest laws, but was that not the cause of the final rift?'

He looked down at his hands.

'It was Jane.'

'Jane? Your little sister?'

'Not so little now. Nearly fourteen and grown into as pretty a maid as any in the village.'

Alan had always been particularly fond of the girl, his parents' only other surviving child. Because of the difference in their ages, she had become almost a daughter to Alan and Beth since the death of her parents. I realised now that I had seen nothing of her since coming to

Leighton.

'Where is she?' I looked about, as though I expected to see her tending the hens.

'We have sent her to Beth's cousin in Burford. To keep her away from Mordon.'

An explanation was beginning to appear.

'What did he do?'

'She was down by the mill stream, searching for one of the hens that had escaped. He seized her and tried–' He swallowed. 'He tried to violate her. I was in the manor kennels, but I heard the screaming. I knew it was Jane. There were two of his London friends with me, looking over the lymers, and they . . . they grinned at each other. They knew. I'll swear they knew. I ran like the devil and found him with her clothes half torn off her.'

He took another long drink.

'I hit him.'

I drew a cautious breath. Men have been hanged by their lords for less.

'And then?'

'He just lay there in the mud, gaping at me like a landed fish. Jane had fallen. Unconscious. With terror, I suppose. I picked her up and ran home with her.' His nostrils flared, and I could see the fury in his eyes. 'By Our Lord's grace, I was in time to stop him. But we did not think she would be safe here, so the next day I took her pillion behind me and rode over to Burford. When I got back, Beth told me Mordon had sent word that I was dismissed. Then the following day – that would be the day you arrived – he waylaid me and told me I must still manage his first hunt for him, since he would not have time to hire another huntsman. It seems these London friends have been promised all the excitement of a deer hunt in Wychwood. Ha!' His tone was full of contempt.

This was probably the longest speech I had ever heard from Alan, but I suspected that he had kept all this to himself and Beth until now. Perhaps it was a relief for him to speak of it.

'You have done the best for Jane,' I said slowly, 'but what of you? Once you have served his turn at this hunt he has ordered, he could condemn you at his own manor court for striking him.'

'I know. And I know it could be adjudged petty treason, to strike my lord, and not just deemed so by Mordon himself. I'm afeared for Beth and Rob, Nicholas, as well as for Jane, if aught happens to me.'

We did not speak it aloud, but the punishment for petty treason is death. Mordon could choose to be judge, jury, and executioner in his manor court.

'You could leave Leighton.' I said it with hesitation, for all Alan's skills lay here.

He simply looked at me and shook his head.

'You could lay a counter charge against him. Accuse him of attempting the rape of a child, at the court in Burford.'

'And whose word would they believe? A rich merchant, lord of Leighton Manor, or a penniless former huntsman? He would claim I made the charge out of spite for being dismissed, and they would believe him.'

'I do not know what is best to do, Alan,' I said, 'but you know that you are surrounded by friends here. May I speak of this to Edmond?'

'Aye.' He shrugged and ran his hand over his face, and I saw the dark shadows of sleepless nights beneath his eyes.

'At least he will do nothing until after the hunt,' I said. 'That gives us some time to think what to do. Have you talked to Sire Raymond?'

'I have not. It would shock the old man.'

'Oh, I think not. He is not so unworldly as he looks. Speak to him. He will understand why you did what you did. And he will be concerned for Jane.'

'Perhaps you are right. Aye, I will see him tomorrow. I would not sully his peace on the Lord's Day.'

'And in the meantime, you still have your duties at the manor, to prepare for the hunt?'

He smiled grimly. 'I have. But I take care to keep out of the way of the new *lord*.' He spat out the last word. 'You and your cousin must expect an invitation to join the hunt. He wishes to ingratiate himself with the better families hereabouts.'

'He has hardly shown signs of doing that. He has a strange way to go about it. Did you not hear how he has diverted our mill stream?'

He nodded. 'Mayhap he thinks that, as lord of the manor, he may do as he pleases, and yet Edmond would still be grateful for the invitation to the hunt.'

'Then he reads my cousin wrongly,' I said. 'However, if we should be invited, I think we will attend. A closer look at this man might prove useful.'

It was time I made my way back to the farm.

'Do not give up hope, Alan,' I said, as he walked with me back to the village street. 'If the man Mordon should attempt anything against you in the manor court, the whole village will rise in your support. He cannot put everyone on trial.'

I walked slowly back up the lane to the farm, pondering all I had learned that morning in addition to what I had been told by Geoffrey Carter back in Oxford, and Edmond's account of the diversion of the mill stream. It was difficult, without having met the man, to understand why he was behaving in this way. Perhaps Alan was right. Having bought the manor, Mordon thought that he had unbridled power over all the neighbourhood and its people.

It was true that in law he had considerable power over those villeins who owed him customary labour and boon days of work on the manor demesne, in return for their small holdings of cottage and field strips, but in fact over the years much of this service had been commuted to a cash payment, in lieu of labour, for a man who spends his best hours at the crucial times of the farming year on the lord's demesne may find it near impossible to plough, sow, and harvest his own crops. Certainly the commuting of service to payment had held here in Leighton for at least two generations. I suppose in the past many of the villeins would not have possessed the coin, but now most families had other small ways to earn. Wives might spin or weave more than was needed for their families and sell the surplus in Burford. Or they might make cheeses for the market. Carpentry or smithing could bring in money. Left to make the most of their own land holdings, some men with small families might have a surplus to sell, either beyond the village, or within it to such as Alan who had no field crops of their own. There was one old man, too old for field work in any case, who made beautiful carved shepherd's crooks, which his daughter took once a month to the market in Witney.

If Master Mordon was bent on reverting to the old way, labour instead of coin, it would disrupt the entire settled economy of the village. I wondered whether his payment of inflated wages to landless day labourers had come about because the villeins had stood firm against sacrificing their established right to commute labour to coin.

When I reached the farm, everyone was just sitting down to dinner, and I realised suddenly how hungry I was. I slipped into the space on a bench next to my mother and gave her a quick hug.

'It is good to see you looking well,' I said. 'We have barely had a moment to speak since we arrived.'

In fact, I could see that she was thinner than usual, and her face was still pale since her illness.

'Harvest always eats up the hours,' she agreed, as she accepted a bowl of rich onion soup from Hilda. 'Still, 'tis a day of rest today, so we must find a quiet spot and you can tell me all that has happened since last summer. We missed you at Christmastide.'

'It could not be helped,' I said. 'The roads were blocked even in Oxford. I cannot imagine how bad it must have been here. I remember some winters when I was a boy – the village was quite cut off, and it was hard even to reach the village from the farm.'

'Aye, but it was usually later. January, not December. I have never seen so much snow so early in all my lifetime as we had last winter. We were indeed cut off, from around Advent to the Feast of St Edward the Confessor, when it began to thaw a little.'

'We will come this Christmas if we can,' I said as I received my own bowl of soup, then my attention was called away by Philip and Jordain, who were disputing some fine point of theology.

'And John Wycliffe would say quite otherwise,' Jordain said, 'for he holds that, if we look carefully at Our Lord's own words . . .'

I smiled and turned to Susanna, who had just taken the seat opposite me. I gave a nod toward the two scholars.

'I have enough of this in Oxford,' I said.

'Who is this John Wycliffe?' she asked, beginning to spoon up her soup. 'They have mentioned him before.'

'Another scholar, about my age,' I said, 'or a little older. He has some very strange ideas, about returning purely to the Bible itself, and casting away all the centuries of learned commentaries by the Church. He thinks the Bible should be rendered into English, so every man may read it for himself. Women too, if they are lettered.'

She paused, with her spoon halfway to her mouth. 'That sounds like dangerous talk. The Church will not like it. Will he not be taken for a heretic?'

'Aye, he might,' I said soberly. 'That is, if anyone pays him any mind. The students attend his lectures in droves, for he is a fine speaker. Talk of his ideas may well spread beyond Oxford.'

She shivered. 'With the Pestilence, and the French wars, and strange ideas in men's minds, the world which seemed steady when we were children has begun to tilt enough to afright one, this way and that.'

I had never heard Susanna speak in such a way, for usually she was wholly occupied with governing her household.

I began to spoon up my soup, rich and brown and

thick with onions. 'What do you mean by strange ideas – some other than those of John Wycliffe?'

'There's a restlessness in the country, since the Pestilence. Men breaking free from their old duties, wanting what their fathers never had, villeins wanting their freedom. This affair of Mordon paying higher wages. In the past, none of our regular labourers would have left us. Loyalty counted for something then. But now?' She shrugged.

'Certainly there are far more masterless men roaming the country,' I agreed, 'and regularly bondmen from the country arrive in Oxford, hoping to earn their freedom by staying a year and a day.'

'Aye, but it is more than that.' Edmond had been listening to us. 'There is a general restlessness, certainly. When so many have seen the death of those they love, 'tis no surprise that they want to seize upon what life is left to them. Here in Leighton it has been no more than a shifting below the surface, like the fermenting of a cask of ale. Yet it needs but a little to make it break out and boil over.'

'Like the arrival of a new lord who is set on ruling with an iron hand?' I said.

'Aye,' Edmond said. 'Just so.'

Chapter four

The following day, Monday, was given over to the final cutting of the barley field, and the carting of all the remaining wheat sheaves back to the barn. We were nearing the end of the field and I suppose we were all growing tired and careless, when there was a sudden yelp from Guy, who dropped his scythe and straightened up, swearing.

'What's amiss?' Edmond called, laying down his own scythe, and started across the field toward him.

Guy was cradling his right arm in his left hand and looking furious.

'Stinking camomile,' he shouted. 'A whole patch of it. Take care!'

I joined them.

'Be glad it wasn't an adder,' I said, for I had seen two myself amongst the wheat on the first day, but fortunately they had slithered away.

Guy shrugged. The skin of his right hand and forearm was already showing red patches. Later, there would be painful blisters.

'Where are your gloves?' Edmond asked, severely. 'Why do you think I handed them out before we started the harvest?'

'I forgot to bring them with me today.'

Guy was shame-faced. He had also discarded his shirt again, which might have provided some protection for his arm. Stinking camomile, or mayweed (as it is sometimes called) is a pernicious weed when it gets in amongst the corn. The rash it causes can be severe.

'Come back to the house with me,' Susanna said. 'I will put some salve on it. That will not cure it, but it will give you some ease.'

As they went off, James and Thomas set to without a word to root out all of the stinking camomile with great care, before throwing it on a bonfire in the yard. The rest of us cut the remaining barley, keeping our eyes open for more of the weed, having no wish to suffer the burning rash, which sometimes led to a fever.

When we had finished, the village women were invited to glean whatever overlooked grain they could find in the wheat and barley fields. Gleaning of the commonly held village fields was the accepted custom, but we had allowed the women and young children to glean in our fields at least as far back as my grandfather's time. It was a small charity, God knows, but one that was appreciated. Later, in a day or two, Edmond's small herd of cows would be driven into the harvested fields to graze the stubble and manure the ground. When the sheep were brought back to the farm from the higher grazing grounds, they would be turned into another field, or follow after the cows, cropping closer to the ground than cattle may do.

'A good day's work,' I said to Martha, wife of the village blacksmith, as she was leaving that evening with two large and well-filled baskets of salvaged ears of wheat.

'Aye, Master Elyot,' she said, wiping her hot face on her sleeve. 'And good plump ears they be. 'Tis as well, for there will be no gleaning on the manor fields this year.'

'The new lord will not permit it?'

'He will not. He has sent word by one of his foreign servants that anyone caught gleaning in his fields will be imprisoned and fined.'

She spoke with bitterness, and had good cause. The manor fields were extensive and offered rich pickings for the gleaners.

'Well, he may live to regret it,' I said, 'for the spilt

grain will seed itself, so next year he will have barley amongst his wheat, and wheat amongst his barley, and oats everywhere.'

'Aye, so he will.' She grinned broadly, and went off cheerfully.

'Foreign', to Martha, meant someone from beyond Oxfordshire, or even from the next village.

It was as well the gleaners had come swiftly to gather up all the spilt and overlooked heads of grain, for over the next two days, as we hurried to stow the barley safely under cover, we watched the thunder clouds building up ominously in the east. Even as the last load was driven into the farm, heavy drops began to fall, speckling the dust of the yard with shining disks as round as silver pennies.

As the afternoon faded into evening, the rain grew heavier, thrown by a rising wind in fistfuls against the windows. My mother had gone home to her cottage before supper, and the rest of us ate by the light of rush dips, which Susanna clipped into their metal holders and placed on the table and the court cupboard standing against one wall.

Afterwards, Rafe climbed onto my lap, while Alysoun leaned against my shoulder and Rowan settled herself on my feet.

'Tell us a story, Papa,' Alysoun begged. 'You always tell us a story when there is a storm.'

'Aye,' Rafe said, nodding solemnly.

'Not always,' I protested. 'Besides, no one else wants a story.'

In the circle gathered round the fire, faces turned toward me. The rain had brought a chill with it, and Edmond had built the fire up after the women had finished cooking.

'Aye, we'd all be glad of a story to pass the time,' Edmond said.

Beatrice glanced up from her mending and smiled at me.

Looking around, I saw that scarce anyone was idle.

Most of the women and Hilda were sewing or mending, though Susanna was knitting. James and Thomas were untangling a bundle of old leather harness, with a pot of creamy polish sitting on the floor between them, somewhat ineffectually helped by Jordain's two students, while Jordain and Philip were looking over some exercise in geometry that Stephen had been working out on his horn book. Guy's arm was badly inflamed and a little swollen. He would not be so careless again, I reckoned.

I was the only one with no task in my hands, apart from Edmond's two little girls, Megan and Lora, who were curled up asleep under the table with one of the shaggy farm dogs who had managed to worm his way into the warmth of the house.

'Aye, Nicholas,' Susanna said, 'with all the books you have, you must know plenty of stories.'

'Well–' I said. I hesitated, wondering what sort of story would suit the present very varied company, and wishing Walter, our family storyteller, were here in my place.

Thoughts of hunting must have been at the back of my mind since my talk with Alan, for I said, 'This is the story of the hunt for a miraculous white stag.'

Alysoun wound her arm around my neck and leaned closer.

'As all good stories begin,' I said, '*once upon a time . . . but although it was long ago, we do know when and even where it happened. This all goes back to pagan times.*'

I drew a deep breath. '*There was a famous Roman general called Placidus, who served the Emperor Trajan, and not only was he a great general, but he was famed for his kindness and generosity to the poor and needy. Moreover, he was also noted for his skill in hunting deer.*'

'Like the deer in Wychwood?' Alysoun asked.

'Aye, my pet, like the deer in Wychwood.'

'*One day, word was brought to the court at Rome that an elusive white stag had been glimpsed in the mountain forests near Tivoli, a little way inland from*

Rome. Now you must know that there are many legends associated with white deer. Some say that they can never be caught. Others say that you must never kill a white deer, for they are magical messengers from another world, and to kill one will bring down terrible disaster on the huntsman and all those he loves. Still others believe that if you follow a white deer for a year and a day, it will bring you to a place where you may live forever in bliss.'

'Like Paradise?' Stephen whispered.

'Like Paradise,' I agreed, reluctant to mention that in some versions of the story the magical place was a pagan fairyland, and not a Christian Paradise.

'Whatever stories had been told to him, the emperor ordered Placidus to hunt the deer and bring it back to Rome. "Alive, if you may," he said. "If not, bring back his carcass, and I will have him stuffed, for I know of no other who possesses a white stag, alive or dead." Now, I do not know whether Placidus warned him of the dangers of killing a white stag. Perhaps he did not know himself, but he bowed and said, "My lord, it shall be as you wish." Then he sent for his huntsman and his servants, his hounds and his dog handlers, and a few of his closest companions, and set off for the woods around Tivoli.'

'Was that far from Rome?' James asked. 'A day's hunt? Or a longer journey?'

'Not far,' I said firmly. In truth, I did not know, for I had never been to Italy, but a storyteller must have the utmost confidence in his story, or his listeners will not believe him.

'They set off early in the morning, at dawn, and almost as soon as they reached the forest, the lymers picked up the scent of a deer. Placidus was not sure whether it was the white stag, but he sounded his horn, and off they went in pursuit. Even if it was but a common deer, it would prove a good quarry. But suddenly Placidus caught sight of a flash of white between the trees. The dogs had picked up the trail of the white stag! The huntsman sounded his horn, and they galloped after it, deep into the wood.'

Someone had refilled my ale cup, and I drank deeply. It can be thirsty work, this storytelling.

'*On and on they went, weaving between the trees, crashing through the undergrowth. One of the other knights lost his hat, caught on a branch. The horse of another picked up a sharp stone in its hoof, went lame, and had to leave the hunt. One by one the company fell away, till Placidus and his huntsman alone were left to pursue the white stag, although the lymers and alaunts with their handlers struggled valiantly to keep up. On and on, till they had lost their way, and it was beginning to grow dark, though the white stag shone amongst the dark trees of the forest like a shaft of moonlight.*'

Alysoun had climbed on to my lap beside Rafe, her arm clutching me tightly about my neck.

'*Suddenly the white stag halted and turned to face Placidus. He was alone now, but his huntsman was not far behind, and he could hear the cries of the dogs. Suddenly he saw – there between the magnificent branching antlers of the stag, a fourteen-pointer – an image of the crucified Christ, shining whiter even than the stag, casting a path of light that reached out and touched Placidus. "My son," a Voice said, "fear not." But Placidus was afraid. He could not tell whether the voice came from the stag, or from Christ on the Cross, or from somewhere in the air about him.*'

I was seeing the scene myself, now. It was both beautiful and terrible, and I shivered.

'*The Voice spoke again. "Come to me, my son, place your trust in me." And Placidus knew at that very moment that he must abandon the pagan beliefs in which he had been reared, and embrace the True Faith, though at that time true believers were few in number, despised and persecuted. "You shall suffer much," the Voice continued, "but do not despair, for in the end you shall achieve the Kingdom of Heaven." Then, just as the huntsman and the dogs caught up with him, Placidus saw the vision of the Crucifix fade, though the white stag still stood there, one hoof slightly raised.'*

Alysoun began to bite her thumbnail, and I saw that her eyes were swimming with tears. I patted her arm.

'The huntsman raised his crossbow, the dog handlers bent to release the alaunts, which would pull down the white stag once it had been shot. "Stop," Placidus cried. "I forbid you to shoot it." They all stared at him in astonishment. The stag put one foot forward and bowed to him, then bounded off into the forest.'

I heard Alysoun let out her breath in a gulp. 'He was not killed, you see, my pet,' I whispered in her ear.

'When he returned to Rome, I do not know what Placidus told the emperor, or whether he suffered any punishment for refusing to shoot the white stag, but as soon as he might, he had himself, his wife, and his two young sons baptised into the True Faith, and he took a new name, Eustace. Afterwards, the family had many adventures, both his wife and his sons were captured, and he himself suffered, but they were reunited at last, and after his death he became St Eustace. So, should you ever see a white stag, do not kill it, for it may be a holy messenger.'

I sat back. I was not accustomed to telling a story to so many people, but I had been caught up in St Eustace's vision of the unearthly white stag.

There was silence for a moment, then Stephen said, 'Have you ever seen a white stag, Master Elyot?'

I shook my head. 'Never. But you must ask Alan Wodville. He has been a huntsman since boyhood. If there is a white stag in Wychwood, no one is more likely to have seen it than he.'

'I shall ask him tomorrow,' Stephen said.

Edmond stood up and stretched. 'You tell a good story, Nicholas. But, Stephen, I fear we are unlikely to see Master Wodville tomorrow. There will be no work on the harvest, I am certain.'

He was right. Caught up in telling the tale, I had not noticed how the force of the storm had increased, but everyone now saw the flash of lightning through the half open shutter, and heard the roll of the approaching thunder. The flames of the rush dips flickered in the intruding fingers of the wind. Rafe, who feared thunderstorms, took a firm grip on my sleeve as Edmond crossed to the window and pulled the shutter closed, bolting it securely. Even so, it rattled in the wind.

'Harvest or not,' Margaret said, 'it is long past the time for these children to be abed.'

She helped Susanna gather up the two little girls from under the table, where they had slept through storm and story and all. Stephen somewhat reluctantly hobbled away to the room he shared with Philip on the ground floor.

'Come,' I said, as I struggled to stand up. Alysoun slid from my lap, but Rafe clung round my neck like a monkey from Africa. 'You may stay with me tonight, Rafe, while the storm lasts.'

'And me,' Alysoun said jealously.

I sighed. 'Very well.' There would be little sleep for me that night, with two wriggling children sharing my bed.

The storm reached its peak around midnight, and Rafe sat up in my bed, white-faced, while the thunder crashed about the farm.

'The lightning may hit us here,' he said anxiously. 'We do not have St Peter's and St Mary's to catch it.'

The blessed protection of two church spires in Oxford was certainly lacking on the farm. Even the village church stood lower down the hill, and its short tower would hardly serve as a lightning catcher.

'Ah, but here we have the whole of Wychwood to protect us,' I pointed out. 'Some of those huge trees are far, far taller than the spires of our Oxford churches. Great oaks, centuries old, standing firmly on guard. Just think of it! No lightning will bother our low-built farmhouse, when there are all those tall trees to choose from.'

'Perhaps,' he said reluctantly.

Alysoun turned over, grunted, opened one eye, then fell asleep again. Finally Rafe relaxed as sleep overtook him again. I tried to ease the two of them over far enough that I might sleep without clutching the edge of the bed like a shipwrecked sailor clinging to a plank. Here in the bedchamber of my boyhood, the bed was narrow, tucked in under the sloping eaves. There was a rustling in the thatch above my head as some small creature – bird or mouse, or even a squirrel – burrowed in for comfort from the storm. By the sound of the rain hitting the shutters of my unglazed window, there was sleet mixed with the rain, a sorry change after the heat of recent weeks. The crop of oats would be taking a battering out there.

A watery sun broke through the retreating clouds the following morning, and to be sure the clean scent of freshly washed earth and grass rose up as I threw open the shutters. I leaned out to see the hens already turned out of their coop and foraging for worms in the softened earth, though I drew my head in quickly as the thatch dripped on me. Edmond, already dressed and out in the yard, was heading out of my line of vision to the right. Off to see how serious was the damage to his crop of oats.

The children were still asleep after their disturbed night, so I dressed quickly and ran down to join Edmond. He was standing at the edge of the field, arms folded, frowning. He had good reason. Much of the crop was flattened, beaten down by the heavy rain.

'What do you think?' I said. 'Can much of it be saved?'

He shrugged. 'We needs must leave it a few days. Some of it may spring back up, and if we have some sun, it may dry out.' He sighed. 'Too much to hope for, that we would get all safely in before the weather broke.'

'Still,' I said, 'the wheat and barley are in, the most valuable crops. And we will certainly be able to harvest some of the oats.'

'Mayhap.' He sighed again. 'If we are forced to use the manor mill for grinding this year, instead of our own, we will have that payment to make. The fellow Mordon would squeeze every man dry if he could. And then, the ploughing–' He hesitated. 'You see my draught oxen there?' He pointed to the small paddock where the two great beasts were grazing contentedly on the fresh grass.

'Aye?' I wondered why the sight of two such fine animals should make him gloomy. 'A new yoke of oxen since last year, are they not? They look a strong hearty pair.'

'Aye, they are that.' He gave a grimace. 'And cost me a fair penny. More than I had to spend, but when one of my old beasts died, and the other was past the work, what could I do?'

I glanced cautiously aside at him. 'You did not . . . were you forced to borrow?'

In the past, should such a case arise, Yves de Vere would have been prepared to advance a small loan, to a man he was sure to repay it within the twelvemonth. But now?

'Two months ago,' Edmond said, 'when I lost my former team, the new lord of the manor had come briefly to view his new property and order the building works he required. He called on me, and I mentioned the oxen, for it was at the front of my mind. "I can lend you the cost of a new team," he said, and fool that I was, I agreed.'

'What do you mean?' I asked.

'Without asking, I assumed he meant a loan on the old terms – repayment within the year, no interest charged.'

I felt as though a cold finger had touched my spine. 'The Church does not allow the lending of money at interest,' I said.

He gave me a wry sideways smile. 'We all know what that means. The Church looks away and asks no questions. Mordon's lawyer brought me papers to sign, which I thought was unnecessarily formal, but after all, the man had just met me. Like the fool I say I was, I signed without reading carefully.'

'What did you agree to?'

'I must pay him one fifth of the loan every month for

a year.'

'What!' I tried to calculate what that meant in interest, but I needed ink and paper. 'That means you will have paid back the loan in five months, then in the next five months, pay it all a second time. After that, pay another two-fifths of the amount as well. I cannot work that out, but it is more than a hundred per cent in interest.'

'Aye. A hundred and forty per cent.'

I clutched hold of a fence post, for I felt almost dizzy.

'You cannot pay that, Edmond. It is monstrous.'

'I am bound. I signed.'

'How much have you paid so far?'

'The second payment is due next week.'

I realised I had been holding my breath. I let it out in a gasp. 'Philip is very skilled in the law. Let him look at the agreement, to see whether there is a way out.'

Edmond shrugged. 'He may look and welcome, but I have read it carefully . . . as far as I could .. . if belatedly .. . and I do not think it is possible.'

He turned away from the oat field and we began walking back to the farm.

'After I realised I had been trapped, I began making enquiries about Master Mordon. It seems he is more than merely a pepper and spice merchant. He has another business, quietly, on the side, making loans to a few select folk.'

He gave a dry laugh.

'No paupers, you understand, who would never be able to repay. It seems he has also made loans to the king himself, for the expenses of the French wars. You see that I am in very exalted company! So the king's debt to him played a part in Mordon's securing the manor of Leighton and the hunting privileges that go with it. For all that anyone knows, the manor itself may have cost him nothing in coin, but have been the repayment of a royal loan.'

'I wish you had come to me, Edmond,' I said. 'I might have been able to help with the cost of the new oxen.'

'Nay,' he said, resting his hand on my shoulder. 'You have your own family and your own business. It is not for you to undertake the burdens of the farm. You have done enough, bringing your friends to help us rescue the harvest. We should have some surplus now, which we can take to market. That will help with the payments. Believe me, I will never again sign a paper without reading it carefully. But you know how it is – it was very long, written in lawyer's language, half French, perhaps half Latin, for all I know of the language.'

I nodded. 'Enough to trap any Englishman. That is why the king has ruled that cases in court must be conducted in English from now on. Nevertheless, I think we should have Philip study it. He was able to solve a legal problem for me before.' And I told him how Philip had discovered precedents for freeing Emma from her stepfather's attempt to bind her to the monastic life.

After we had broken our fast, Edmond fetched the agreement and Philip sat down at the kitchen table to study it. All the remaining men went out to the barn to start the threshing of the wheat, a task that could be undertaken while the sun began to dry out the oats.

'We will pick some of the beans,' Susanna said. 'There will be plenty ready now for salting down in crocks. Even the children can help with that.'

So we divided into two parties, and I soon began to work up a considerable sweat, for threshing the ears of wheat with a jointed flail is hard work, like beating someone to death, someone made of stone. It uses quite different muscles from swinging a scythe, and before long my shoulders ached painfully, and sweat ran down my back and even trickled into my eyes. Dust and chaff rose up in a cloud around us, making us cough and sneeze, working its way into the gaps in our clothing, where sharp fragments of straw lodged painfully, digging into our skin. It was a relief when Alysoun came to call us to dinner.

Before we returned to the house, we stood about the well, pouring buckets of water over each other. As I ran my fingers through my hair, plucking out bits of straw, I reminded myself just how easy a life I had in my bookshop, able to buy flour for Margaret's bread making – flour from grain which had been sowed, grown, cut, dried, threshed, winnowed, and ground. At times one forgets the labour that goes into the making of flour for a simple loaf of bread.

Philip had cleared his papers off the table for the laying of dishes for dinner. He had not managed to discover any loophole in the agreement, which had been drawn up by a skilled lawyer. However, he handed Edmond a stiffly folded square of parchment, sealed with a large round of red wax, into which an unusually massive seal had been impressed.

'This arrived while you were at the threshing. A liveried servant delivered it,' he said, his tone sarcastic. 'Is it the new fashion, that a pepper merchant may clothe his servants in livery, like a knight of the realm?'

I sank down thankfully on a bench, easing my painful shoulders against the wall, and raised my eyebrows enquiringly at Edmond. From the look on his face, I realised that he recognised the seal.

'It is from Master Mordon,' he said with distaste. 'I wonder what he wants of me now? Will he try to encroach on our land, as he has stolen our mill stream?'

He broke the seal carelessly so that bits of the wax cascaded on to the floor, where Rowan licked one up experimentally, chewed it as if in deep thought, then spat it out.

Edmond was frowning over the letter.

'Nay, it is not some demand or other. It is an invitation to attend his first hunt for deer in Wychwood, which is to take place next Friday. We are all invited, even the women and children. My household and guests, it says.'

'We can hunt?' Alysoun asked in amazement.

'Nay, my maid,' Edmond said. 'Some ladies will go a-hawking, but only a very few will ride to the venery. There will be a feast in the forest first, that is the custom, and you will be invited to that. Afterwards you will be able to admire all of us fine huntsmen, as we gallop about in search of the deer. He means to have a hunt *par force de chiens*.'

'From what I have heard of the man,' Margaret said dryly, 'I am surprised he has not organised a *bow and stably* hunt, to be sure of an easy kill.'

'What is that, Mistress Makepeace?' Stephen asked. 'A *bow and stably* hunt?'

'The deer are fenced into a small area, Stephen,' she said, 'and the hunters take up their positions in a line along one of the fences. Then the huntsman and his servants drive the deer past the hunters, who shoot them as they run by.' She sniffed with some contempt. 'It is no more difficult than throwing a hoop over a peg at Oxford's St Frideswide's Fair.'

'I think it sounds cruel,' Alysoun said hotly. 'The deer would have no chance to escape.'

'Well, they will on Friday,' Edmond said. 'I do not expect our new neighbour and his London friends will have much skill at true hunting in a forest like Wychwood. Not many deer will be killed.'

'Good,' Alysoun said.

'And *par force de chiens*?' Stephen was determined to have all clear. 'That is with dogs?'

'Aye,' I said. 'Lymers who track the quarry and alaunts who bring it down.'

'Will you accept the invitation, Edmond?' Margaret asked.

I could tell from her expression that Susanna must have shared with her some of what Edmond had told me that morning. I watched him debate with himself as to what decision he should take.

'Aye,' he said at last. 'I think we should go, all of us. If for nothing else, at least to have a care that Mordon and his friends wreak no more damage in Wychwood than can be helped. With Alan no longer serving as huntsman . . .'

'Ah, but remember,' I said. 'He is held to his position until he has managed this first hunt. He will take care that all is in order.'

'The villagers who will be hired to help,' Susanna said thoughtfully, 'they dislike him.'

'But he pays well,' Edmond reminded her grimly. 'More than the law permits for day wages. They will be glad to pocket his coin.'

I saw that both Alysoun and Stephen were following this exchange keenly. They might be young, but both were sharp for their age.

'Do you think it wise to take the children?' I said cautiously. 'I do not like what I have heard of the man.' I had not shared what Alan had told me of his sister, but I worried about the safety of the children near such a man.

'Oh!' Alysoun exclaimed. 'Of course we must go! I have never been to a hunt.'

'Very well,' I said, but I was determined to pass on a warning to Margaret and Susanna about the man Mordon, so that they could keep a close watch on the children during the day of the hunt. They must not be allowed to wander off on their own. It should not be difficult to keep them in check, with warnings of being run down by the galloping horses.

In the days remaining before the hunt, the field of oats was still in too poor a state to allow any cutting, so we spent an exhausting time threshing the wheat. The roughly separated grain was shovelled into heaps to await a day with a good winnowing wind, when it could be separated from the chaff. The straw we began to build into a stack in one of the barns, ready for use during the winter. The women and children spent the time picking more beans for drying, and in the afternoon of Thursday set to and baked raised pies, plum cakes, and custard tarts to take to the hunt breakfast the next day.

'I'll not be beholden to Master Mordon for our food,' Susanna had said briskly as we finished dinner. 'No doubt he will provide lavishly, him with his London cook, but I have no wish to appear a pauper, dependent on his alms.'

I made no answer to this. It is of course the obligation of the host to provide the hunt breakfast, but I could understand Susanna's reservations.

We returned to the threshing in the afternoon, all of us with aching shoulders and backs, but it was a task that must be done. Best to do as much as we could while we were here to help. Alan had joined us, and several of the day labourers, so we had made good progress with the wheat, when Edmond called a halt.

As we were crossing the yard for our usual sousing at the well, Geoffrey Carter drove up to the farm.

Edmond frowned. 'I wonder what is to-do,' he said. 'I am expecting nothing by cart. He will be come from Oxford, I'm thinking.'

Jordain and Philip exchanged worried glances. Word from Oxford might mean unwanted news for either of them. Yet when Geoffrey jumped down from the cart, it was to me he crossed.

'I've a letter for you, Master Elyot,' he said, reaching into his scrip and groping about until he found what he was looking for.

Had Walter a problem at the shop? I wondered. He would not open while we were away, but he would keep a watch over all. Perhaps the storm we had suffered here had caused problems in Oxford, though my premises lay well away from the areas prone to flooding from the two rivers. The roof was sound enough. Still, like Jordain and Philip, I felt a slight tremor of worry.

'Ah, here 'tis,' Geoffrey said, 'I knew it was somewhere.'

He handed me what seemed more a packet than a letter, the outer layer consisting of good quality parchment, sealed with a device that seemed somehow familiar, though I could not at once place it.

The writing, however, I knew. It was addressed to 'Master Nicholas Elyot, to be sent by the hand of Mistress Farringdon, St Mildred Street, Oxford'.

I found myself flushing, and slipped the packet into

my own scrip.

'I thank you, Geoffrey,' I said, giving him a silver penny for his trouble. 'Mistress Farringdon gave it to you, did she?'

'Aye. She said she had received it but two or three days before, by a carter from the south. That would be Jim Wangate, I'd guess. He covers those places south of Oxford. Anyways, she knew I'd be coming this way, so she give it me to bring you. No need to pay me, she did that already.'

He held out the penny, but I shook my head.

'Keep it, for ale money, or ribbons for your wife.'

'Will you step inside?' Edmond said.

'Nay,' he said, 'I'm away home, to settle Ned here before supper.' He slapped his horse's shoulder affectionately. 'He's needing a good feed of oats. They told me as I came through the village that there's to be a hunt tomorrow. That new man planning to show us all how 'tis done, is he?'

Edmond laughed. 'We shall see. Will you be there?'

'Aye, and most of the village.' Geoffrey grinned. 'Those that aren't paid to serve will be watching the sport. Happen we might learn a thing or two.'

He climbed up on to the seat at the front of the cart and clicked his tongue to the horse Ned. As he headed away down the farm track, we could hear him whistling.

'Seems we'll have quite an audience tomorrow, then,' Edmond said ruefully. 'Not that either of my horses are built like noblemen's hunters. I've no wish to make a fool of myself before the whole village.'

'I daresay the village will be hunting too,' I said. 'Alan will give them permission, even if Mordon fails to do so.'

Edmond possessed two horses, mainly used for hauling carts about the farm, or sometimes when one of the family needed to ride into Burford. Edmond would be riding one tomorrow. James and Thomas had spun a coin for the other, and James had won.

'Aye, well,' I said, 'Rufus is no aristocratic steed either, but he is sturdy and untiring. That's what is needed in the hunt, not some delicate mount who will flag in half an hour.'

'That's very true. Let us clean up before supper. The others have got ahead of us.'

Indeed, the others, seeing that the carter was no concern of theirs, were already clustered about the well.

'Will you not open your letter?' Edmond asked, curiously.

'Not while I am so dirty,' I said, affecting a casual air. 'I recognise the writing and I do not think it can be anything needing urgent attention.'

All through our ablutions, followed by supper and a time sitting together in the evening, I was conscious of the packet in my scrip. It was with difficulty that I managed to stop myself slipping my hand into my scrip and fingering it.

At last, however, we all withdrew to our bedchambers, earlier than usual, for we needed to be up betimes in the morning. Most would need to walk to the manor, save the few of us who would ride to the hunt: myself, Edmond and James, together with Philip and the two students. Jordain had been offered Edmond's second horse, but politely declined.

'I can amble about on horseback,' he said, 'but I am not the man to go galloping about through woodland, wielding a bow and a spear. You must hold me excused, else I should finish by tangling you all in my poor horsemanship and probably cause someone a hurt.'

When at last I was able to retire to my small chamber under the eaves, I waited until I had shed my clothes – still prickly with bits of straw – and donned my night shift. Then I sat down on my bed, with a rush dip standing on a stool at my side, and drew out the packet Geoffrey Carter had brought for me.

Using my small knife, I lifted the seal. It would be that of Sir Anthony Thorgold. I had not consciously remembered it, but I must have seen it when I visited him earlier in the year, to appeal for his help on Emma's behalf. The beautiful flowing script on the outside was unmistakeably Emma's hand.

I unfolded the outer layer carefully, and discovered that there were several sheets inside. I unfolded these in turn, and flattened them out on the bed beside me.

Three were drawings.

One showed her grandfather's house. It was a meticulously detailed drawing, including every window, corner and crenellation. She had even managed to give an impression of depth, a trick only the best artists can achieve. The grounds around the house were also shown, though in less detail, the trees lightly sketched, so that the house took prominence. The whole was done simply in black ink, with nothing but thick and thin lines, and some hatching, to give texture. Of course, at her grandfather's home she was unlikely to have coloured inks, although his own scribes might possess red ink for initial capitals in legal documents.

In the second picture, the estate's servants were occupied with their tasks in the farm yard. It was a busy scene, with much to examine. A woman collecting eggs, while hens pecked around her feet. A man sharpening a scythe on a circular grindstone like the one in Edmond's barn. One maid milking a cow while another carried a bucket toward the house, just glimpsed at the end of the picture. Two lads wrestling with an escaping pig. A puppy (who looked remarkably like Rowan) about to trip up a pompous man, perhaps the estate steward, who could not see it over the ample swell of his well-fed stomach. At the edge of the scene, on the opposite side to the house, a recognisable tall man with a quill behind his ear was looking on in some bewilderment. I grinned. I hoped that I did not always look so bemused.

The third picture was a harvest scene, men and women bent over, weary with labour, the field half cut, but still stretching away in the distance, with so much bone-aching work still to do. Two rabbits and a hare were bursting out of the field, and almost out of the picture, at the very front.

I looked at the three pictures, laid side by side. There was no denying that she possessed a remarkable talent. How unfortunate that her sex and her rank prevented her from employing it.

As a kind of self-discipline, I had kept the fourth sheet, the letter, till last. Now I unfolded it and tilted it toward the light of the rush dip.

Dear friend, it began. I smiled. She had chosen her opening wisely.

As you will see, I have arrived at my grandfather's house without mishap and find him well. He wishes me to send you hearty greetings. There is little for me to occupy myself with here, and so I have been wielding my pen and ink to pass the time. As evidence of my humble skills as a scrivener and illuminator, I am sending you three of my drawings.

I laughed aloud – 'humble skills' indeed.

Like any poor suitor for employment, I hope that they may serve to recommend me for a position as scrivener, should the house of Master Elyot, bookseller of Oxford, be willing to engage me.

It is my hope that you and your family find yourselves in good health and that the harvest proceeds apace, as it does here.

Your friend, Emma Thorgold.

I laid the letter down and stared across into the shadows of the room. Now what, exactly, did she mean by this?

Chapter five

After a restless night, I rose before dawn, to a chorus of birdsong. Although it was well past the season for the pairing of bird with bird, it seemed the winged population of the farm welcomed the aftermath of the storm, the oppressive heat banished, earth and heaven washed clean. I dressed hurriedly, but with some care. I had no wish to appear too rustic in the eyes of Edmond's new neighbour and thus to bring disgrace on him, but I had no garments with me that might pass muster with this Master Mordon and his grandiose ideas of his own importance. I did, however, have a pair of good russet hose and a dull green cotte, slit at the sides for riding. Lord de Vere had always advocated clothing for the hunt which blended well with the woodland, since it was less likely to alarm the quarry. He would have approved of my choice, I was sure.

In the kitchen I found only Margaret, Susanna, and one of the maidservants, busy shaping the morning's loaves.

'You are too early, Nicholas,' Margaret said. 'There will be no breakfast for another hour.'

'That is no matter,' I said. 'I did not expect it. I have remembered that one of Rufus's shoes seemed somewhat loose. I want to take him down to Bertred Godsmith in the village before riding him to the hunt. I've no wish for him to suffer harm. The shoe might come half adrift and cause him to stumble or even fall. I should be back before we need to set out.'

'Aye,' Susanna said, 'Bertred is likely already astir. He will have been summoned to the hunt.'

This was what I had counted on. It is always wise to have a blacksmith at hand during a hunt, in case any of the mounts needed care. Like many of his calling, Bertred Godsmith was also something of a horse doctor, and the demands of the hunt can often prove a strain on the horses, with cuts and bruising, or pulled muscles.

In the barn I saddled Rufus quickly, for he was always patient and biddable, and as I led him outside into the yard the first flush of dawn was brightening the sky. There was very little cloud, nothing but a few wisps, almost transparent, though the heat we had suffered before the storm still appeared to be held at bay. As I rode down the track to the village, I was surrounded by more birdsong, and the trees, which had previously worn the tired droop of late summer, now gleamed, with every leaf freshly washed.

The smithy stood almost in the centre of the village, across the green from the church. The green itself held a small muddy pond, where a few ducks were floating, as if half asleep, and someone's goat was tethered nearby, tearing at the grass and regarding me sideways from a cold yellow eye.

Susanna was right. There was smoke rising from the cottage beside the smithy, and from the smithy fire itself. As I slid from the saddle, an overgrown boy peered from the open door of the smithy and Bertred himself emerged from the cottage, a chunk of cold pie in his hand.

'You be about mighty early, Master Elyot,' he said, through a mouthful. 'Need me, do you?'

'Aye. We are bidden to the hunt today, and I'm not sure about the horse's off fore.' I nodded toward Rufus. 'He's not mine and I don't want him coming to harm. Will you take a look?'

'I will, surely.'

He stuffed the rest of the pie in his mouth and led Rufus into the smithy doorway. The boy went to the bellows and began pumping, to raise the heat of the forge. I took over Rufus's head, holding the reins close under his jaw, so that he would not twist about and turn his head, while Bertred donned a thick leather apron, its front pocket bulging with the tools of his trade.

As the smith clamped Rufus's off forefoot between his knees, I tried to make out whether the shoe was indeed loose, but could not see past his broad shoulder.

'Was I right?' I asked.

'Aye, 'tis loose, right enough, and worn down on the outside edge. It will be setting him off balance afore long. I can fix it firmer. Or I can fit him with a new shoe. Which is it to be? If he's not your horse, mebbe you'll not be wanting to spend the money.'

'Fit a new shoe,' I said. 'I don't want him going lame. As well as the hunt, he has to carry me back to Oxford. Best check the other three shoes as well.'

Bertred let Rufus's foot drop and set about hunting through his half-made shoes to find one which could be shaped to fit. When he had found one to his satisfaction, he seized it with his long-handled tongs and began to heat it in the fire. Soon there was the ring of hammer on anvil, followed by the throat-catching smell of singeing hoof as he shaped and tested the new shoe, finally securing it with nails, driven through the side of the hoof, the excess length snipped off and bent flat. Then he checked the other shoes.

'They'll do,' he said, 'but you mebbe should let me take another look before you ride back to Oxford. When do you leave?'

'Oh, not for another week at least,' I said. 'We are here lending a hand with the harvest.'

'Aye. I heard.'

Of course. Everyone in the village would know.

'Will you be at the hunt?' I asked.

He grimaced. 'Aye, the new *lord* has commanded me.' He gave the word the same sarcastic emphasis I had heard from others. 'I owe him no service, whatever he may think, but I'll be there.'

Like Geoffrey Carter, Bertred Godsmith was a free

man, master of his own living, indeed like many others in recent years, even in small villages like Leighton-under-Wychwood. Fewer and fewer villagers were held in villeinage to an overlord, tied to customary labour and boon days. The de Veres had respected this and paid the blacksmith for his services. If the new man at the manor did not understand the way of it, he would soon learn his lesson, for Bertred was a big man and proud of his independence. He would not see his rights trampled under foot.

I paid for the new shoe, and told Bertred I would see him later at the hunt. He had a small portable forge and anvil that he would take with him, in case any emergency farrier work was needed. As I rode away I saw the boy – who had spoken never a word – pick up the old shoe and throw it on a heap of scrap iron. From time to time, Bertred would melt this down to make new shoes in various sizes, to be shaped and trimmed like the one he had fitted to Rufus.

Back at the farm I found everyone at breakfast, despite the fact that we would soon be enjoying a lavish meal in the forest. I ate little. Ever since I was a boy I have felt somewhat sick before the excitement and danger of a hunt, for in truth it could be dangerous. A blow to the head from a low-hanging branch when you were galloping at speed, or a heavy fall, or any other of a number of accidents could kill you. None of us, however, mentioned these possibilities before the children. I collected my hunting spear, my bow, and a quiver of arrows from my bedchamber, where I stored them when I was in Oxford, having no need for them in town. I tested the bowstring and arrows, and checked that I had a spare string. All seemed in order, but I decided to leave the spear behind. Unlike some, I never carried a crossbow to the hunt, finding it too heavy and unwieldy on horseback.

Soon after this we set out, all but Edmond's two little girls, Megan and Lora, who were deemed too young to risk in the forest and were left behind with all the maid servants, save the one girl, Elga, who would help carry some of the food we were providing for the hunt breakfast. All the horses had saddlebags filled with the less fragile items, while the rest of the food was placed in baskets brought by the women. Philip lifted Stephen before him on to his horse, to save the boy the long walk. I thought our lively procession would make a fine subject for one of Emma's drawings as we made our way down to the village and the turn to the manor house. The girl Elga was alight with excitement, not being much more than a child herself.

'I have never seen a hunt, Master Elyot,' she said as we set off. 'Imagine! That I should be off to a hunt in the royal forest!'

I smiled at her. She would enjoy the hunt breakfast in the open greenwood, but I knew she was unlikely to see much of the actual pursuit and killing of deer.

I had left Emma's drawings and letter behind, slipped between the pages of one of the books I had brought for Stephen to read. He was already engrossed in the other. By the time he moved on to the second one, I should need to find another hiding place, for I was reluctant to leave them lying about, for anyone to see.

What did Emma mean, about employment as a scrivener? She knew I could not employ her. Was she merely teasing? Probably. Although I should have preferred to see her face as she said it. I should have preferred to see her in any case. Although she was but over the border of south Oxfordshire, she might have been in Cornwall or Northumberland, she seemed so far away. How should I reply? It would be easy enough to send a letter – by Geoffrey Carter to Mistress Farringdon, who could then despatch it by the other carter to Emma's grandfather's house – but I could not imagine what I could say in response to such an odd letter.

My troubled thoughts were interrupted by our arrival at the road leading to the manor. As I had noticed on the evening we arrived, the neglected and overgrown bushes had been cut back, so that the way up to the manor house looked much as it had done in Yves de Vere's time. We were to gather at the manor and meet our host, then proceed, along with his household and guests, into Wychwood by a path which led out from behind the house into the fringes of the forest.

'Do you suppose we will take our meal in the usual place?' Edmond had ridden up beside me. 'That clearing by the stream?'

'Probably.' I nodded. 'I do not suppose Master Mordon could have found it for himself, but if Alan Wodville is in charge of the hunt, he will have marked it out for him. There is nowhere else so well suited.'

As we drew near the manor, we could see the signs of busy activity all about both house and stables. I was curious about those 'improvements' Geoffrey Carter had mentioned when he had come to Oxford. Most likely they were mostly withindoors, but I could see that the rampant ivy, which had climbed over the outside of the building, even fingering its way into the windows, had all been cleared away. The daub between the timber framework had been freshly lime washed, and there was new mortar between the bricks of the chimneys, all of which were smoking, even on this August day, a sign of careless wealth. The stables and other outbuildings had likewise been restored and newly thatched, so the man Mordon had done something worthwhile at least. Left as they had been by the absentee heir, both house and outbuildings would soon have begun to collapse past saving.

I noticed Alan standing amongst a group of hunt servants, gesticulating and looking worried. He would be anxious that the hunt should go well, even if he was carrying on his duties by force. It had always been a matter of pride with his family that the hunts from the manor should be conducted in a seemly fashion, with good sport, a successful haul of game, and no more than a few minor hurts amongst the hunters. With a crowd of unknown and untried strangers to be managed, it was little wonder that he looked worried.

Edmond, Philip, James, the students, and I dismounted as we reached the house, and Philip lifted Stephen down. The womenfolk, Thomas, and Jordain, following more slowly on foot with the children, would be here before long. We nodded to friends amongst the crowd – some from the village, some from neighbouring manors. It seemed Master Mordon had sent out his invitations widely. Another reason for Alan to look worried. Too many horsemen crowded together, galloping through the dense woodland, was a likely source of collisions, falls, and injury. The new man had little sense of such dangers, it seemed, preferring to flaunt his right to the chase before as many people as possible.

A well-built man, of middle years, in a lawyer's black gown, came hurrying down the steps from the house and strode over to Alan, where he seemed to be giving him orders. Alan stood perfectly still, his face blank, then he nodded once, briefly, and turned away. There appeared to be no sign of our host.

'Time we were on our way,' Edmond murmured in my ear, as the others of our party came up. 'What is the delay?'

I shook my head and shrugged. 'I saw a party of servants leaving, loaded down with cushions and rugs, and a handcart of plates and flagons, so I suppose they are gone to set up the hunt breakfast.'

'But we cannot make a start without our host. Where is the man?'

As if in answer, the door to the manor house was opened again, and after a pause, a man stepped forth. He was a big man, but heavy with fat, not muscle. In his middle years, perhaps fifty, with the oily, well fed – not to say over fed – look of a successful merchant. I hoped he had a strong horse, to bear such a weight.

But what drew the eye, and caused me to clap my hand over my mouth to hide my incredulous grin, was not so much the man as his clothes. He had dressed for the hunt in purple hose and the kind of shoes with exaggerated pointed toes such as foolish gallants half his age could sometimes be seen wearing, strolling about Oxford, instead of the sturdy riding boots such as the rest of us wore. His long houppelande was of so bright a crimson it hurt the eye, and was trimmed at neck, hem, and trailing sleeves with braid of gold thread, beneath which a shirt of fine white silk could be glimpsed. He wore a gold chain about his neck, and his hands were heavy with jewelled rings. Crowning all was an enormous capuchon of bright yellow, the long liripipe twisted atop his head like the nest of some monstrous bird.

He paused at the top of the steps that all might gape in admiration.

Despite the hand clasped over my mouth, I could not entirely suppress my snort of laughter. Behind me, I could hear Guy and Giles sniggering, while Edmond had been obliged to turn his back, and Philip was gazing intently at the sky, as though he was concentrating on some sight of great interest, far above the smoke of the manor chimneys.

'He is proposing to hunt, dressed like *that*?' Giles whispered.

'He will fright all the deer,' Guy said, smothering a laugh. 'We shall never be able to draw near enough for a clean shot.'

Edmond had his face under control now. He took me by the elbow, urging me forward as Mordon descended the steps in a stately fashion. Seeing him now, as it were, on a level with the servants milling about, I guessed that the elaborate headdress was intended to make up for his lack of height.

'What's afoot with you?' I muttered to Edmond.

'I'd best present you to our host,' he said, 'before we set off.'

We made our way through the crowd as more people descended the steps from the house. By their equally unsuitable dress, these were his guests come from London. There were more women than men amongst them.

'She that is wearing the dark blue cotehardie,'

Edmond whispered, 'that is his wife.'

The woman must have been twenty years younger than her husband, nay more, and would have been pretty, had her face not been marred by a discontented frown. This was one person who seemed not to be looking forward to a day in the greenwood. At her elbow was a young man of her own age, perhaps filling something of the position of a squire to this Mordon who was no knight. He might have been a merchant's clerk, although there was nothing clerkly about him. It appeared he was to take part in the hunt, since he carried a bow. And to my surprise, so did the woman.

When we reached Master Mordon, Edmond presented me, and I bowed – ironically rather more deeply than his rank merited. He gave a curt nod, his eyes passing over me dismissively, and seeking some object of more interest over my shoulder. In spite of myself, I found I was flushing with annoyance. Edmond noticed, and patted my arm.

'Even a nod,' he said with a wry smile as the man moved away, 'is more than he affords to some.'

Herded into some sort of order by Alan Wodville and his assistants, people began to mount and ride round the side of the house to the track leading into Wychwood. Alan rode ahead, no doubt to ensure that all was in order for the meal. A huge stallion was led forward from the stables and Mordon heaved himself inelegantly astride. His houppelande was so long it seemed it might cause the horse to stumble. He ignored his wife, who was helped on to her palfrey by the young man. Did she intend merely to ride to the meal, or did horse and bow mean that she planned to join the hunt?

'What do you think?' I asked Edmond, as we mounted and prepared to follow. 'Will the lady ride to the hunt?'

He shrugged. 'All I know is that she comes from a noble family in Northamptonshire, so she may have been bred up to hunt. In some of these great families a few of the bolder women ride to the chase. It is said that Mordon bought her of her father, wanting an aristocratic alliance for his descendents. His first wife died of a fever, and this one has given him no children, so it seems he made a bad bargain.'

Alan's nephew Rob appeared from the direction of the outbuildings, accompanied by the eager baying of the alaunts, held on a tight leash by their handlers. They, at least, were eager for the day's sport. The tracking lymers, trained to silence, padded alongside.

As we rode in our ill assorted crowd to the forest, a flock of crows rose squawking with indignation from the trees. A tawny owl, disturbed from his daytime rest, swooped across in front of Mordon's horse, caused it to shy and swerve. He hauled it back with a vicious jerk, and landed a stinging blow from his whip across its hindquarters. It jumped and fretted, but was so savagely held back, its chin nearly touching its chest, that it could not move. The man rode like a fat porker, but it seemed he was master of the big stallion.

It was several years since I had been in Wychwood. The last time I had ridden to the hunt here had been in Yves de Vere's time, before the Death, when I had brought Elizabeth and Alysoun to visit my parents. Alysoun must have been about a year old then. Despite the recent neglect of the manor house, the nearby woodland had been cared for, and it was clear that this was not simply since the arrival of the new man. Undergrowth had been kept down, smaller trees removed to give light to the rest, so that they should produce fine straight timber. The manor's hereditary forester was a cousin of Alan's, and I knew that in the past the two families had worked together to maintain the woodland at its best for both the production of timber and the breeding of game. I wondered whether the forester still retained his position under the new regime. Perhaps his post came instead under the royal warden of the entire forest. Rights of chase in the forest also carried responsibilities for those who held them, but the whole forest belonged to the king.

The path through the outer fringes of the forest was a

wide area of turf, and the trees here were widely spaced, straight and well grown, forming an aisle like the pillars in a church, but at a short distance from the path, on either side, there were occasional thickets of bushy undergrowth. A townsman like Mordon might suppose that they were a sign of neglect on the part of the forester, but in fact these clumps of untrimmed bushes had been left deliberately for the wild boar, who would use them for covert.

There were still some boar in Wychwood, though they had been over hunted in recent years. It was not unknown for the king to send out orders to the royal huntsmen to provide several hundred deer and boar, to be produced at court, with very little warning. In such a case, any noble who had rights of chase in a royal forest must give way to the king's men. For some reason I do not understand, the herds of deer seemed to recover quite quickly from these massive depredations, but the boar did not. All over England, it was said, the boar were declining. As for wolves, I had not heard of any being caught in Wychwood in my lifetime.

Not far into the wood, the trees drew back, opening out to reveal a wide, grassy clearing as neat and tended as a lady's bower. The turf was short – surely it must have been scythed – and at the far side of the clearing a swift, chattering stream ran silver over pebbles, eventually emerging from the wood near the manor house to join the debatable mill stream. Off to the left side of the clearing, a temporary paddock for the horses had been created with withy hurdles. In the centre, the manor servants had set up one large trestle table, covered with a cloth of white linen, while several more cloths had been spread on the short grass, surrounded with cushions. The most favoured guests would sit at the table on stools, while the rest of us (amongst whom I included myself) would sit on the ground.

There was even a fire, sheltered from draughts by an iron screen, where a cook's boy was stirring something in a pot suspended from a framework of iron spikes and hooks, while other servants were laying out dishes – silver for the table, pewter elsewhere – and linen napkins. Flasks stood along each cloth, surrounded with silver or pewter cups. These were embossed with some sort of device, though I was too far away to make it out.

Mordon had already dismounted and was shouting orders as a groom ran up to take his horse, which had simply been left standing, his hooves practically on one of the table cloths. We followed the groom and turned our horses into the enclosure. I noticed that Stephen was looking about him, wide eyed.

I grinned. 'I hope you are hungry, Stephen,' I said. 'Look over there.'

Two more handcarts were being trundled up, piled high with food of every sort, from fancy breads to dishes of delicacies like roasted larks on skewers.

'Look,' Stephen said, his voice lowered to a whisper, 'there is even a *swan*!'

There was, indeed, a swan.

All swans in England are heavily protected, most reserved for the king, but I have heard that the livery companies in London have the right to some.

'It must have been sent from London,' I said to Stephen. 'In the hot weather we have been suffering, it may not be fresh. I should have a care, if you are offered any. The meat may be rotten.'

I doubted whether a lame child, clearly of no importance in the eyes of a man like Mordon, would have any chance to taste the roasted bird, which was being carried with great ceremony to the centre of the table. As is the way with these ostentatious dishes, it had been made to look as much like the live bird as possible. The neck had been twisted with wire to hold it upright, the wings had been pinned back on to its sides, and the feathers painstakingly reaffixed to its body – by what means I am not sure. The attempt was not altogether successful. Perhaps it had suffered in being transported from the manor kitchen to the woods. The neck drooped sideways, the head hanging at an unnatural angle, one of the dead eyes turned skyward. A patch of feathers had been rubbed off, and one of the servants was attempting to restore them. I thought the whole thing repulsive.

Fortunately our own party arrived with our contributions to the meal, and these more humble (but at least edible) provisions were soon laid out on one of the cloths spread on the turf. Food from the manor was also provided for us, but I noticed that some of the other guests, come from Shipton and Ashton, had also taken the precaution of bringing their own supplies. Those of highest rank were soon seated at the table, but their households joined us on the cushions.

The hunting dogs had been tied up near the horses and were making a fair clamour, for certainly they must be able to smell the food. No huntsman, however, will feed the dogs before a hunt, for he has no wish for them to lose interest in pursuing the quarry. A sleek, well fed dog is of no use at the hunt.

'Well,' said Margaret, as we passed around the pies and cakes we had brought with us, 'this brings back memories of times past, does it not, Nicholas?'

'Aye,' I said, washing down a mouthful of game pie with some of Mordon's wine. 'But I never remember such crowds of people in Yves de Vere's day. Nor such elaborate fare. And clothing.'

She grinned. 'Perhaps we are under dressed for such a grand gathering.'

'He will scare every deer from here to Burford,' Giles grumbled. 'Is the man quite mad?'

'Best keep your voice down, lad,' Edmond said, for there had been a brief lull in the chatter and it was possible Mordon might have heard.

'It is Alan who will be fretting most,' Susanna said.

'Aye.' Jordain set down his wine cup. 'I am thinking we might have done better to spend the time trying to salvage the oat crop.'

I studied my own cup, trying to make out the device.

It seemed to be a coat-of-arms. Had Mordon earned the right to one? It appeared to depict a crude set of scales and some anonymous blobs. Peppercorns, perhaps.

Edmond shook his head. 'I must live neighbour to the man, Jordain. I do not want to risk offending him by refusing his invitation to the hunt. There is still the matter of the mill stream to be settled.'

'It seems you are not the only one with matters to be settled,' Philip said, 'from all I have heard. Dismissed servants. Free men threatened with villeinage. Villagers forced to labour they do not owe, yet forbidden the right to glean. Charges at the mill doubled. Disputes over land holdings and rents. Maidens assaulted.'

I glanced at him, surprised. Had he heard about Alan's sister? Or were there other assaults? During our days of field work it seemed Philip had kept his ears open to the villagers' talk.

'Even his own party seems somewhat discontent,' Susanna murmured, nodding her head toward the table.

I turned and glanced where she indicated. Most of the neighbouring gentry and even the party from London looked bored or contemptuous, eating in silence while Mordon held forth, waving one of those skewered larks to emphasis some point. Hardly anyone else seemed to be speaking, although Mordon's wife and the young man had their heads together at the end of the table.

Despite the pleasant day, sunny but not unduly warm, despite the elaborate preparations and the ostentatious food, an uneasy atmosphere hung over the hunt breakfast. Matters would improve, I was sure, once the hunt itself was underway. There would be none of this awkward politeness barely covering an under-layer of discomfort. Once we were mounted and the tracking lymers were set to their task, all our minds would be turned to the pursuit of the quarry. It was the very start of the deer season and Alan had promised us good sport.

As people finished eating and drinking they stirred, rose from the stools and cushions, and began to mill about.

I noticed that the favoured guests from manors round about lost no time in leaving the table and joining their own households or seeking out friends amongst the local people, leaving the London party somewhat isolated. Sir Henry Talbot, who held a manor not far from Burford, made his way to us, kissing Margaret and Susanna, and bowing to Edmond and me. He had been a lifelong friend of my father, never standing upon rank.

'Well, Edmond,' he said, 'how goes the harvest with you? Word is, you had some difficulty securing enough day labourers.'

Nothing remains long a secret in the country.

'Better than I had hoped,' Edmond said. 'Nicholas has brought a party of friends to lend their aid. Without them I would have been sore pressed.'

'Hard times, hard times,' Sir Henry said, 'ever since the Death.' He grinned at me. 'So you are not grown too fine in your Oxford ways, Nicholas, to swing a scythe?'

I grinned back and held out my hands to him. The ink stains had been augmented by blisters and calluses raised by scythe and flail.

'Nay, Sir Henry, I have not forgot the skills of my father and grandfather. Without wheat, who shall eat bread? And without barley, who shall drink ale?'

'Aye, that's a good lad!' He clapped me on the shoulder. I suppose to him I still seemed the boy he remembered. He lowered his voice. 'And what think you of this new man? I've heard tales. Causing trouble, is he?'

Edmond shrugged. 'He has yet to learn our country ways, I suppose, but, aye, he has been causing trouble in many quarters.'

'And as for his dress!'

Sir Henry rolled his eyes, and we all laughed.

'One of the students fears he will fright away all the game,' I said.

'Aye, he will, and provide a clear target in that bright red houppelande.'

Sir Henry himself was dressed modestly in similar

clothes to my own, brown and green, like any experienced hunter. He looked around now.

'Where has the fellow gone? I begin to think we shall never be on our way. Sitting over that fool of a roast swan while he discoursed on the fame of his pepper shop.'

Sir Henry's tone conveyed a country gentleman's contempt for such an occupation as the selling of pepper.

'Did you eat of the swan, sir?' I asked, curious.

'Never fear! I like nothing better than a roast goose I've shot myself that morning over my own marshes, but some rancid fowl stuck all about with feathers–! This is a hunt breakfast, not a meal at court. And at court at least the bird would be fresh.'

He shrugged. 'I have come for a day's sport, with but my one manservant. Tomorrow I'll ride home to watch over my own harvest. And there, you may be sure, we eat no fancy delicacies, all show without and rotten within.'

I looked around to see whether I could spot Master Mordon, but that yellow turban and eye-blinding houppelande were nowhere to be seen.

'Well, I think I shall fetch my horse,' I said, 'to be ready as soon as we are able to make a start. I suppose Mordon wants to lead the hunt.'

'That is what he has been saying.' Sir Henry shrugged. 'I fear your student has the right of it. If he leads, we shall trail along behind, like the tail of a blazing comet, through a wood quite devoid of game.'

Suddenly a scream pierced the peaceful woodland, and the idle conversations stopped abruptly as everyone turned toward the direction of the sound. It seemed to come from the opposite side of the clearing from the horse paddock. The handcarts, baskets and bundles had been left there, out of the way of the meal. Alan Wodville was nearest and started forward, but Edmond and I were close behind, followed by Sir Henry and Philip.

'An adder, do you think?' Edmond said, as we ran after Alan. 'There could be little else here to fright a woman. No boar would come near, not with all these people and our noise.'

It might be an adder. But most countrywomen would not be so frightened by a small snake as to scream like that. The London women might be, but they were all still clustered by the table.

As we neared the carts, there was a thrashing amongst the bushes, sounds of a man cursing, and a whimpering cry from a girl. It was clear enough what was afoot even before young Elga burst out, her hair tumbled, her face streaked with tears. She was clutching her gown at her throat, but we could all see that it was ripped down to her waist.

I grabbed one of the table cloths which was lying in a cart and wrapped it around her, while Edmond steadied her with an arm about her shoulders. He was white with anger.

'Who did this, lass?' he demanded, but the girl only wept the more.

'I have a shrewd guess,' Alan said, pushing through the bushes.

There was the sound of a struggle, accompanied by more swearing, then Alan dragged Mordon out into the open.

'You bastard!' Alan said, shaking the man till his teeth rattled and his carefully folded liripipe tumbled down about his ears. 'Not content with my sister, you would defile every helpless maid you can lay your hand upon.'

Mordon was red in the face, but every mite as angry. 'I'll see you strung up for assault, you churl!' he said. 'Take your hands off me.'

'Assault!' Alan shouted. 'It is you who have assaulted this maid, and this time there are witnesses.'

Mordon spat contemptuously, barely missing Alan's face. The man's lowbred origins were revealing themselves.

'Her? 'he said. 'She's nothing but a worthless serving wench. She probably feels the honour of attention from her lord.'

'You are not her lord.' Edmond's tone was steady,

but cold. 'She is free, and a member of *my* household.'

'Enough,' Sir Henry said. 'You have misbehaved grossly, sir, but if the day is not to be ruined for all, I think we should say no more now. You will apologise later to the maid.'

Mordon glowered at him, but looking round at all of us he clamped his jaw shut.

Few had followed us all the way to the carts, although we were the cynosure of all eyes. Edmond led Elga over to our womenfolk, and Sir Henry was urging Mordon back to his own party when the man whirled about and jabbed a finger at Alan.

'Do not think I will forget this, fellow.' His face was still suffused with the red flush of anger, although the comical disarray of his headgear robbed the threat of some of its impact.

When I joined our household, the women were discussing what was best to do.

'I will take you home,' Susanna said, her arms around the girl, who was still sobbing, but more quietly now.

'Nay,' Beatrice said. 'You should remain. Your absence might cause comment. I am a stranger here. I will take Elga home and we will have a quiet afternoon together. We can salt more of the beans, can we not, Elga?'

The girl gulped and nodded, and they set off together, back along the grassy ride, Elga still wrapped in the linen cloth.

Edmond wiped his face. 'Jesu! That was unpleasant. What was that about Alan's sister?'

As we walked toward the paddock, I gave him a brief account of what Alan had told me about his sister. Since he had shouted it out before all of us, I felt I no longer needed to keep silence about it.

'That child!' Edmond exclaimed. 'She is even younger than Elga.'

'Best we get to horse.' Sir Henry had come up behind us. 'Mordon has sent for his stallion. After the hunt, I will speak to him further.'

Edmond gave a grim nod, but we said no more about the matter, busying ourselves with checking our horses' girths, and mounting, ready to set off on the hunt. Rufus was no hunter, but he could sense the excitement in the air, snorting and tossing his head in anticipation.

The clearing was now a mass of circling horses, all afire and nervy. The women and children, and the men who were not riding to the chase, had withdrawn to the edge of the open space to allow the horses more room and all remnants of the meal had been cleared away. Alan was astride his powerful stallion, his most treasured possession, and had sounded his horn to warn that we would shortly be off. A servant handed Mordon a horn on an embroidered baldric, which he slung over his shoulder and across his chest. At a distance it looked as though it was bound with gold, but surely it must be brass. There was the wink of red stones in the sunlight filtering slantwise through the trees, but probably they were no more than coloured glass. Certainly the man had demonstrated that he was rich, but who would lavish real jewels on a mere hunting horn? I hoped he knew how to use it. If he sounded calls that conflicted with those Alan would use to control the hunting party, it must lead to confusion and chaos.

A large number of villagers had now joined the party of observers, slipping silently into the woods and forming an outer circle beyond those who had been invited to the breakfast. Some carried their own hunting gear of bow or spear. I had already noticed some villagers amongst the servants at the meal, and others acting as hunt assistants to Alan. One of these I recognised as Matt Grantham, the man Mordon was attempting to reduce to villeinage on account of some of the land he held. Over near the empty paddock, Bertred Godsmith and his boy were setting up his temporary forge, ready if they should be needed.

'There are too many of us,' I muttered to Philip, whose hired horse was shifting uneasily from side to side, next to me.

'Aye.' He looked worried. 'We shall never be able to

keep together, and even if we do, there will be injuries.'

'Well, let us ease our way to the front,' I said. 'If we can get clear of the crowd, we shall have a better chance.'

He nodded and we began to edge our horses through the throng until we were quite close behind Mordon and Alan. I was surprised to see Mordon's wife nearby, and the young man still in close attendance.

'I see Lady Edith does intend to ride to the chase.' Sir Henry had joined us, no doubt with the same intention of keeping to the forefront, clear of any unskilled riders. 'She's a bold woman, so I've heard.'

'Who is the man always with her?' I asked. 'Do you know?'

'Some cousin or other of Mordon's. Inherited a small estate in Buckinghamshire and so thinks he outranks Mordon, though 'tis Mordon holds the purse strings. What's the fellow's name?'

He scratched under his hat with the butt of his whip. 'Dunston? Dunstable? Aye, that's it. John Dunstable. His great-uncle was squire to one of the last king's knights.'

That could mean almost anything. The history of our present king's father and his knights was best forgotten.

Alan's nephew now made his way to the front, herding the hunt dogs and their handlers past Mordon's great stallion, who shifted uneasily as the dogs brushed past his legs. Some of the dogs were barking excitedly, but the tracking lymers, as always, were silent. The alaunts, trained to pull down a wounded beast, were making the noise, though their handlers hushed them and struck a few with the slack of the leather leads to silence them.

When all was as much in order as one might hope from such a motley gathering, Alan lifted his horn to his lips and sounded the signal, a quick double note – *To the deer! To the deer!*

The lymers, knowing the signal, leapt to the scent, their handlers running beside them. Later they might be loosed, but for now they were kept on their leads.

I leaned forward, gave Rufus his head, and we broke

into a gallop behind Mordon and Alan. The hunt had begun!

Chapter Six

Alan had been tracking the deer for the previous few days, and again early that morning. He was now leading us toward the part of the wood where the herd had last been seen. At least, he was attempting to lead us, but Mordon constantly jostled him roughly aside, his big stallion shouldering across the path and blocking Alan's way. I could hear the huntsman muttering curses under his breath, but not so quietly that Mordon would fail to hear them. He glared at the huntsman, but continued to behave aggressively, ignoring the respect due to the huntsman's skill and experience.

To begin with there was an open ride through the trees, a way which had been cleared by the forester and his servants to aid the removal of felled trees. Our whole company was able to stay more or less together as we galloped over the turf. The dogs were silent now, noses down on the scent, the only sound the dull thud of the horses' hooves on the turf and the panting of the dog handlers, running along either edge of the ride, the alaunts held back, the best of the lymers loping just ahead of Mordon and Alan. I hoped that Mordon had sufficient control of his mount to prevent him from running down the dogs and crushing them.

Sir Henry and Edmond were close beside me, but I could not see Philip now, or James or Guy. Giles was not far behind me, and riding so near to him that their horses' shoulders almost touched I saw, to my astonishment, the

Lady Edith. I had never hunted with a woman in the company before and had supposed she would have kept to the rear. Instead, she stayed with the leaders, riding astride like a man, and seemingly fearless. As I glanced over my shoulder I saw that John Dunstable was immediately behind her, and was trying to force Giles off the path. I felt a spurt of anger. Hunting is dangerous enough without playing the fool games Mordon and his man were indulging in. I wanted to shout a warning to Giles, but feared he was too far back to hear me through the thunder of the hooves.

I found that I was beginning to fall a little behind. Rufus was not built for speed and the pace set by Mordon and Alan was almost too much for him, though even so I found myself grinning with excitement at the heart-pounding gallop. In this wide avenue there were no low hanging branches, so one could give oneself up to the chase with little fear of injury. Then I became aware of some confusion ahead. The two leading horses had slowed to a stop, as had Sir Henry. The rest of us reined in, a tumble of sweating and excited horses and breathless riders. The lymers were milling about, some straining forward along the ride, others turning eagerly aside towards dense woodland, where the only way through was a zigzag route between the trees, which grew close together here.

Alan sounded the *Come back* on his horn, a series of long repeated notes. The hounds gathered about his horse as more of the hunting party caught up with us, Lady Edith and Dunstable pushing through to the front, with little concern for others. As well as the dog handlers, Alan's other assistants were taking conference with him, amongst them Matt and his brother, both carrying bows. Several of the dog handlers sank to the ground, trying to catch their breath. Mordon and Alan appeared to be arguing.

'What's to-do?' Edmond asked Sir Henry, who had reined back beside us.

He grimaced. 'Your huntsman wants to follow the main avenue until we are close to the herd. Safer, he reckons, with this large company, many of them inexperienced. However, the hounds have scented a short cut through the wood and Mordon is demanding to go that way, as though he thinks that following the avenue is some kind of insult to his courage. Fool! Taking some of these folk through close set woodland will mean injuries. Bound to.'

While the argument up ahead continued, more of the riders came up, and villagers who had been following the hunt on foot drifted silently into the fringes of the wood on either side of the ride. Many of them also carried bows, for they had the right to shoot down any lesser game, does or fawns, which came their way, as long as they left the stags to the hunt party. They would be given a share of the meat, provided Mordon observed the custom of the manor, and good eating it would be, for the beasts would be well fed and fat at this time of year. Some of the venison would be eaten fresh, but most would be smoked or salted for the winter, a precious provision laid aside for the hungry months.

I could see Alan leaning down from his horse, giving instructions to his hunt assistants and the dog handlers. He was just raising his horn to his lips, to signal the resumption of the chase along the broad ride, when Mordon suddenly jerked his horse aside into the woods, and gave a blast on his own horn, the urgent sound of the *Gone Away*, which sends a shiver up the spine. I had not expected him to know the hunting calls, but the hounds recognised it, for it was their signal to pursue the quarry. Some leapt away after Mordon so suddenly that they tore their leads from their handlers and bounded away into the trees, following the scent they had discovered, the short cut to the herd of deer. Within moments they were out of sight.

Alan swore loudly and swung his horse in pursuit. Most of the remaining lymers and the alaunts, the handlers, the hunt servants and even some of the village followers crowded after him. Several more of the hunt servants, however, urged on by Alan's angry gestures, continued along the ride, taking some of the dogs with them and following Alan's intended route. By the time Edmond and I had our horses under control, a crowd of riders was in front of us, including the Lady Edith, Dunstable, and Giles, while Sir Henry was just behind us. He too was swearing as we turned aside to follow Alan. The rest of the horsemen continued up the ride. I thought I glimpsed Philip and Guy amongst them, but in the confusion I was not sure.

'No way,' Sir Henry gasped, between breaths. 'To keep. Folk. Together. No clear path.'

He was right. Within a few minutes the whole company of hunters had spread out and dispersed through the woodland, each trying to find a way through the trees, which here grew so close together. I soon lost sight of the last of the dogs, though I could hear the calls of a hunting horn in the distance, but whether it was Alan's or Mordon's I could not tell. Giles, Edmond, Sir Henry, and I kept together, but apart from the crashing of brushwood I could not be certain of anyone else's whereabouts. With the noise we were making I thought every deer within a mile of us would be off and away before ever we could draw near.

I crouched close over Rufus's neck, for there were low branches a-plenty in this part of the wood and I had no wish to be brained by one, and perhaps swept to the ground under the hooves of a following horse. I had just dodged one with barely inches to spare when I heard a crack and a yelp of pain. I reined Rufus in and looked over my shoulder.

Giles had pulled up and was swaying in the saddle, looking as if he was like to fall at any minute. There was blood on his forehead, and his cap was skewered on a twig of the oak tree beneath which he had halted.

Sir Henry and Edmond joined me as I rode back to him.

'Didn't duck low enough,' Giles gasped, shamefaced. He was dabbing his bleeding head with a handkerchief.

'How bad is it?' Edmond asked. 'Should you go back?'

'Nay.' Giles shook his head, then thought the better

of it. ''Twas just a glancing blow. I saw it, and nearly missed it.'

'I said there would be trouble, coming this way.' Sir Henry reached up for Giles's cap and unhooked it from a sharp twig protruding from the branch. 'Your good fortune this did not spear you in the eye.'

He handed the cap to Giles, who poked a finger through the hole in the brim. 'Aye,' he said, 'better my cap than my eye.'

'You were fortunate not to take a fall.,' I said. 'but are you sure you are fit to ride?' In Jordain's absence, back with the observers, I felt some responsibility for the boy.

'Quite sure,' he said, jamming the damaged cap back on his head.

'No need for us to rush,' Edmond said. 'We shall never overtake the leaders now. Have you any idea where they are, Nicholas?'

I shook my head. 'I think they were headed in that direction.' I waved my arm ahead and to the right. 'At least, that is where the most noise seemed to come from, but it can be deceptive in woodland.'

'Aye, I think that is the way,' Sir Henry said. 'Let us try in that direction, but keep our ears pricked.'

We set off again at a gentle canter. There was no point in a faster pace. If the huntsman and the main party had managed to overtake a stag despite all the noise and commotion, it would have been despatched long before we could hope to reach them.

Sir Henry was picking a route through the trees in the general direction which we hoped would lead us back to the hunt, with the three of us following behind him. I kept to the back, still somewhat afraid that, after the blow to his head, Giles might turn dizzy and fall, even now. I had half my attention on him and half on the way through the trees, for there were still branches dangerously low, so that it was only from the corner of my eye that I thought I caught a glimpse of something red a little distance away on the left, mostly concealed by the undergrowth where a covert had been left for boar. Perhaps some of the villagers were still making their way on foot, trying, like us, to catch up with the hunt.

Yet even as I twisted my head to look again, it was gone. Odd, for I thought all the villagers had been wearing green or brown. And red is an expensive dye. But before I could give it further thought, Giles swayed in the saddle, and looked like to fall. I rode forward and seized him by the arm.

'Take care!' I said, and called to the others to stop.

''Tis nothing,' Giles said, as they rode back. 'Just a moment of dizziness.'

Then he gave it the lie by leaning over his horse's side and vomiting, fortunately on the side away from me.

'From now on, we hold the horses down to a walk,' I said firmly, and so we did, while I kept my reins in one hand, the other retaining my grip of Giles's arm.

Before we had ridden much further, we heard the hunting horn again, close at hand now. A long wavering, wailing note, bidding farewell to the spirit of the stag and praising the dogs for their skill.

''Tis over,' Edmond said. 'Despite everything, they have made a kill.'

I nodded. In view of all that had happened it was surprising that Alan had managed to track down and kill a quarry, but his family had all the skills of the hunt bred into them, blood and bone. After such a triumph, Mordon should grant Alan his position as manor huntsman again, unless he was even more of a fool than I took him to be. Yet he also seemed like a man who would nurse a grudge lifelong. Not only had Alan struck him after the assault on his sister. He had this very day humiliated him before both his important friends and the watchful, hostile eyes of the villagers.

As we came out from amongst the trees, finding the hunting party gathered on the turf of the ride, the undoing of the stag had already begun. The dogs were growling and fighting over their *curée* – the humbles, chopped and mixed with bread and blood, then spread for them on a piece of the stag's hide – their reward for the day's work.

Alan had set aside, on a broad dock leaf, the share left in the woods. It was another pagan custom that lingered on – an offering to the spirit of the woodland, whose meaning was lost in time. Perhaps it was meant to signify a lack of greed on the part of the hunters, presenting a share to the forest. Or perhaps by returning a part of the stag to his native woods, it was intended as a token of peace to the creatures of the woodland. It was known as the *corbyn bone*, the fee paid to the crows and ravens, dark, winged spirits of the woods, gathering watchfully in the surrounding trees. Alan had lodged it in the crook of a branch, too high for the dogs to reach, and was now dismembering the quarry according to the exact ritual of the hunt.

Close on our heels, Lady Edith and Dunstable arrived, and she exclaimed in annoyance that she had missed the kill. Most of the London party were here, I saw, some of them having had the good sense to keep to the wide avenue, instead of crashing through the trees, although a few were still drifting out of the wood. I could not see Mordon anywhere. Philip and Guy were away on the far side of the crowd, and I raised my hand to them.

'Our host appears to have failed to witness the kill on his own first hunt in Wychwood,' Edmond said, not without a touch of satisfaction.

'Man's own fault,' Sir Henry grunted. 'Should always follow your huntsman's advice. He knows what's best to do. Your man would have taken us all along the main ride until we were near the herd, and there would have been a clean kill of the quarry, without all this senseless roaming about. One of the hunters could have been killed amongst those trees, and the lad has certainly a bad bump on the head. Would not surprise me if there are a few more injuries as well.'

As he was speaking, we could hear the creak of a cart coming along the ride. It was drawn by a mule, and the hunt servants began to load the butchered carcass into to it, ready to be carried back to the manor. Before they were done, two of the villagers came out of the wood, carrying another kill slung from a pole – a yearling stag by the look of it. Several more of the villagers were with them, including Matt Grantham, who must have decided to do some hunting on his own account. They all looked pleased. Venison to enjoy now and provide for the winter.

All of this was taking time, and Giles had dismounted. He was sitting on the ground, leaning back against a tree, with his eyes closed. His horse, after blowing wetly in his face, had begun to crop the grass at the base of the tree.

''Tis odd,' Edmond said, looking about. 'Where has Mordon gone? Even if he was left a little behind, he should be here by now. That stallion of his is a lusty beast. I'd not have expected him to have failed to arrive, however poorly his master rode him.'

'Aye, very true. But–' I remembered the glimpse I had had of something red, over beyond one of the coverts. I told Edmond what I had seen. 'I thought at the time it was one of the villagers, for it was not a horseman. Too near the ground.'

Edmond shook his head. 'None of them would wear red, you know that, Nicholas.'

'Aye, but Mordon would not be on foot,' I pointed out. 'Unless . . . perhaps he has had a fall. We'd best go back. He went off at such a pace, there may have been no one near him. And we were so spread out in the wood–'

I rode over to Alan, who was washing his bloodied hands and forearms in a bowl of water one of the servants had brought him.

'Where is Master Mordon?' I asked. 'He is nowhere here. Has he returned to the manor?'

Alan shrugged as he rubbed his hands dry on the sides of his cotte. 'I haven't seen him since he called most of the dogs away into the wood. I've given it no mind.'

He rolled down his sleeves. 'My work for him is

done, once we have carried the kill back to the manor and returned the dogs to the kennels. After that, I owe him nothing.' He glanced round defiantly at Lady Edith and the rest of the party from the manor. He had spoken loudly and they had all turned in his direction. 'He may go hang, for all I care. It is nothing to me.'

He gave me a long penetrating look, which I could not quite fathom. Perhaps he was thinking of his young sister. Then he walked over to his horse and mounted. The cart had been reversed and was starting to trundle back to the manor. Hunters, servants, and villagers began to sort themselves out, riding or walking back in the same direction. The hounds, having devoured their share of the quarry, were buckled once more on to their leads. Their handlers, who had had the most exhausting day, followed after the mounted hunters.

Lady Edith showed no concern at the absence of her husband, but was setting off with Dunstable back to the manor.

I rode over to her.

'My lady,' I said, bowing in my saddle. 'I fear Master Mordon may have suffered an accident. I will ride back into the woods and see whether I can find him.'

She looked me coolly up and down, as if I were some unprepossessing fellow asking for employment in her household and not meeting with favour. She shrugged. 'If you wish. That horse is near too much for him. By now he has probably been carried into the next county.'

She turned away indifferently and set her horse to follow the others. Her constant shadow Dunstable grinned at me contemptuously. 'Do not expect to be thanked if you find him,' he said.

'A family and household of unspeakable elegance and charm,' Edmond muttered.

'Unspeakable, certainly,' I said. 'Will you come with me?'

He nodded.

'And so will I,' said Sir Henry. 'If the man has had a

fall, it will need more than you, Nicholas, to heave him on to his horse again.'

Giles got, somewhat unsteadily, to his feet. 'And I,' he said.

'You will *not*,' I said. 'You must go straight back along the ride to the clearing where we had our meal and join Jordain and the others. They have seen nothing of the hunt and will be preparing to go home. Go back with them, or Jordain will skin me. Did you not see Guy and Philip amongst the riders here?'

'Aye.'

'Then if you are able to speak to them, tell them all to go back to the farm. Edmond and I will come as soon as we may.'

He was reluctant, but his head was clearly still hurting, so he mounted and set off down the ride, at the tail end of the hunt party.

Sir Henry, Edmond, and I turned our horses away from the smooth grassy ride and back into the unkempt area of woodland from which we had emerged.

'Do you think you will be able to find the place again, Nicholas?' Sir Henry asked. 'There is no clear path the way we came.'

I looked about somewhat helplessly, wishing that I possessed one tenth of Alan's woodcraft.

'I think we came from over there, did we not? There are a few broken branches.'

'Aye,' Sir Henry said, 'and see, our hoof marks in this patch of softer ground. If we go carefully and keep a sharp watch, we should be able to find our way back.'

It took us a great deal of time.

Parts of the way were clear, where the ground was soft enough to mark our passing, or the leaf litter showed signs of being disturbed, but frequently we lost all trace of the way, or mistook some other riders' route for our own, and were forced to dismount and cast about. Several times we went quite wrong and had to retreat some distance and try again. The afternoon began to draw toward evening.

'I recognise that stand of three oaks,' Edmond said, 'with the hazel coppice over to the right. We passed this way a while after Giles struck his head.'

We continued to follow the traces of our passing until we reached the place where Giles had received his injury. There was still a fragment of his cap fluttering from the branch.

'We have gone too far now,' I said. 'It was after Giles's accident that I saw . . . whatever it was I saw. We must turn back.'

It was easy enough to follow the way back again, for by passing twice over the same ground we had begun to mark out a clear path with our horses' hoof prints.

'It was over to the left,' I said, peering in the failing light.

Then at last I saw it.

'There! Beyond the thicket. Whatever it is, 'tis still there.'

We turned our horses and headed toward the covert, but before we reached it, we heard the jingle of harness off to the right. Mordon's horse, his reins trailing and his saddle askew, was calmly cropping the tufts of grass that sprang up between the roots of the trees.

'He must have had a bad fall,' Edmond whispered, as though finding the horse somehow made a slight suspicion into solid fact.

Sir Henry pointed ahead. 'You were right, Nicholas.'

Stretched out, face down in the leaf litter, his crimson houppelande dragged upwards to reveal two meaty thighs in their purple hose, was the new lord of Leighton, Master Mordon.

We all stayed, stock still, reluctant to move any nearer.

'If he has lain here unmoving since you first glimpsed him, Nicholas,' Edmond said, barely above a whisper, 'then he is deep out of his wits. Or else–'

'Or else dead,' Sir Henry said grimly. He was the first to go forward, with Edmond and me slowly following.

The man lay very still, his arms sprawled awkwardly, his head hidden by the ruin of his yellow capuchon. There was something odd about his position. When a man falls from his horse in woodland, it is usually because he has been swept from the saddle by a branch, in which case he will fall backwards over his horse's hindquarters and end by lying on his back. Either the blow from the branch or the impact of his head as it meets the ground can send him out of his wits. Or worse. But Mordon was lying face down.

I stepped up close and pulled his houppelande down over his buttocks, in a kind of futile attempt to make him more seemly. That was when I saw it, distinct even in the poor light. A large patch of darker red on the red of his houppelande. In the centre of it, a ragged tear in the cloth. I knelt amongst the leaf litter and touched it. It was wet and sticky.

'Blood?' Sir Henry said.

I nodded.

I pulled the houppelande up again. The white shirt beneath was even more widely stained, and like the outer garment was roughly torn. Lifting the shirt, I revealed the man's skin. There was a great jagged wound in his lower back.

With a grunt, Sir Henry lowered himself to kneel on the ground beside me as I tried to find a pulse below Mordon's ear. There was nothing. His body was still warm, but growing cooler. Sir Henry rested his hands on his thighs and leaned forward, to get a better view of the wound.

'Arrow,' he said. 'Punctured a lung, I'd say. And maybe grazed the heart. He'd not stand a chance.'

'No arrow here now,' Edmond said, peering over our shoulders.

'Nay, that's why 'tis such a devil of a mess. Whoever shot him retrieved the arrow. Dragged it back out again. Going in, it would have been a clean wound. On the way out, the barbs of the arrowhead would have torn the flesh like this.'

As he explained the wound with such authority, I remembered that in his younger days Sir Henry had fought in the French wars. He would be familiar with every kind of wound. I sat back on my heels.

'It could have been anyone,' I said. 'Almost every one of the hunters was carrying a bow. And most of the villagers as well.'

'But why remove the arrow?' Edmond said.

'Perhaps it was distinctive,' I said, 'and could have identified whoever shot it. And whoever it was, he would had been terrified of being discovered.'

'Accidents will happen at the chase,' Sir Henry said, getting to his feet with a groan, and briefly grabbing Edmond's arm for support.

'I wonder whether it *was* an accident,' I muttered. 'In these bright colours, no one could have mistaken him for a deer.'

'Unless he rode in front of the quarry just as the arrow was loosed,' Edmond said, without much conviction.

'Hmm,' I said.

'Time to think of that later. It will be dark soon,' Sir Henry said. 'Edmond, can you catch his horse?'

While Edmond went off in pursuit of the stallion, who had moved further away, Sir Henry and I turned Mordon over. His face wore a look of blank surprise.

'Didn't see it coming, then,' Sir Henry said.

'Nay. Someone came up from behind . . . Everything was in such confusion here in the wood. *Could* it have been an accident?'

He smiled grimly. 'What do you think?'

I shook my head. 'Unlikely.' I paused. 'In the short time he has been here, the man has made many enemies.'

'Well, we must take him back to the manor, and see to it that the coroner is sent for. He will not like it that we move the body, but we cannot leave the poor fellow here in the forest, prey to any beast.

I nodded, thinking how a man of wealth, power, and mighty arrogance can be reduced so swiftly to a poor fellow.

Edmond returned, leading the stallion, who no longer seemed so mettlesome as he had earlier in the day. When I had straightened the saddle and tightened the girth, Edmond and Sir Henry heaved the body upright between them.

'The girth was slack,' I said thoughtfully. 'Some groom was careless this morning, in saddling the horse.'

'Should have checked it himself,' Sir Henry said dismissively, but I wondered whether there had been more than one scheme afoot to do Master Mordon harm.

'If you will hold the horse steady, Sir Henry,' I said, 'Edmond and I will try to sling him over the saddle.'

With such a heavy man, and a dead weight, it was not a simple task. Edmond and I were both red of face and short of breath by the time we managed to heave Mordon across the saddle on his stomach, his head hanging down on one side of his horse, his feet on the other. As we manoeuvred him into a position where he would be balanced, his hunting horn swung out and hit me on the shoulder. It was crushed out of shape. It must have been beneath him as he fell to the ground. His hunting knife was still in the sheath at his belt – a fancy toy, ornamented with uncut semi-precious stones. Clearly the killing had not been for robbery, for the knife must be worth more than a year's wages for a labourer. We could not find his whip, but it had probably flown off as he fell and was now hidden amongst the leaf fall. Someone could search for it by daylight.

We set off along the way back to the tree where Giles had been struck, Sir Henry going first.

'I think I can find the way back to the ride from there,' he said, 'but we had best make haste, for it will be full dark soon.'

I came next, leading Mordon's horse, while Edmond rode alongside him, a hand out to steady the body should it start to slip. Fortunately, Sir Henry's instincts proved right, and before long we were riding easily along the turfed way which would take us directly back to the manor house. As we neared the edge of the wood, a barn owl flew across our path, perhaps the same one which had startled Mordon's horse in the morning. I gripped the leading rein tightly, fearing he might shy again, but he plodded on, undisturbed. Perhaps without the harsh hand of his master he was a quieter, steadier horse than he had seemed before.

The lights of the house began to show through the trees, and we came out into the grounds surrounding the manor. We could hear voices and laughter from within, and the sound of a lute being played. The three of us exchanged a glance.

'It seems the master's absence has not yet caused much concern,' Sir Henry said dryly.

'So it would seem,' I said.

There was screaming and shouting a-plenty, however, when Edmond and I carried Mordon's body in through the front door of the manor house, while Sir Henry called for grooms to come and see to the horses. All the London party was gathered in the Great Hall, the oldest part of the house, and a number of the guests from surrounding manors were also there, presumably intending to stay the night in Leighton and return home in the morning. Servants had set up trestle tables and were beginning to lay out an elaborate supper, supervised by Lady Edith, who had donned a gown of white velvet sewn with pearls, over which she wore a cotehardie of cloth of gold, embroidered with exotic birds and flowers, which looked as though they had sprung from the pages of some bestiary, never having been seen on this earth.

I jerked my head toward one of the tables which had not yet been laid, and Edmond and I carried Mordon's body over to it. Placed on his back, with his limbs carefully arranged, his arms crossed over the swell of his considerable belly, he looked more like a man asleep and less like the sprawling corpse we had found in the wood. The arrow had barely penetrated to the front of his clothes, so for the moment there was no blood to be seen. Edmond dusted away some leaves and fragments of twig which still clung to Mordon's houppelande.

Up to this moment, Lady Edith had been standing at the far end of the hall, surrounded by her guests, but now she came striding down the room, a look of fury on her face, that such lowly persons as my cousin and I had dared to enter her house uninvited. Sir Henry hurried in front of us, holding out his hands to stop her, but she swept him arrogantly aside and advanced on us, her mouth open to warn us away.

Instead, her eyes fell on her husband, and that was when the screaming began.

Soon the rest were crowding around, women screaming, men shouting, demanding to know whether Mordon was injured or dead. Edmond and I retreated behind the table, leaving it to Sir Henry to answer their questions.

He explained how I had caught a glimpse of red earlier, but had thought nothing of it until Mordon failed to appear, and how the three of us had searched the woods until we had found both man and horse, the man lying on the ground, already dead.

'A bad fall,' one of the men said sagely. 'That horse was too much for him. And crashing through the trees like that, no wonder. He should have stayed with us and followed the ride.'

Several more were nodding their agreement.

'He fell,' Sir Henry said, when he could make himself heard, 'but the fall was not the cause of his death. I believe he was dead, or nearly dead, before ever he fell.'

Lady Edith had ceased screaming and was now weeping copiously on Dunstable's shoulder, while another woman, perhaps one of her waiting women, put an arm about her.

'What do you mean, Sir Henry?' It was the lord of Shipton manor. 'How did he die?'

'He was shot from behind with an arrow.'

Sir Henry turned and murmured to us, 'Turn him over

lads. Best they know the truth before any more wild speculation.'

With some difficulty, Edmond and I rolled Mordon on to his side. The table was too narrow for us to turn him on to his stomach. The hall was ablaze with torches in sconces along the walls and large free standing candelabra placed here and there about the room. In all this light the large patch of blood on the houppelande could be seen clearly. Even now it had not dried completely but had a dull sheen in the candlelight. There were horrified gasps from the company, and a few whispers of 'Murder!'.

Lady Edith screamed again and came toward us, as if she was about to accuse us of the foul act.

'Murdered! Aye, we all know who has murdered him! You all heard him say that he hoped my lord would hang. Well, he had already set his hand to it, and it is he who will hang. That huntsman! It is he who has murdered my lord!'

It took a long time to quieten her. Some of the company agreed that it must be the huntsman who had done this. Everyone had seen the quarrel that morning, and how Alan had rough handled Mordon. It seems some also knew of the earlier quarrel, when Alan had struck Mordon to the ground. Others were more circumspect. Surely the huntsman had been within sight of many for most of the hunt? Even though not many of the hunters had been able to keep pace with him, there were the hunt servants, the dog handlers . . .

'Churls!' Lady Edith cried. 'They would hide the truth, for my lord knew their thieving ways.'

Her hair had come loose and her cheeks were flushed an unhealthy crimson. When her women tried to calm her, she threw them aside, and slapped two of them. Sir Henry tried to calm her.

'The coroner must be sent for. He will call an inquest, which will decide the truth of the matter. You should not make accusations, my lady, until more is known. May I send one of your men at once? He should go first to Burford, to enquire where the coroner may be found. I think the writ of the Oxford coroners does not run this far. It will be the county coroner we need.'

Lady Edith ignored him, but Dunstable bowed to Sir Henry and assured him that he would see to the matter. As he hurried out of the hall, Lady Edith began calling for the lawyer, whose name, it appeared, was Sir Thomas Baverstoke.

'Do you think we may leave?' Edmond whispered. 'At home they will be frantic with worry, wondering what has become of us.'

I nodded. 'There is no more we can do here. We shall be needed for the inquest, but let the man's household take matters in hand now. I wonder why she has sent for the lawyer.'

Edmond shrugged. 'Somewhat soon to be thinking about the will, would you not say?' He gave a sardonic smile.

'I should be glad to go,' I said, starting to ease my way, crab-like, out from behind the table. Somehow the press of people had thrust it back almost to the wall, with Edmond and me trapped behind it. Sir Henry saw what we were about.

'Aye,' he said, attempting (without much success) to heave the table away from the wall. With Mordon's weight on it, it was too heavy for him. 'Get you home. I was to stay here this night in any case. I can answer any of their questions. Did you not say you hoped to save what you could of your oats, Edmond? Let you carry on with your harvest. The coroner cannot be here by tomorrow. Best use the time to advantage.'

Frustrated by our attempt to escape around the edge of the table, Edmond and I were forced to crawl underneath, emerged in time to hear the lawyer saying, 'I will see to it at once, my lady.'

Sir Henry was no longer by the table, but striding across to the lawyer. 'What is this devil's scheme, sir? You have no right in law. You, of all men, should know that.'

'When there is convincing evidence of a man's guilt,' the lawyer said smoothly, 'it is quite in order to secure his person. Moreover, with the lord of this manor now deceased, and no male heirs, the rights of *infangenthef* and *outfangenthef* fall to his widow. She has given orders that the felon Alan Wodville is to be seized and held in confinement, awaiting the decision of the coroner's court and his appearance before the court of this manor. He is clearly the culprit and cannot be permitted to remain at large, since he is likely to take to his heels and flee.'

I gasped. 'Surely they cannot do that? The arrow could have been fired by any one of dozens of people. Mordon had already made a great many enemies. Why single out one man?'

Sir Henry nodded. 'You overstep the mark, sir. We will await the coroner. Besides, the rights of *infangenthef* and *outfangenthef* have become debatable of late. And they cannot be asserted by the widow until heritage of the manor is confirmed. Moreover, the crime was committed within the royal forest and not within the fee of this manor.'

As a substantial landowner, Sir Henry presided over his own manor court and knew his law, but the man Baverstoke ignored him and began issuing orders to the manor servants to make haste at once into the village and seize the person of Alan Wodville.

'If he is not at home, search the village until you find him. Let no man attempt to conceal him from the law.'

'At this hour, maister,' one of the servants objected, 'all the village will be abed.' He was a local man, and looked far from happy about obeying Baverstoke's orders.

'Then rouse them out of their beds,' the lawyer snapped. 'This is a case of murder. We cannot allow the murderer to escape.'

There was some muttering at his words, prejudging the killer without any evidence other than a public quarrel. The gathering began to shift and divide into separate groups – the outsiders and Mordon's household gathering about Lady Edith and the lawyer, the local people drifting down toward our end of the hall and forming an uneasy group around Sir Henry. However, there was nothing we could do to intervene when the lawyer despatched half a dozen servants to hunt out Alan. I saw that he had thought better of sending any local men.

'Best you go home,' Sir Henry said to us quietly when they had left. 'I will send you word in the morning of what has happened here. I do not like the way matters are proceeding. I shall stay until the coroner arrives.'

He looked across at the body of Mordon, lying once more on his back.

'There seems little care for the murdered man,' I said thoughtfully. 'Rather more for fixing the guilt, unproven, on Alan Wodville. Mordon has not even been decently disposed.'

'Aye.' Sir Henry pursed his lips in distaste. 'I will see that he is laid out in the manor chapel. Get you away now.'

We slipped out of the house and went to retrieve our horses from the stables. They, at least, had been given more care than Mordon – unsaddled, rubbed down, and provided with a feed of oats. By the time we were on our way down the lane to the village, the moon had risen and we could see well enough.

There was a commotion in the village outside Alan's house. He was held between two men, swearing furiously. Beth stood in the doorway, weeping, while Rob tugged helplessly at the arm of one of the men who was starting to drag Alan away in the direction of the manor. Pale faces peered from behind half open shutters in the houses on either side and across the street.

'Do not lose heart, Alan!' I shouted across the noise, augmented now by the barking of village dogs. 'We will not let you be wrongly convicted.'

'I never touched the bastard!' Alan shouted back, then was silenced when one of the men struck him across the face.

Chapter Seven

Edmond and I returned to an anxious household at the farm. The children had been sent off to bed, but once we had settled the horses, we found all the adults gathered in the kitchen, where Susanna was heating some soup over the fire, and Margaret was treating the injury to Giles's head.

'Did you find him?' Jordain demanded. Clearly Giles had told them all that he knew.

'We found him,' Edmond said grimly, sinking down on to a stool by the fire and starting to ease off his riding boots with a groan. Hilda knelt on the floor beside him to help.

'Ill news, then,' Margaret said, glancing across at me as she stoppered her jar of woundwort salve.

I passed a hand wearily over my face and sat down opposite Edmond. I was too weary even to trouble with my boots, but when she had removed her father's, Hilda began to unlace mine.

'Aye, ill news indeed,' I said. 'We found Master Mordon dead, and already growing cold.'

Susanna stopped ladling the soup into bowls. 'He fell from his horse, then? Struck his head or broke his neck?'

'Nay.' I shook my head. 'Dead of an arrow in his back. At least, there was no arrow, but Sir Henry swears that it is an arrow wound. It was withdrawn after the killing, tearing the flesh further.'

Beatrice clamped her hand to her mouth and shivered.

'An accident, do you suppose?' Philip said, taking her other hand in his and raising it to his lips. She gave him a shaky smile.

'It could have been,' Edmond said, 'and the bowman made off with the arrow for fear he might be known by it.'

'But surely,' Jordain said, 'tricked out as Mordon was, in crimson and purple and yellow, no one could have mistaken him for a deer. More like an African parrot.'

'Just my thought,' I said. 'Thank you, Hilda.'

I wriggled my stiff toes. One was poking through my hose.

'Surely it cannot have been an accident,' I said, 'unless Mordon rode across someone's shot at the wrong moment.'

'The party at the manor have decided that it was deliberate murder,' Edmond said, 'and have fixed on Alan Wodville as the murderer. Between them, Lady Edith and that lawyer have claimed the right to seize and imprison Alan. He was being arrested as we came through the village.'

'Sir Henry tried to stop them,' I said. 'Swore they were acting illegally, but they ignored him. However, Sir Henry remains at the manor tonight and will keep a sharp eye on whatever they are about.'

'But why should Alan–?' Susanna began, then stopped.

'Where is Elga?' Edmond asked.

Two of the maids were slicing bread and setting out the remains of the hunt food on the table, but there was no sign of Elga.

'I sent her to bed with the children,' Susanna said. 'She is still much distressed.'

Edmond nodded. 'Certainly everyone at the hunt saw Alan shouting at Mordon about his attack on the girl, and swearing at him for his lewd ways, but why should he kill him?'

'There are others with as much cause,' she said. 'Mark Grantham, for one, ever since Mordon made a claim on him as one of his villeins, because of that new land of his. There are others in the village in dispute with him. Lads severely punished for trapping conies on their own land. He has even tried to claim villein service from Geoffrey Carter and Bertred Godsmith, who are both free men, and their families before them for generations. And there are all the other matters – the higher tolls at the manor mill, the ban on gleaning.'

'For that matter,' Edmond said with a grim smile, 'you might say the same of me, for he has robbed me of my mill stream and most of my day labourers.'

He did not mention his debt to Mordon, and the monstrous rate of interest.

'Again, hardly a reason for murder,' I said, 'but rest easy, cousin. You were never out of sight of me, Sir Henry, and Giles here, until long after the man was dead.'

'So that absolves the three of you as well,' he said. 'But what of Philip and James and Guy? They were somewhere in that mad throng crashing through the wood.'

Guy looked momentarily alarmed. 'Sir, I had not even met the man! Nor had Master Olney.'

'That leaves me under suspicion, then,' James said.

'Never fear, son.' Edmond got up and clapped him on the shoulder. 'I spoke in jest. Shall we eat this soup? I for one have the hunger of a wolf. How many hours is it since the hunt breakfast?'

'Too many,' Susanna said. 'Come, sit. We have bread left from this morning, and some of the pasties. And I had set aside a tart of the early plums for this evening. Fetch the cream, Hilda.'

As we ate our welcome supper, we turned over again the little that was clear about the killing of Gilbert Mordon, but could make no more sense of it. Had the killing been deliberate murder? Or no more than an unfortunate accident? If it had been an accident, it was not unreasonable that the man who had shot the arrow, finding Mordon dead, should have been seized with panic, removed the arrow, and kept his lips sealed. The fear which had surrounded Mordon in life would not necessarily disappear with his death.

'If that was the way of it,' I said, 'then the killer must have been alone when it happened, or with none but trusted friends nearby.'

'Aye, but if that *was* the way of it,' Giles said, 'would he continue to keep his lips sealed, if an innocent man is accused of murder?'

'It *cannot* have been Alan,' I said, thumping the table in frustration. 'I am certain he would never have been out of sight of the hunt servants and the dog handlers, even if none of the other hunters had kept pace with him.'

'There you put your finger on the crucial point, Nicholas,' Jordain said. 'Accident or deliberate killing, it must have happened by stealth and Alan is the one man who could never have been alone this entire day.'

We were all late abed that night, but must be up betimes the next morning, to see what might be salvaged of the oat harvest. A day's work on the farm had been lost on Friday, while we had been absent at the hunt. Now but one day remained before the Sabbath's enforced leisure. The weather continued to look changeable, so every minute in the field counted toward the stores for winter.

Before I went down to break my fast, I took out Emma's letter and read it again. She was surely teasing, when she spoke of working for me as a scrivener – was she not? I could not employ a woman. Yet there was a certain irony about it. Confined as a novice to Godstow Abbey, she had the freedom to use her talents as scrivener and artist, however much she resented what she saw as her imprisonment there. Now, restored to her rightful place as her grandfather's heir to a substantial manor, she found herself imprisoned quite otherwise, by the bonds of propriety and convention. She might, certainly, write and illuminate books for her own pleasure, but she could not become a professional scrivener. I was an official *librarius* licensed by the university of Oxford. I must observe the rules. Indeed, I did not know that there actually existed a *rule* against employing women as scriveners. It had probably never occurred to anyone that such an unlikely thing would ever be thought of.

Tomorrow, after Mass, since there would be no field work, I would write an answer to Emma's letter. Geoffrey Carter would be off on his rounds next week, which would take him to Oxford in a few days' time. He could carry my letter to Mistress Farringdon.

A day's grace for the field of oats had not been entirely wasted. A fair amount of the flattened stalks had straightened again, at least partially, plenty to occupy us for the whole of the day. It was slow work, for whole areas had been twisted together by the storm, so that we could not move across the field in an orderly row, but must each struggle to disentangle a clump at a time, working close with sickles instead of the long-handled scythes. It was irritating and tedious, and to cap all, every insect on the farm seemed to have moved into the thick clusters of stems. Before long my forearms were covered with scratches and bites, and the more determined insects were biting through my hose.

Where patches of oats still lay on the ground, Susanna and the other women worked their way even more slowly through them, lifting the fallen stems and salvaging what they could. If the grain they recovered was damp, it would need to be spread out on trays of loosely woven withies to dry in the barn. My mother had come to help again, though I hoped she would allow herself to rest from time to time, for it was tiring, back-breaking toil. Even the children were set to gathering the heads which had been scattered on the ground. Anything that could be saved, would be, even if it must be used at once to stop it rotting.

As we walked back to the farm at the end of the day, Edmond heaved a sigh.

'Not all lost, it seems. I have had better crops of oats, but we should have just enough to see us through the winter, without having to buy in. We could never have saved what we have, without you and your friends, Nicholas. If the rain holds off, we should finish the oats on Monday or Tuesday. Then there is nothing more but the beans and peas, and the women can harvest those, while the lads and I turn the beasts on to the stubble, before the autumn ploughing. I hope my new team will prove worth the cost and the worry they have brought me.'

He turned to Jordain and grinned. 'A far cry from your usual daily labour in Oxford, I am thinking, this field work has been.'

Jordain laughed. 'I think it has done us good. We spend too long crouched over our books or disputing the finer points of philosophy in Latin. It has reminded me of my youth. And look at that lad! Such a change in him!'

Stephen was ahead of us, swinging along swiftly with just one crutch. I had not noticed before, but he seemed to have discarded the other altogether. He was laughing at something Thomas had said, his face tipped up to the older boy. Jordain was right. His face was flushed a healthy colour and his eyes were bright. I thought he had even gained a little weight, with the field work and the good farm food. I suspected that at home in Oxford he led a very restricted life.

Edmond's mention of his new team of oxen reminded me of the nefarious bargain he had been tricked into, over the repayment of the loan to Gilbert Mordon. The man had not only robbed him of his mill stream. With a sudden sickening lurch of my heart, I realised that my cousin had as good a reason as any man to wish Mordon dead, if it meant he would be set free from his debt. Yet he had been within my own sight for the whole of the time when Mordon must have been killed. Sir Henry and Giles could also swear to it, should Edmond's name ever arise, as one who would not be sorry to see an end to the man.

The women had gone ahead of us to prepare the evening meal, for as usual on these harvest days we had eaten sparingly at midday, taking our main meal, for a change, when the day's toil was done. Elga had been in the field today amongst the other women. She looked pale, but otherwise worked as hard as any. Thanks to Alan, no serious harm had come to her, beyond a severe fright.

As we reached the yard, to be greeted with yelps of joy by Rowan, who had been confined, once again, to the barn, a horseman rode in from the lane. Sir Henry.

He dismounted and handed his horse's reins to James, who ran to his assistance.

'Thank 'ee, lad,' he said.

'You have news for us, Sir Henry?' Edmond strode across, and bowed a welcome.

'Little enough. The coroner has been sent for, but it's not known for sure where he is at present. Gilbert Mordon has been laid out in the chapel at the manor, but cannot be coffined until the coroner has seen him, so let us pray it will not be long. The worst of the heat is over, but 'tis still summer, and he should be buried soon.'

'What of Alan Wodville?' I said. 'Have they carried out their threat of imprisoning him?'

'They have, but dare not do more, for I have said that I will report them to the sheriff if any harm comes to him. The Lady Edith and the lawyer Baverstock are very hot to have him accused, found guilty, and hanged without delay, but I and one or two others from the county will make sure nothing untoward occurs before the coroner holds the inquest. No one is making any attempt to find the real culprit, for I do not believe it was the huntsman.'

'Nor do we,' I said, as we walked toward the house, followed by Philip, while the rest of the harvesters went to wash at the well. 'It is certain that Alan was always in company the whole day, never on his own. Even if we did not know the man's character, that he's no murderer by stealth, he would simply never have had the opportunity.'

'So also I have maintained to them,' Sir Henry said, 'till I ran out of breath. I could have saved it, for all the good it did. They are bent on accusing the huntsman.'

'Come away in, Sir Henry,' Susanna said, standing on the threshold. 'Will you take supper with us? 'Tis but simple fare.'

'I should be glad to, mistress. Glad to be away from that house, with everyone within staring suspicious at everyone else.' He beamed at her and kissed her cheek, as an old friend to the family. 'Ah, Nicholas, many's the time I've discussed a pint of ale in this kitchen with your father. Mistress Bridget! Have you been set to work by these young folk? For shame! Nay, do not get up.'

He pressed my mother back in her chair with a gentle hand on her shoulder, and kissed her too.

Once we were seated with cups of ale to wet our dry throats, while the meal was readied, I said, 'Was it just Lady Edith and the lawyer who were so strong against Alan Wodville? Or did others in the manor party support them?'

'That sly fellow Dunstable did so. Not as loud as Lady Edith, but as strong for hanging the huntsman. The others? Many, I think, wished they were safe back in London and could shake our Oxfordshire dust from their garments. They wanted no part of it, one way or another. But there were others eager to blame young Wodville. For ye see, do ye not, if the blame falls on him, everyone else is innocent as pure spring water. So it is to the advantage of everyone else who rode to the chase yesterday if someone can be named as scapegoat, whether he be guilty or not.'

'Hence their haste,' Jordain said shrewdly. 'For if the blame can be laid on Alan, and he is dealt with swiftly and ruthlessly, no one need go looking for any other to blame.'

'Yet we are certain,' I said, 'all of us here, that Alan was never alone, from when he rose before dawn to arrange all for the hunt, until the two carcasses were carted away, long past Mordon's death, when he made his way home to the village.'

'I am sure you have the right of it,' Sir Henry said, and drained his ale. 'Thank you, lass.' He smiled at Elga as she refilled his cup. 'Are you quite recovered?'

He was a blunt man, Sir Henry, and clearly saw no reason to curb his tongue. The maidservant coloured painfully, lowering her eyes, and her hand tightened on the handle of the ale jug, so that the knuckles shone white. She dropped a curtsey and whispered, 'Aye, I thank you, Sir Henry.' Then she backed away hastily, probably fearing further questions.

'He needed a whip taken to him, that fellow Mordon.' Sir Henry buried his nose in his cup. Half his ale seemed to disappear in one gulp.

'I wonder how Lady Edith felt about his behaviour,' Edmond mused.

Susanna set down a wide platter of beef collops in a rich sauce in front of him, next to a stack of pewter plates.

'His lady cared not a fig for him,' she said briskly. 'Anyone could see that. She despised him. She was raised as a gentlewoman, and he was a boor. She had her eye on that young gallant Dunstable, though from what I gathered, hearing the gossip of the London ladies, he has barely a groat to rub against a sixpence, and has been dependent on Mordon for his living these three years past. A fine head of hair, though, and a shapely leg.'

Hilda gaped at her mother, and Edmond snorted into his ale so that it went down the wrong way and Jordain was obliged to thump him on the back until he had recovered enough to serve the collops.

Over a meal, which was excellent, despite Susanna's self-deprecation, talk turned to other matters, mainly the harvest. Sir Henry was anxious to return to his own manor, for he had intended to ride back there today, had he not been delayed waiting for the coroner.

'My steward and my reeve are both excellent fellows,' he said, stretching out his legs after devouring a second helping of rhubarb tart, lavishly swamped with cream, 'but a man likes to keep an eye on the harvest himself. Like everyone else since the Death, I am short-handed. I am fortunate that I have not the blight of villeins running away, like so many others. I have only lost two, younger sons, who could have taken on a good yardland each, for I have plenty to spare, with so many dead, but they would go off. I'll not pursue them. An unhappy villein is little use on the manor.'

I knew very well why few of Sir Henry's villeins had taken to their heels. He was famously – nay, notoriously – soft-hearted toward the villeins on his estate. The two who had gone off to seek their freedom in Burford or some other town might well find life much harder as free men who must find work and food and lodgings for themselves than as villeins under Sir Henry. Still, the thought of shaking off villeinage had tempted many a man away from the land since the Death, and there would be many more hereafter.

'I have sent word to my son by one of Mordon's servants,' Sir Henry said. 'He has the harvest on his own manor to look to, but he will ride over and cast a glance over mine. No harm in showing my men that I have not forgotten what they should be about.'

Talk only reverted to Mordon as Sir Henry was leaving.

'I shall see you in church tomorrow,' he said. 'And will let you know whether there is any word of finding the coroner. And I will look in on your young huntsman. They have him locked in one of the cellars, but – unfortunately for him – not the one where the barrels of ale and wine are kept. One of the waiting women was concerned enough to see that he had a palliasse and a blanket, and I had a word with the cook myself.'

'If you have a chance to speak to him,' I said, 'be certain to assure him that we all believe that he is the one person who could not have shot Mordon. His friends will stand by him and ensure that the coroner knows this.'

'I will do so.'

Sir Henry swung himself on to his horse.

'The problem,' I said, patting the horse's neck and looking up at his rider through the summer twilight, 'is that although we know Alan Wodville could not have killed Mordon, we have no idea who did. So many people disliked – even hated – the man. Many might have wished him dead, but who had the opportunity? No one seems to be trying to discover the truth.'

'Well, when you can spare a thought from the harvest,' he said, 'you may turn your minds to the problem. You know these people better than I. And all your Oxford learning must have taught you to use your brains!'

He was chuckling as he rode away.

'He means to mock us for our Oxford learning,' Jordain said, 'however kindly, but he is right. Surely by reason we may come somewhat closer to the truth.'

Four of us had accompanied Sir Henry to the stable and now walked back together to the house – Edmond, Jordain, Philip, and I. The sky was a translucent blue-black, clear of cloud, the first stars beginning to glint far overhead.

'It should not be difficult to discover who was always within sight of others for the whole of the time when Mordon went missing,' Philip said. 'And who might have gone off on his own.'

Edmond shook his head. 'I am not so sure. For a time, after we turned aside into the wood, all was confusion. The horsemen were riding hither and thither, trying to find a safe path through the trees. The villagers following the hunt on foot were spread out in all directions, seeking quarry of their own.'

'And some, at least, found it,' I said. 'There was that young stag brought in. I wonder how many were together then.'

'It is not only a matter of who had the opportunity,' Jordain said. 'There is the crucial question: Was it some kind of accident, hastily covered up? Or was it deliberate murder? Planned beforehand? Or an opportunity seized when it offered?'

'It could hardly have been planned beforehand, could it?' I said. 'No one could have foretold that the hunt would split apart like that, because of the dogs finding a second scent. Or that Mordon would hasten off after them, ignoring his huntsman's instructions.'

'Very true,' Jordain said, 'unless someone knew that he was inclined to such behaviour. He was an arrogant, self-willed man. Perhaps someone knew him well enough to guess that something like that might happen.'

'That would rule out all the villagers.' Edmond looked relieved at the thought. 'They have experienced his unreasonableness and his unjustified claims, but they could not know his full character.'

'And there is also not only the question of who had the opportunity to do the deed,' I said. 'There must have been a reason compelling enough to commit murder. Who had such a reason? Several people have mentioned Matt Grantham, fiery of temper and threatened with villeinage, but Matt must know that any court would find against Mordon, on the evidence of all his neighbours that he is a free man. And, in any case, he is a man more likely to strike Mordon in the face with his fists than to shoot him covertly in the back.'

'Of course,' Philip said, 'we must remember that it need not have been deliberate murder. It *could* have been an accident, and the removal of the arrow merely the action of a frightened man, perhaps alone, with no one to swear that it was an accident.'

We had reached the side of the farmhouse, where a path of light streamed out from the open kitchen door, warm and welcoming. From inside we could hear the quiet voices of the women and the clatter of the dishes as they cleared away the meal. I thought with a shiver of Mordon, laid out cold in the chapel of the manor. Only yesterday he had been swaggering in the full pride of his riches and his new lordship, never suspecting that his end was but a few hours away. He had died suddenly by violence, and unshriven.

'That arrow,' I said slowly. 'I wonder why it was so urgent to take it away that the killer – killer by accident or design – stayed to drag it from the body. It cannot have been easy. As Sir Henry said, the barbs caught and tore the flesh. There must be something distinctive about that arrow. I wish we could find it.'

'By now,' Jordain said, 'it has probably been reduced

to ashes in one of the manor fireplaces.'

'Aye,' I said despondently. 'You are probably right.'

The air was definitely cooler as we walked down to the village the next morning. You could not have said that it was autumnal, but ever since the storm it had felt as though summer was slipping away. There is something sad about the coming of autumn, with the reminder that winter, with all its privations of cold and hunger, is lurking on the threshold, yet, for those of us in and about the university, autumn and the Michaelmas Term also hold the promise of new beginnings. New young faces would be crowding the streets, newly made graduates would be taking on the mantle of teaching. There is a quality about the constant flow of boys coming eager to the halls and colleges that perpetually renews the world of Oxford. Some would fall by the wayside over the years, but others would flourish and prosper in the rich soil of learning and debate. They would grow and stretch their wings, some to fly out even to the wider world of Court and Church, as lawyers, Crown officials, diplomats. It was a world I might once have joined myself, but I would never regret the exchange I had made. Alysoun and Rafe, clasping my hands and skipping down the lane, were proof that I had made the best choice. They were my legacy.

Sire Raymond stood at the church door, smiling a welcome as we approached. He was never a priest to stand upon the ceremony of his calling. Intelligent and even learned, he hid his abilities behind an honest modesty. It was clear that he was gratified, if perhaps somewhat alarmed, to see that a large party was also approaching, from the direction of Leighton Manor.

'Well!' Margaret murmured close to my ear. 'It seems our humble village church is to be honoured by the presence of gentry.'

'Apart from Sir Henry and a few of our own neighbouring lords,' I said dryly, 'I am not sure how many of that party are gentry. I imagine that many of the

Londoners are no more than shopkeepers like me, though perhaps on a larger scale. They may be rich, but it is not coin that makes a lord.'

She laughed. 'Coin they certainly possess. Will you note the silks and velvets amongst their garments?'

'Some most unsuitable for an August day in the country.'

Sir Henry abandoned the manor party and walked over to join us.

'We are honoured, sir,' Edmond said, 'but is there no Mass said today in the manor chapel?'

He shook his head. 'The priest come from London with the Mordons is unwilling to hold Mass there, with his late master's body lying before the altar, open and plain to view. It is a very small chapel.'

'Understandable,' Margaret said, wrinkling her nose with distaste.

The priest, whom I had noticed in the hall of the manor, but not at the hunt, had borne down upon Sire Raymond, and was gesticulating.

'I think he hopes to conduct the service himself.' Sir Henry regarded the two clergy with amusement. 'Will Sire Raymond give way, do you suppose?'

Edmond shook his head. 'Our priest has a sweet nature, but this is his parish and these are his parishioners. He can be stubborn when he so chooses. I think he will be unwilling to hand them over to a stranger. No doubt he will allow the other man to assist.'

As we made our way to the front pews reserved for our family, we found Will Dowland, the churchwarden, scuttling about, trying to fend off several of the manor party who were bent on seizing the highest ranking position in the church. Edmond went to Will's assistance, shepherding the intruders to the benches immediately behind ours – still an enviable position. There was a good deal of angry muttering, but no one made overt trouble, except Lady Edith, who merely stood at the end of our row, waiting for us to give way to her. I lifted Rafe on to my lap and moved a few inches, so that she was obliged to take the small space next to me. I had no wish to sit elbow to elbow with the widow all through Mass, but I summoned up a smile for her. She glanced at me as before, with an expression that said as plainly as words that I was not fit to share the very air with her, and certainly not one of Yves de Vere's oak benches.

The two priests had reached some kind of compromise. Sire Raymond conducted the Mass, with assistance of his two altar boys, but the other priest joined in the words of the service. One of the altar boys was Rob, Alan Wodville's nephew, pale of face and red of eye, but severely composed as he carried out his duties, with all the dignity of outraged youth. I wondered whether he and Beth had received any word of Alan's present condition.

The Mass seemed interminable that Sunday, and I fear that my mind wandered from its proper devotions. The memory of Friday's killing would not leave me, and my thoughts circled round themselves, repetitive and annoying. I tried to remember how long Mordon had been in sight after we had entered the wood, and how long after that I had noticed the blur of red out of the corner of my vision. It was impossible to judge just how long we had been thrashing about in the undergrowth between the trees. And where was everyone else at the time? Had I noticed anyone heading in the same direction as Mordon? The Lady Edith, now holding herself tautly away from the touch of my sleeve, had been near me at the first, as had the man Dunstable, who was now sitting immediately behind me. But I had soon lost sight of them amongst the trees, as I had of almost everyone else, apart from the three I had stayed with throughout the hunt.

As we had agreed amongst ourselves the evening before, two facts were important: who had been out of sight of the rest of the hunt but near Mordon, and who had reason enough to kill him? That was on the assumption, of course, that it had been a deliberate killing. It was tempting to believe that it had been an accident, and the removal of the fatal arrow merely the act of a man frightened of the consequences, if there had been no one nearby to bear witness that Mordon had ridden across the path of an arrow already loosed.

Tempting, indeed, but was it plausible? The flight of an arrow is swift. To have crossed in front of it before it reached its intended target, Mordon would have needed to be very close indeed. And if he had been that close, tricked out in garments so garish to the eye, so violent in contrast to the greens and browns of the summer woodland, he *must* have been seen. Nay, I could not believe in the comforting solution that it had been an accident.

So it must have been intentional murder. Perhaps not planned beforehand, for we could not have known in advance that the hunt party would be dispersed amongst the trees. Someone seizing an opportunity. Someone with a grievance or a hatred so intense that it had led to murder. Yet even then . . . if it was the act prompted by a sudden impulse, the intention might have been merely to wound, not to kill.

Rafe had fallen asleep, his thumb in his mouth. He was slipping sideways, so I eased him up against my chest, for my arm was growing numb. He was a sturdy child for his age, and like Stephen he seemed to have gained weight here in the country. Lady Edith must have sensed my movement, for she glanced aside at me, frowning. I ignored her. I knew that Sire Raymond did not mind if the young children fell asleep during the long service. They would be blessed, even as they slept, simply by being here.

If I accepted that the shooting of the arrow was intentional, whether to wound or to kill, it might have been done by anyone, for hunters and villagers had all carried bows. I thought I had noticed a few of the villagers with crossbows, but Sir Henry had been sure that the wound had been inflicted by an arrow, not by a quarrel from a crossbow. Indeed, a quarrel would probably have pierced the man from back to chest, and would have been impossible to withdraw. I did not think any of the mounted hunters had carried a crossbow.

This still meant that the field of possible killers was too wide, far too wide. Mentally, I shook myself. Why was I wasting time worrying at the problem? I was in God's house, attending holy Mass, and should pay attention to the sonorous words, singing around our small church in Sire Raymond's sweet voice, with the harsher bass of the visiting priest as an undertone. The service was nearing the end.

It was no affair of mine, this killing of Gilbert Mordon. I had met him for the first time but a few short hours before his death and had barely exchanged a word with him. It was the business of the coroner and the sheriff to determine what had happened and who was responsible, not mine. Theirs and their jurors' business to pass judgement.

Yet Alan Wodville had been seized and accused – loudly and publicly – by the woman now sitting beside me. I could understand that she had some justification for making her immediate accusation. Her husband had dismissed Alan from the position of manor huntsman held by his family for generations, although I did not know whether she was aware of Mordon's assault on Alan's young sister. Despite being turned off, Alan had been held to all the responsibility of organising Mordon's first hunt at his new manor, and he had carried out his duties carefully if resentfully, until Mordon had thrown all into confusion.

Then there had been that all too public confrontation when Alan had caught Mordon assaulting another young girl, as of right. He had handled his former lord violently, shouting accusations and swearing at him before his guests, both the wealthy and the well born. Aye, Lady Edith did have some justification for leaping to the conclusion that Alan had made the murderous attack, although she had far overstepped her authority in having him seized and imprisoned. She was not yet confirmed in any rights on the manor of Leighton, though it might well be that her family in Northamptonshire had such rights of life and death on their own lands. But only over their villeins, surely? Not over a free man like Alan.

My thoughts had wandered again. Everyone was standing for the final blessing. I heaved Rafe on to my shoulder as I rose, and he opened sleepy eyes. Alysoun tugged at the hem of my cotte, and I smiled down at her. Sire Raymond made the sign of the cross over each part of the congregation, then led his fellow priest and the two boys down the short nave and out at the west door. Sunlight poured in as it was opened. While we had been inside, the day must have brightened. I turned toward Lady Edith, but she was already gone, joining her party who had been seated behind us and sweeping away after the priests, brushing aside the villagers who bowed and curtseyed politely as she passed, paying them no heed.

We waited until most of the church was clear, before starting to move slowly toward the door. Rafe was fully awake now, so I set him on his feet, and Margaret took him by the hand. Outside, there was no sign of the other priest, who must have left with the party from the manor, but Sire Raymond was there as usual, greeting each of his parishioners by name.

When I reached him, he stayed me with a hand on my arm, until most of the congregation had gone.

'Nicholas,' he said, 'I do not like what I hear about this taking of Alan Wodville. His wife came to me yesterday, to ask if I might help. Do you think I might be allowed to see him?'

I waved to Sir Henry to join us.

'What is the news of Alan?' I asked.

'He fares not too badly. I visited him this morning and found him somewhat tousled, but fed and rested. He has not been ill used. Not yet, at any rate. Wiser heads have prevailed. We have persuaded the lady that to do any harm to a man merely suspected, with no evidence to connect him to the killing, will do *her* harm in the eyes of both the coroner and the sheriff. She acted, I believe, on the hot impulse of the moment. The mention of the sheriff gave her pause. If she is to take seisin on the manor in her lord's place, she would be wise not to make trouble with the king's sheriff beforehand.'

'Very true,' Sire Raymond said. 'But Wodville remains a prisoner?'

'For the moment. Let us hope the coroner may be here by tomorrow. The man Mordon cannot remain much longer unburied.'

'Does the lady wish him to be buried here, at our village church?' Sire Raymond glanced anxiously aside at the small churchyard. He would need to allocate space for the grave. 'She does not . . . she would not expect him to be laid to rest in the de Vere chapel?'

I frowned. Some of the de Vere tombs lay in the stubby south transept of the village church. Although it was known as a chapel, it was hardly that, nothing but a corner containing three tombs. Yves de Vere had been buried before the altar, under the flagstones of the nave, for there had been little room left for a tomb near his ancestors. Besides, when the Death was mowing down half the village, no one had been able to give thought to erecting a fine tomb in the chapel. It would be an outrage if Gilbert Mordon should be placed there.

'Nay, I think not,' Sir Henry said. 'She has spoken of burial in the manor chapel.'

Sire Raymond gave a sigh of relief. 'That would indeed be best. Later today I shall visit Alan Wodville's family and assure them that he is not faring too ill.'

As Sir Henry and I turned away down the short path leading from the church to the village street, he took me by the arm.

'I do not know whether you have had any further thoughts on the nature of this killing, Nicholas?'

I gave a rueful smile. 'Thoughts, aye. As tangled as the undergrowth we ploughed through in Wychwood. Conclusions? Never a one, though I am almost certain it could not have been an accident.'

I told him my reasons, based on the flamboyant

nature of Mordon's clothing.

He nodded. 'My thinking also. However, I think we may narrow it a little further. This morning, before coming to Mass, I seized the opportunity to take another look at that injury. The light was poor in the wood, with evening coming on, when we found him. In bright daylight, I noticed something further which had escaped me before.'

He paused.

'The angle of the arrow. Straight through the man, a level shot. Such an arrow could not have been shot by a man standing on the ground, and shooting upwards. It was loosed at much the same height as it penetrated, I would guess, and from quite close by. A horseman, I'd say, who had no difficulty in approaching Mordon, and so was known to him. I do not believe it could have been one of the villagers, on foot.'

I nodded. 'I am sure you have the right of it. A man on foot, shooting upwards – the arrow would have entered at a steep angle. Indeed, might not have penetrated so deeply as to prove fatal.'

We stopped on the verge of the village street.

'It was a man on horseback,' I said. 'One of the hunters.'

Chapter Eight

In the afternoon I took myself off to my bedchamber up under the eaves, to pen my letter to Emma. I always carry writing materials with me, so I drew from my scrip my portable inkwell, untrimmed quills, penknife, and a sheet of inexpensive parchment, a little ragged at the edges, for it had been in my scrip for some time.

I used the knife to neaten the sheet, and shaped the quills as I like them, moderately broad at the tip, with a slight slant. In preparing everything to my satisfaction, I managed to spin out the time until I must finally put the words down, for I had not yet decided what I should say. As a boy I had done my lessons for Sire Raymond on a little table beneath the window, and here I laid out pens, ink, and parchment in a neat row, drawing up the same stool I had used in those far off days. I thought of that boy I had once been, bent eagerly over the borrowed books, passionate to learn everything he could lay his hands on, seeing the world open up before his eyes.

What would that boy have thought of me now, a man grown? Probably with some little contempt, for having thrown away all that he had once thirsted for. Yet how far time and circumstance may change us! Indeed, my world had narrowed down, but it was a world I loved, a world where I was content. Jostling in the world of ambition and fame, would I have been as content? I doubted it.

I smoothed out the parchment with the edge of my hand, for it was inclined to curl. It stared up at me, creamy, open, inviting words I could not find. I began to chew the end of my quill, a habit I deplore in myself and scold in my scriveners. I held it out and looked at it gloomily. Tattered and unsightly. As a boy I would never have come so near to ruining a quill. My supply then was limited, for goose feathers were not readily available in the village. Often I had to make do with chicken feathers or the feathers of wild birds like gulls or ravens, found by chance. None served as well as goose feathers, so I treasured those I owned. Nowadays, with a ready supply, I was grown careless. I could even afford good quality feathers to fletch my arrows, though I rarely used a bow now, save for practice at the town butts. I had never so much as notched an arrow to my bow during the ill-fated hunt in Wychwood on Friday.

I brushed the crumpled plume into something like order, and dipped the quill in the ink pot, wiped the tip on the rim to avoid blots. I would begin as Emma had done:

Dear friend,

And what to say now? Well, I could say something of our work on the harvest, then try to find some response to her curious letter. Should I mention the death of Mordon? Surely I must, for if she did not hear of it until the time when next I saw her, she would wonder why, having written to her, I had not mentioned it.

I have received your letter, brought hither by carrier from Mistress Farringdon, for which I give you thanks. Your drawings are very fine, and they recall for me my visit to your grandfather's manor.

Well enough, although I sounded somewhat pompous.

Our party made a safe journey, though tiring, from Oxford here to my cousin's farm, and I trust your own journey did not overtax you.

I was beginning to sound like some ancient dame. What was amiss with me? Should I begin again? But I had not brought many sheets of parchment. Best not to waste this.

Most of the harvest has gone well, as long as the good weather held. The wheat and barley are all cut and partly threshed. A bad storm hit us before we could gather the oats, so we now must save what we can. The children run wild here in the country, and Rowan is in some disgrace today for chasing the cock and pulling out one of his tail feathers. It would make a good subject for one of your drawings.

That was better. A simple account of our activities. But I had mentioned drawing again, so I could not avoid the issue.

Would that I might employ you as a scrivener! Though perhaps it would put poor Roger's nose out of joint. But, dear friend, you have another role in life now. No longer Sister Benedicta, confined to Godstow Abbey, yet free to work in the scriptorium. Now the Lady Emma, heir to a goodly manor. Your grandfather must have other plans for you.

I was not happy with this. It sounded cruelly dismissive. Even 'dear friend' sounded like a sop to soften harsh words. But it was written now. Let it stand. Could I somehow take away the sting? I began to chew the end of my quill again.

You have a great talent, both as an artist and as a scribe, but what can I do? We are trapped, both of us, in what the world expects of us. Perhaps you might make another book, for your own pleasure? I will help you all I can, supply parchment and coloured inks and gold foil, discuss with you what binding would best suit. It would give me much joy to do so. Would that please you? Of course, it may be that you will not return to Oxford, but remain with your grandfather.

Did that sound like an ultimatum? I hoped not.

Jesu! I had never written a more difficult letter in my life. Should I have repeated 'dear friend'? What would she make of that? It was the phrase she had used herself, so surely she could not take exception to it. Safer, much safer, to turn away from any matter that touched us and write instead about Mordon.

On Friday, two days gone, we joined a party to hunt the deer in Wychwood, the first hunt of the season. The new owner of Leighton Manor had invited my cousin and his household, and we went right gladly, for we used to hunt there as boys, in Lord de Vere's time, although the new lord, Gilbert Mordon, had shown himself ill-natured and haughty to all hereabouts. The hereditary huntsman of the manor, a lifelong friend, had been dismissed of his post by Mordon, though required to organise this first hunt before leaving.

I stopped again. Should I tell Emma all the details of why Alan Wodville had quarrelled with Mordon? Nay, my small piece of parchment would not hold so many words.

During the hunt, when all the party was dispersed amongst the woods, somehow it came about that Mordon was shot with an arrow and killed. The killer is not known, although Mordon's widow ordered that the huntsman should be seized and imprisoned, since he had been seen in angry dispute with her husband a short time before. Yet he is the one person never out of sight at any time and could not have done the deed.

There was little room left to write more.

We have sent word to the coroner and sheriff, for if the matter be not placed in the hands of the law, I fear for my friend. The lady is very hot against him. We must remain here until the matter is resolved, for Cousin Edmond and I, together with Sir Henry Talbot, were finders of the body.

I may hope to see you on my return to Oxford.
Your friend, Nicholas Elyot.

There, that concluded it with the doubtful death of Mordon, nothing further touching on her talk of working as my scrivener. Nothing as to how matters stood between us, if indeed they could be said to stand at all. I ran my fingers through my hair. Of course she was not serious about coming to work for me. It was folly on my part to think so. The lady merely meant to tease.

After I had folded and sealed my letter, impressing the wax with my seal, I realised I had not asked her – as I had meant to do – whether her grandfather had yet resolved the matter of her confinement to Godstow Abbey by the actions of her stepfather, Falkes Malaliver. As her nearest kin, Sir Anthony Thorgold should be able to break Malaliver's gift of Emma as an *oblata*, at least that was Philip Olney's legal opinion. If need be, I did not doubt that Sir Anthony would make a generous gift to the abbey, in recompense for losing their unwilling novice, for she was his only kin. He had had no part in Malaliver's plot to divert Emma's inheritance into his own hands, but would ensure it could not happen. Nothing more had been heard of the man since Emma's flight from the abbey, but I was not altogether easy in my mind that he would not make some other attempt.

Most of our household had decided to enjoy the day of leisure with small tasks – mending harness, knitting winter hose, reading the book I had brought for Stephen. He had finished it, and it was now being passed about amongst those who could read with pleasure. I found Jordain bowed over his papers on the kitchen table.

'Working?' I asked.

'Preparation for the Michaelmas term.'

'Let it rest. You have done little but labour in the fields since you arrived. I am walking down to the village to find Geoffrey Carter. Do you come with me. 'Tis a fine afternoon, too fine to spend indoors.'

He grinned. 'Very well. I will let you tempt me.'

Outside we found the children throwing a ball for Rowan. Susanna had contrived it for them from some scraps of leather and stuffed it with straw. As soon as they saw what we were about, they clamoured to come with us.

'Not this time,' I said firmly, for I had another visit in mind, where children might not be welcome. 'Another day we will all go down to the village, or perhaps we may cast a fishing line into the stream. We sometimes caught a trout in the mill stream when I was a boy.'

Fishing, I thought, would be a pastime suitable for all, even for the youngest, and for Stephen, who could sit and hold a fishing rod as easily as anyone.

Jordain and I took our time walking down the lane to the village.

'Already the summer flowers are fading,' he said, 'despite the clear skies and the August sun.'

I nodded. There was a soft perfume in the air of fading greenery and of the cut stems of harvested grain. Even the sweet scent of the hay still lingered 'Aye. Somehow harvest always marks the beginning of autumn, before summer is fairly done.'

We walked a little further in silence.

'So what is it you want to talk to me about?' he asked.

'Ah, you did not think I invited you purely for the pleasure of your company?'

He grinned. 'The visit to the village is but an excuse. We were there this morning. It is the murder of Gilbert Mordon that is worrying you, is it not?'

'Not merely an excuse, I have a reason. I need Geoffrey Carter to carry a letter to Oxford for me.' I hesitated, but Jordain and I have never had many secrets from each other. 'I received a letter from Emma Thorgold. I have written an answer to it.'

He nodded. 'I thought I knew her hand, on that letter you had. I remember it from the book of hours you bought from the bookbinder Stalbroke.'

'Stalbroke was merely the intermediary. I bought it from Godstow Abbey.'

'She is well, Mistress Thorgold? Or Lady Emma, should we call her now?'

'She seems well. I have told her about the events at the hunt, the death of Mordon.'

'Aye, as I said, it is worrying you.'

'It was Edmond and Sir Henry and I who found the body, so, aye, it is worrying me. Not that I care a farthing for the man himself.' I paused. 'Nay, that is unkind. No man should die thus before his time, by violence and unshriven. He had surely another twenty years of life ahead of him. With age he might have become kinder. More tolerant. What worries me is the accusations being made against Alan Wodville. He is an old friend. I have known him even longer than you, though not as well. We grew up here as boys.'

'But surely–' Jordain stopped and sat down on an old fallen tree beside the path. 'It is clear that he could never have been alone, he was surrounded by others the whole time of the hunt. It must have been a man alone who did the deed, or a man accompanied by no more than a single trusted friend.'

'Everything points that way,' I agreed, 'yet Alan is but a simple villager, while the Lady Edith and her London friends, including that lawyer Baverstoke, have so fixed on him that they are convinced he shall be found guilty. And they have money and power to enforce their will.'

'The coroner will surely see the force of truth.'

'I know nothing of the present coroner for this part of the shire. He is a new man since I lived here. William Facherel, he is named. You and I both have some familiarity with the Oxford coroners. Experienced and skilled men, although their inquest on the death of young Farringdon was conducted somewhat hastily. But of this new fellow I have heard nothing.'

I braced my foot against the log on which he was sitting, and clasped my hands about my knee.

'Who will the coroner summon for the jury, do you suppose? Everyone who was present at the hunt? In Oxford, they summon jurors from the nearest three or four parishes, but that cannot be the custom here. The next parishes are too far away.'

He nodded. 'Probably everyone from the hunt, save the women and children. So I should guess also.'

'Then the greater number will come from the village, but the party from London is also large. I suspect they will speak the loudest and their voices will carry more weight.'

'And you believe they will speak out for the guilt of the huntsman?'

'Do not you?'

'Aye. Probably. It is in man's nature. Alan Wodville is a stranger to them. Let the guilt be fixed on him, and then they will be away home to London. I doubt they will ever be seen in these parts again.'

'Except,' I pointed out, 'the Lady Edith, if she is indeed heir to the manor.'

'That is very true. And she has had these few days to persuade her friends to her own conviction of Alan's guilt, did they not already believe it.'

'As a woman, she cannot be a juror.'

'But she can be summoned as a witness. You may be sure she will do her best to blacken him.'

'Aye.' I turned and sat down beside him. 'I have been trying to make out *why* she is so fixed against him. I think it is not merely because of his quarrel with her husband. I think it is because, in going to the rescue of the little maidservant Elga, Alan exposed – before the faces of his important friends – just what manner of man he was. His wife? She probably knew or guessed it already. But then she was humiliated not merely by his behaviour but by the public revelation of it. That, she cannot forgive Alan Wodville.'

He nodded. 'I think you have the right of it. As long as it remained secret, she could hold her head high in her pride. Humiliation would not come easily to such a woman.'

I sighed. 'If the inquest goes as we suspect, then Alan will be forced to stand trial before the sheriff. Lady Edith cannot hold such a trial in the manor court, whatever she may claim. In our present king's time, an end is being put to such practices. It will be trial before the sheriff.'

'That surely is to be welcomed. Better than a manor court conducted by Lady Edith.'

'Better than that, indeed, but not quite to be

welcomed. The present High Sheriff of the joint shrievalty of Oxfordshire and Berkshire is John de Alveton.'

'I have heard the name,' he said.

'Aye, and so also have I,' I said. 'He has held the post before – in '35, '41, and '42. In '41 he held office for a mere nine days. That was the year the king set afoot an enquiry into the many complaints about corruption amongst the county sheriffs. I was only a boy. It was the year before we went up to Oxford. But I remember very clearly my father and his friends talking about it. There had been complaints against de Alveton, for taking bribes – both for turning a blind eye and letting a guilty man go free, and for pinning a guilty verdict on an innocent man. Though the word was, in that case, such a man could probably buy a pardon.'

Jordain pulled a face. 'I remember that enquiry, but I did not know the sheriff of Oxfordshire was involved.'

'Oh, he was by no means the most venal. He lost his office that year, but was let off with a fine. He was High Sheriff again the following year. And here he is, back once more. There were others far worse, who milked their shires through extortion and fraud, while with de Alveton it was petty bribes. But in this case, with all the coin on Lady Edith's side, the outlook seems bleak for Alan, if it comes to trial.'

Jordain cocked his head to one side. 'You think you can help him? Prove his innocence?'

I spread my hands and shrugged. 'I think I must try. Will you help me? In the first place, we must gather everyone we can to assert that Alan was always in company for the whole time of the hunt.'

'He must have been. Unless–'

'Unless what?'

'I was not there, of course, since I did not join the hunt. I was still back in the clearing where we took our meal. But as it has been described to me . . . when the hunt first broke into two groups, one following the ride, the other turning aside into the thicker woods . . . was Alan not alone for a time then?'

I drew a shocked breath, then closed my eyes, trying to see again that moment of confusion.

I shook my head. 'Nay, there were hunt servants and dog handlers with him all the while. Some went one way, some the other, but he was never alone.'

'The only certain way,' Jordain said slowly, 'is not simply to prove Alan could not have shot that arrow, but to ascertain who did.'

'Aye.' I laughed grimly. 'Find the owner of a vanished arrow, and we have the murderer. An arrow, which you have said yourself is now probably nothing but ashes.'

I stood up, and brushed fragments of dusty bark from my cotte. 'I wonder,' I said, 'what was so distinctive about that arrow that the killer risked all to remove it from the body?'

'I shall be off to the south tomorrow,' Geoffrey Carter said. 'I should deliver your letter to Oxford two days after that, or three at most. I have a load of woollen broadcloth to collect in Witney and carry to a clothier in Northgate Street, and nothing else but a few small errands on the way.'

I gave him the farthing he asked for carrying the letter, with my thanks.

'You know my journeyman scrivener, Walter Blunt,' I said. 'I have not written him a letter, but could you take him a word from me?'

'Aye, if 'tis not out of my way.'

'He has lodgings above the fruiterer's shop in Fish Street,' I said, 'not far from Carfax.'

'I know it.'

'Will you tell him that I may be delayed here by the inquest on Master Mordon? And mayhap by the trial as well, if there is to be one. Walter should reopen the shop if I am more than two more weeks here. There will not be much custom until the start of term. He will be able to manage, with Roger's help.'

'I will tell him so.' He squinted at me. 'Who do you think will be called for the inquest? I shall lose my load in Witney, and the fee, if I must stay here.'

'I think you should set off,' I said. 'As one of the finders of the body, I must stay. But you were not present at the hunt, were you?'

'Aye, I was there, with the rest of the village.' He winked at me. 'Kept my distance from the deer, but snagged two conies for the pot, while the lordling's eyes were elsewhere. And he'll not be claiming sole rights of warren now, will he?'

The shooting and snaring of rabbits who strayed from the manor's farmed coney warren had always been allowed to the villagers by Yves de Vere and his ancestors, but I had heard other hints beside this one of Gilbert Mordon's claim to own every rabbit in the neighbourhood, farmed rabbit or wild. Geoffrey Carter was another man who would not be sorry to see the last of the incomer. Could he have fired the shot? It was not impossible. Like every man in the village, he was trained to use the bow. From the age of seven they would practice at the butts at least once a week, for at any time a man might be called to serve under his lord in the king's wars. From fifteen he must provide himself with bow and arrows, in case he should be summoned for military service. As Jordain had said, rather than try to prove who did not shoot the fatal arrow, better to try to discover who did.

'Is that your business in the village finished, then?' Jordain asked, as we headed down the path from Geoffrey's cottage.

Before I could answer, his wife Joan turned in at the gate. She looked weary, but content.

'Good day to 'ee, Master Elyot,' she said, bobbing a curtsey, 'and to 'ee, maister.' She smiled at Jordain. Her basket was filled with bottles and jars, with a bundle of rags tucked in beside them, some of them bloodied.

'A new arrival this day, Joan?' I asked. I turned to

Jordain. 'Our village midwife. Her mother brought me into the world.'

'Aye, so she did.' Joan grinned. 'And by all I've heard, you greeted the world squalling your head off. There's a new mouth to feed at Matt Grantham's. Another lusty lad.' She shook her head. 'A blessed babe, born on the Sabbath, but how much of a blessing to Matt and his woman? That's the tenth, and all of them still living, every year another babe, but only the two eldest old enough to work in the fields. How can they feed them all? It's past my reckoning.'

'If Matt needs work,' I said, 'there's a deal of threshing yet to do at my cousin's. He would be glad of more hands.'

She tucked an errant wisp of hair back under the tight edge of her wimple. 'I'll tell him, Master Elyot. It has been a bad time they've had of late, with this threat of villeinage hanging over them. If Matt was forced into villein work on the manor demesne, and could not take paid day labour when he is not working his own land, then I'm thinking they would starve. Do you think that will be set aside now, that claim that he is a villein, all on account of a small parcel of land?'

'I am sure there were never grounds for reducing Matt to villeinage,' I said firmly. 'On the evidence of all the parish, he would have been judged a free man, had it ever come to court. It was never more than an empty threat, and even that is gone now.'

As we made our way along the village street, Jordain said quietly, 'This new father, this was the man Mordon tried to claim was his villein?'

'Aye,' I said grimly. 'And Matt Grantham is as freeborn as you or I.'

'So yet another man who had reason enough to kill.'

'Reason indeed, but I do not see Matt shooting a man furtively in the back. More like he would slam a fist into his face or throttle him with his bare hands.'

'Still–'

'Oh, aye. He had reason. But as well, I cannot see Matt having cool enough wits to remove his arrow. Even had he shot Mordon, he would most likely have kicked him where he lay, then stormed off and drunk himself senseless at the alehouse.'

'Not a kindly man, then.'

I laughed. 'There is no real harm in Matt Grantham. And he mostly uses his fists only when he's downed too much ale. 'Twas too early in the day for that.'

'You have another errand in the village?' Jordain asked, for I was leading the way to the far end of the street.

'I want to see how Beth Wodville fares, and if she has had any word of Alan.'

'I remember her, she was at the Lammas supper and the harvesting. A slight, fair-haired woman, a little frail for the work.'

'She is, but that does not stop her from working as hard as any of the village women. The Wodvilles have had some uncertain times since the de Vere family died, not knowing what the future might bring. The de Vere heir, away in Leicestershire, he kept Alan on in some of his duties as huntsman, just to see to the hunting dogs, and the few hunt horses that were left. Alan and Beth must have thought all would be well once the manor found a new owner.'

'They have no children?'

'Beth lost two, stillborn, and another at a few months old. Then they took in Alan's nephew Rob when the boy was orphaned. And of course his sister, Jane, was more like a daughter, being so much younger.'

'This is the child Mordon tried to defile?'

'It is. Alan has taken her away to Burford.'

We had reached the Wodville's cottage, which looked forlorn, as though no one was about. I knocked at the door and was greeted with silence.

'Beth!' I called, 'It is Nicholas Elyot. I have come to see how you are faring.'

There was a sound of movement from within, then I

heard the latch lifted and the door opened slowly. Beth was no longer her trim and pretty self. Her gown looked as though she had slept in it, she wore no wimple and her hair hung loose and tangled to her shoulders. Her eyes were red and swollen with weeping. The lad Rob had been serving the priest in church that morning, but I realised that I had seen no sign of Beth. Impulsively I reached out and took both her hands in mine.

'May we come in?' I was sure she had no wish to be a spectacle for the village street.

She nodded, withdrawing her hands gently from mine and holding the door wider for us.

'You will take a cup of ale?' she said, her voice no more than a hoarse whisper.

I saw that Jordain was about to refuse, but I smiled and nodded. 'That would be kind, Beth. It is a dusty walk down from the farm.'

I turned to Jordain. 'Beth is famous for her ale. She uses some secret herbs in the making, which she will reveal to no one.'

Beth gave a watery smile as she went to fetch the ale, but did not speak. In truth, I had no need of ale myself, but I could see that she did, having wept herself hoarse almost to speechlessness.

'Now,' I said, when she took a seat on a stool and began to twist her hair nervously into a knot behind her head. 'I have come to tell you to leave off weeping. Alan is in no danger, of that I am sure.'

'Oh, Nicholas,' she said, 'if I could but believe that were true! But the Lady Edith has him in prison and she is determined he shall hang for the murder of her husband. I swear to you, he never killed that man, though he had good reason to hate him.'

'Of course he did not kill him! Alan was one of a handful of people who were never out of sight of company. The hunt servants and dog handlers will swear that they were with him the whole time of the hunt.'

'But who will listen to them? Poor folk? Servants?

Those grand people from London will say that they are lying to protect him.'

'I think not, mistress.' Jordain set down his ale cup and smiled at her reassuringly. 'Anyone who understands the role of a huntsman in pursuit of a deer will know that he would have been surrounded at all times. The killing of Gilbert Mordon was done by stealth.'

'And,' I said, 'there is something that it is unpleasant to discuss, but you are a woman strong of courage, Beth. Whoever shot Mordon stayed long enough to withdraw the arrow, he did not take to his heels at once. It cannot have been done quickly, for it was a grisly business, tearing the flesh. So the killer must have been out of general view for some time.'

She turned somewhat pale at my words, no doubt imagining for herself what I had just described, but despite her frail appearance, I knew that she was stout of heart.

'But unless the true killer can be found,' she said, 'they will still arraign Alan for the murder.'

I shook my head. 'I think not, but to make all sure, the true killer must be found. Since he took care to remove his arrow, there must have been a reason. He must have thought that the arrow could identify him. Now I wonder, has Alan ever mentioned to you anyone who uses unusual arrows? Anything distinctive at all?'

She bit her lip, thinking, but shook her head. 'Nay, he has never told me anything of that, yet he may know of such arrows. If you could but speak to him, you could ask.' Her voice broke. 'But no one can speak to him, imprisoned as he is.'

'Never fret,' I said. 'Sir Henry Talbot has seen him this very morning. He is provided with a bed and food, and is well treated. Sir Henry is seeing to that.'

I knew that Sire Raymond meant to visit her to bring this comfort, but on the Sabbath he would be occupied in the church until late.

Like sunshine after cloud, her face brightened. 'Sir Henry has seen him! Oh, Jesu be thanked! I thought he was quite shut away. They would not let me see him. I went to the manor and begged, but I was turned away by that lawyer.'

'Sir Henry stays at the manor until the inquest is held,' I said. 'And I am sure that after the inquest, Alan will be set free again. The Lady Edith has no jurisdiction to hold him prisoner.'

'I pray you may have the right of it.'

'I intend myself to visit Alan,' I said. 'With Sir Henry to speak for me, I think it may be managed. It is growing too late today, but tomorrow morning I shall go to the manor as soon as I have broken my fast, if my cousin can spare me from salvaging what is left of the oats. They were badly beaten down by the storm.'

Beth gripped her hands together and raised a resolute face to me.

'I will put my trust in you, Nicholas, and not stay here weeping uselessly. Perhaps your cousin would be glad of my labour at the oat harvest, so that you may be spared? Even if Alan escapes the charges against him, he has lost his position as manor huntsman. Lady Edith will never employ him. So we must scrape a living as best we may.'

'Edmond will be glad of you, I am sure,' I said. 'But put your trust in God, Beth, and not in a weak man like me, groping for answers where all is hidden.'

She smiled then, a true smile, the first we had seen. 'I shall put my trust in you, Nicholas, as God's instrument.'

We were a quiet company at supper that evening, and went early to bed. With both Friday and Sunday lost to labour on the farm, it was needful to make the most of the dry weather in the oat field the next day, for clouds had begun to build again toward the end of the afternoon. Ever both the farmer's friend and enemy, the changeable English weather!

'I shall walk over to the manor early,' I said to Edmond, as we carried our rush dips upstairs to bed. 'My business with Alan should not take long, if Sir Henry is able to bring me to him. Then I shall come straight back, ready for field work again.'

He nodded. 'Take more time if you need. There is the matter of gathering witnesses to the fact that Alan was never alone at the time of Mordon's death.'

'True,' I said. 'While I am at the manor I had best take the opportunity to speak to the dog handlers. Those who served as Alan's assistant huntsmen were some of them manor servants, others were villagers who know the hunt business. I will try to speak to any I can find about the manor. Most of the villagers he employed I think I can remember. Them I can visit tomorrow also. The sooner they are all apprised of what they must tell the coroner, the better.'

'I wonder how soon he can be here. Mordon must not remain much longer unburied.'

'Nay.' I shuddered.

Although I was early in my bed, I took a long time finding sleep. Certainly the day had lacked the physical labour which often brings sleep the moment one's head touches the pillow. But rather it was the whirling of thoughts in my head which would not let me rest. If this unknown coroner was a man of sense, our argument that Alan was never out of sight of company should convince the man that the huntsman was not the killer. But men in the pride of such offices like to show their ability by settling such matters swiftly and with decisiveness. A coroner hates an open verdict. Much better to be able to point the finger and say: 'This is the man. It was done thus. Here is the weapon of such-and-such a value to be rendered to the crown.' Not for nothing was the coroner called the 'crowner'. My mind went chasing away, like a hound after a hare. What would be the value in coin of a single arrow, probably now destroyed? A ha'penny? Less, surely. Would the royal official concern himself with something so trivial? Perhaps the bow which shot the arrow would also come into the reckoning of the *deodand* owed to the crown, and the value of a fine bow is considerable.

I threw myself over in my bed, and pushed aside the single blanket in irritation. Why was my mind concerning itself with such things? Behind the jumble of thoughts about the killing of Mordon, I sensed a certain separate unease within myself. Why had I written that letter to Emma? The more I thought of it, the more I regretted it. It was pure folly, one moment pompous, the next . . . Perhaps I should go to Geoffrey Carter's house at dawn and demand the letter back again.

Annoyed with myself, distracted and uncomfortable, eventually I fell asleep.

It was no surprise, then, that I woke late the next morning. The moment I opened my eyes, I could tell from the light pouring in through the open shutters that I was too late to retrieve my letter from Geoffrey. He would have left at dawn, or even before, to gain the most advantage of the day. By now he would be well away.

I sat up and swung my feet to the floor, my head in my hands. My mouth was dry and my head ached, as if I had drunk deep the night before, so troublesome had my wandering wits been, without even the assistance of ale. Well, there was nothing to be done about my letter. Instead, I must think of my visit to the manor.

I dressed carefully, donning the clothes I normally wore only for church on Sunday. My bedchamber contained no glass to see myself, for as a boy I had never needed one. The small ivory comb I had brought with me from Oxford lacked some teeth, but I tugged it as best I might through my somewhat tangled locks. Like my children, I have hair which curls randomly and tangles readily if I do not pay it mind, and I had been too distracted to do so of late. The comb teased out a small gleaning of straw fragments and husks. Truly, I was a disgrace to my family.

When I descended to the kitchen, I found the rest of the household halfway through breakfast.

'I thought you planned to rise early,' Jordain said with a grin.

I shook my head. 'I did not sleep well. I'll not sit down. Susanna, if you will cut me some bread, I will eat as I walk.'

She began to slice a new loaf, its warm yeasty smell filling the air. 'There is some cold bacon, too,' she said, folding the bread around a piece, 'and stay at least for a sup of ale.'

'Aye, I will that. My mouth is as dry as a threshing floor.'

I took the cup she handed me, and drained it swiftly, but would not sit down to eat. I had already wasted too much of the early morning, lying slug-abed.

Birds were singing as I made my way down to the village, not the urgent songs of the spring wooing but the slightly melancholy cadences which told of another year's life gone, the young birds flown from the nest. The migrating birds would soon set off on their mysterious travels, like restless pilgrims who cannot endure to remain long at home. The birds always native to our English shires would be feeding up now in preparation for the lean months of winter. I watched a flight of starlings pass overhead, making for Edmond's wheat field. The gleaners would have missed some of the fallen grain, and the cut stems would have exposed the low creeping creatures which would fill an avian belly.

In the village I exchanged greetings here and there, but did not linger, pressing on to the turn which led to the manor. Here there was the usual morning bustle about the yard and barns and stables, almost as if tragedy and death had not laid hands on the place. Only, the servants were perhaps somewhat more quiet than is usually the case at a busy manor. There was no whistling, no singing, hardly a word exchanged as men and women went about their business.

I thought I would take my chance with the dog handlers now, for once the hounds were fed, they would be taken out to exercise, and I might miss my chance. Aelfric, the most senior of them, though he was hardly more than two and twenty, was just coming from the kennels carrying an empty bucket.

'A word, Aelfric,' I said.

He looked at me dubiously. 'I've my work to do, Master Elyot.'

'This will take but a moment,' I said. 'On Friday, at the hunt, when the party split between the ride and the woods, you went into the woods with Master Wodville, did you not? I was a short way behind you then, though I lost sight of you later.'

'Aye.' He drew it out, reluctantly. 'I followed Master Wodville, as he bid. Took half of the dogs with me. T'other half went up the ride with Gudrun, as we was meant to go.'

I nodded. 'Then you stayed with him right to the kill. When we caught up with you, you were leashing the dogs and feeding them. Sir Henry and I were delayed when one of our group caught a blow from a branch, but we were not far behind. So you were with Master Wodville the whole time.'

He shifted his feet and looked aside. 'I couldn't rightly say.'

'What do you mean? You must have stayed with him. Where else would you go? The lymers scented a stag and you all went off in pursuit.'

He shook his head, but did not speak. I saw that he glanced anxiously in the direction of the house.

'Who shot the stag?' I asked.

As if he could not hold back the words, he burst out, 'Master Wodville. There wasn't any other hunters near by then. Good clean shot to the breast. I sent in the alaunts, but there weren't no need. Beast were already dead.'

'So you *were* with him the whole time. And the rest of the handlers, those who went into the wood.'

He swallowed nervously, and muttered, 'I suppose I were.'

'And the others?'

'Aye.'

'What ails you, Aelfric?'

'Told not to say aught, weren't we?'

'Who told you?'

'Lawyer fellow. Him in the black gown.'

I drew a deep breath. It seemed Alan's enemies were already at work.

'At the inquest, Aelfric, you must tell the truth, sworn to it on the Bible. If you lie, your immortal soul will be in peril. Neither Lawyer Baverstoke nor any other man can compel you to such mortal danger. You must speak truth, and so must the rest of the men. Do you understand?'

He was sweating now. He put down his bucket and rubbed his face with his sleeve. It was threadbare, and already mended at the elbow.

'Told we'd be turned away if we spoke in defence of Master Wodville,' he whispered, leaning close.

So that was the way of it.

'You do not need to speak either for or against the huntsman,' I said. 'All you must do is tell the simple truth of what you did, where you were, and what you saw. Did you have Master Wodville always in sight?'

'Aye.' It came grudgingly, but he looked at me instead of the house.

'And the others?'

'I cannot speak for 'em. They must speak for theirselves.'

'Indeed they must. But will you tell them that they will be under holy oath at the inquest? That they *must* speak the truth?'

'I'll tell 'em.'

'Good.' I looked about the yard. I could see two maids coming from the barn with buckets of milk, while a cattleman and his boy urged the cows toward the gate leading to the pasture. Household servants were shaking out bedding and sweeping the steps, but I saw no sign of any of the hunt servants.

'What of the general hunt servants Master Wodville employed?' I asked. 'I can see none here.'

He shrugged. 'Turned away, all but two as looks after

the horses, but they're general stable lads.'

'Then tell them as well. Most were men from the village, but some I did not know.'

'Two-three from over Shipton way. Worked for old Master Wodville in the past. Not too pleased, they wasn't. Turned away without pay, and a long trudge home.'

That might make them the more willing to speak up for Alan, I thought. The party at the manor had made a mistake in not paying fair wages. It would have been little enough. A single earring of the Lady Edith's would represent ten years' wages for such men. Sir Henry knew Shipton better than I. He might know these men.

'I thank you for your time, Aelfric. And remember, at the inquest, no harm can come to you from speaking the truth.'

He spat into the dust of the yard. 'Harm enough, if I lose my place.' He picked up his bucket, turned, and walked away.

Chapter Nine

I found Sir Henry in the orchard, stomping about under the laden trees and punting fallen apples with a heavy stick into the long grass. The place looked unkempt. No one had bothered to gather the windfalls, which Margaret – or any of the womenfolk I knew – would have pounced upon for early pies, or made into preserves. Even windfall apples bear unblemished portions which make good food. This was sheer waste, given over to the smeary trails of slugs and the eager buzzing of feasting wasps. Every time Sir Henry lobbed an apple with his stick, an angry cluster of the insects rose menacingly into the air, then settled again on the nearest half rotten fruit.

'Have you not been stung yet?' I asked.

'They know better than to try.' He batted away a wasp more courageous than the rest. 'Do you see this? The trees have had their spring pruning, but I'd say never a man has been near the orchard since. Fruit left to rot. And they should have sheep here, keeping the grass down. Takes the goodness from the trees.'

'Or turned the swine in here, to benefit from the windfalls,' I said. 'Yves de Vere's servants were kept on, and his villeins did their customary work on the demesne as long as his heir held the manor,' I said. 'At least that is what Edmond has told me. That is why the spring pruning was done. Since then?' I shrugged. 'I'm told Mordon dismissed most or all of the servants, and the villeins would do only the work they were given by the reeve. Under the new lord, I do not know who that would be.'

'Whoever it is, he has no care for the orchard. This used to be one of the best in this part of the shire.'

He flung his stick away. It sailed to the far edge of the orchard, hit a tree, and fell into the thick grass. He strode over to me, his boots swishing through the long, feathery stems, which sparkled with the morning's heavy dew.

'I should be back on my own lands,' he said bitterly. 'I cannot expect my son to see to everything at this busy time of the year, when he has his own estate to care for. Instead I must kick my heels here until the coroner comes.'

'Is there any word?'

'Aye, one of his servants arrived late last night. He should be here tomorrow. Let us pray the inquest will be over before the end of the day.'

'Not if he decides against Alan Wodville.'

He made a disgusted noise. 'There is no case against the man. Are you here to see him?'

'I am.'

We turned together toward the house.

'Fortunately, one at least of de Vere's servants is still here,' Sir Henry said. 'The cellarer. It seems he is so knowledgeable about the stores of expensive French wine that even Mordon was not such a fool as to part with him. He knows me of old, and will give us the key to the cellar where your man is held.'

Sir Henry led me into the house through the back premises, thus avoiding any danger of encountering Lady Edith and her friends.

The cellarer, Warin Hodgate, was a man ripe in years but still upright and impressive. Had he worn richer garb, instead of his sober gown of good but plain cloth, a visiting stranger might have taken him for the lord of the manor, in preference to Mordon, with his vulgar but costly mountebank's clothes.

'I have here the key, Sir Henry,' Hodgate said, without needing to be asked. 'Good day to you, Master

Elyot.' He gave me a dignified but restrained bow. He had known me as a boy, scrumping apples from the orchard we had just left. I suppose, in his eyes, I was not much changed or raised in rank since those days.

'How does the huntsman fare this morning?' Sir Henry said.

'In body, well enough. Distressed in mind, though. He is anxious for his wife.'

'I saw her last evening,' I said. 'And she is equally distressed for him, but otherwise in good health. She is made fearful by what is being said here.' I nodded my head towards the other part of the house.

Hodgate gave a short bark of laughter. 'They may say what they wish. There is no possibility Master Wodville raised a hand against the man.'

The man not *my lord*. It seemed Hodgate was not afraid to speak out.

'I saw Aelfric on my way here,' I said, 'and ascertained that Mordon was always in his sight. However, he – and the others – are afraid to affirm this at the inquest. They have been threatened.'

Sir Henry looked at me in shock, but Hodgate seemed unsurprised.

'There have been a number of threats made,' Hodgate said, cool but grim.

'They must tell the truth under oath,' Sir Henry said.

'That is what I told him, and put the fear of hellfire in him, but he fears also for his living.'

Hodgate began to lead us toward the steps down to the cellars, which lay beneath the undercroft, halfway below ground, where stores might be kept cool.

'They are a strange lot, this household,' he said. 'Do you not find them so, Sir Henry?'

'Strange here in an Oxfordshire manor. They would not seem so strange in London, amongst the great merchant houses, with a sprinkling of lesser men circling about them, hoping for gains, and a few from noble families, brought into an alliance. As the wealth of our merchants in coin begins to outstrip the wealth of our nobles in land, such alliances are become more common.'

'You are thinking of the Lady Edith,' I said.

He inclined his head. 'I am. But there is one other here who puzzles me.'

We had paused at the top of the steps.

'Who is that?'

'You will have observed him, Hodgate. A small, quiet man, as soberly dressed as a lawyer, but not a lawyer – cotte, hose, and short gown, all in dark colours, greys and browns. Unremarkable, you would say.'

'That would be Master Le Soten?'

'It would. I find it strange to see him in this company. I have encountered him twice before, always quiet, always discreet. But then he was at court.'

I raised my eyebrows at this. 'At *court*?'

'Aye. I barely noticed him. I think he is a man who wishes *not* to be noticed. His position at court, I do not know. What he is doing here, I cannot imagine. I find it hard to believe that he was any manner of friend to Gilbert Mordon.'

Sir Henry took the key Hodgate held out to him, and together we started down the steps, leaving the cellarer to his duties. The air grew cooler as we descended, but it was not unpleasant, nor was it damp.

'This man Le Soten,' I said, 'do you think his presence here has any bearing on Mordon's death?'

He shrugged. 'Who can say? But I do find it curious.'

'I have heard,' I said slowly, 'that Mordon had made loans to the king, for the expenses of the French wars, and that Leighton Manor was in some sort a repayment for those loans. Could that have any bearing on Le Soten's presence? He does seem an unlikely guest.'

'Indeed.'

'I think we should speak to him,' I said, 'if we may.'

Sir Henry nodded. 'I agree. Now, this is where the huntsman is held.'

He fitted the key in the lock, which was well oiled

and turned easily. The room in which Alan Wodville had been confined was merely one of the several storage rooms in these cellars, but – as Sir Henry had observed – not one of those given over to wine and ale. A window high in the wall, just above ground level, gave adequate light, showing that the room was bare but clean. There were a few sacks of dried beans and a row of large crockery jars lined up along one wall, which probably held salted peas or beans, or perhaps pickles of some sort. At this point in the late summer, the previous year's stores would be all but exhausted and the manor's supply of storage jars would be scoured ready for the new season's bounty, although by the dust on the shoulders of these jars, nothing had yet been done to preserve this summer's crops. The Lady Edith had been here in Leighton for no more than a few weeks, and so it seemed she had not yet undertaken the supervision of the manor housekeeping. In her London home she would certainly have no fields and gardens from which the winter's supply of food must be gathered. She would purchase all she needed from the shops and markets of the city.

It was strange, however, if she came from a family of landed nobility, that she had not been trained by her own mother in the running of a manor. Unless the family left all such tasks to a housekeeper and a steward. Margaret, I knew, would be aghast at such lack of supervision from the woman who was, after all, the ruler of her domestic realm, as surely as her husband was ruler of his business.

Alan was sitting cross legged on a well filled straw palliasse laid on the floor, with a thin pillow and a folded blanket laid neatly at the end. There was no other furniture but a pisspot and a bucket of water for washing. A tray, with breadcrumbs, and bowl and cup now empty, bore witness that he had been given breakfast, probably more than I had eaten myself. His clothes were rumpled and he had several days' stubble on his chin. The eyes he lifted to us as we entered were anxious. He jumped up.

'Nicholas! It is good of you to come! The witch

allowed it?'

'If you mean the Lady Edith,' I said mildly, 'I did not ask for her leave. Sir Henry is on the best of terms with Warin Hodgate. We came in through the kitchens.'

Alan laughed. 'Aye, you would recall the way, from when we were boys. That old cook used to make excellent gingerbread, do you remember?'

I smiled, but could see that he was merely talking to cover up his present fears.

'I have been to see Beth,' I said. 'She is bearing up well. She tried to visit you, but was turned away by the lawyer Baverstoke, having made the mistake of coming to the front door. Today she will be working in Edmond's oat field. We lost some of the crop, but with patience and care most can be saved.'

I, too, was talking of trivial matters in the hope of bringing him some ease, but knew he could not be diverted.

'Nicholas has been talking to Aelfric,' Sir Henry said. 'The dog handlers will bear witness that they had you in sight the whole time of the hunt. There was no possible way you could have shot Gilbert Mordon.'

'I will also speak to as many of the villagers as possible this afternoon and evening,' I said. 'Both those you employed as hunt assistants, and those who were hunting for themselves on foot. With all the testimony we can bring, the unfounded charge made against you by Lady Edith must be thrown out by the coroner.'

'Nicholas has the right of it.'

Sir Henry clapped Alan on the shoulder. 'The coroner comes tomorrow, and if he has any sense, he will hold the inquest at once, for it is time the man was buried. One more night here, and tomorrow you shall sleep in your own bed.'

Alan essayed a weak smile in acknowledgement of these cheering words, but did not look quite convinced.

'Perhaps. But the coroner – and the sheriff, I suppose – will not leave matters there, I fear. They will want to fix the guilt on someone. Mordon's friends have both money and power. They will demand a reckoning. And unless the true killer can be found, the shadow of the accusation will remain over me. Indeed, over any man at the hunt who cannot be accounted for. Are you in the clear yourself, Nicholas? I should not like you to lift the blame from me, only to fall heir to it yourself.'

'Never fear,' Sir Henry said. 'Nicholas, his cousin, and one of the boys from Oxford were all together with me from the time we entered the trees until we caught up with you at the unlacing of the stag.'

'That fool Mordon!' Alan exclaimed. 'Had he not disregarded the agreed plan for the hunt and gone haring off along that other trail through the wood, this would never have happened.'

'True enough,' I said. 'Now, Alan, can you tell us? Do you know of any man, either local or amongst the visitors, who owns unusual arrows?'

He lifted his eyebrows at this. 'An unusual arrow? Is this what was used to kill Mordon? Bring it to me and I can soon tell you whether I recognise it or not.'

Sir Henry and I exchanged looks of astonishment.

'But, of course–' I said.

When Mordon was shot, Alan was far away in pursuit of the stag. He stayed with the quarry until it was dismembered and loaded on to the cart, together with the smaller deer shot by the villagers. He had then mounted and ridden home to the village, to remain there until seized by Lady Edith's servants and hauled away to this confinement. He had never seen Mordon's body. And it must be that no one had told him that the arrow had been withdrawn after the man was dead.

I turned to Sir Henry. 'You have not spoken to Alan of what we found?'

'Only that we found the body.'

'Alan,' I said, 'we do not have the arrow. Whoever shot Mordon took care to rip the arrow from the wound, tearing the flesh further. It has vanished. We must suppose that there was something about it, something which would identify the killer.'

Alan shook his head. 'Without sight of it, how can I tell? Most of the villagers use whatever feathers they may lay hands on, to fletch their arrows, but I cannot think any one of them has arrows different from his neighbours'. Some better made than others, certainly, but nothing distinctive.'

He ran his fingers through his matted hair and scratched at his unshaven chin.

'As for the visitors, I paid little heed to their gear. None of it was in my sight until the morning of the hunt, and by then I was too much occupied to notice. You ate with them. You probably saw more than I did.'

I shook my head. 'I may have done, but I paid it no heed. Why should any man examine another's arrows?'

Still, Alan made a shrewd point. I must cudgel my brains to see whether there was some memory buried there. And I must ask others who had eaten the hunt breakfast. Impossible to describe the arrow, but someone might have noticed something unusual.

'If anything comes to you,' I said, 'send me word. Now, do you need aught? Have you any message to send to Beth?'

'Tell her to be of good courage, that by tomorrow I shall surely be released.' He made another poor attempt at a smile, for I did not think he believed it himself. 'And ask her to send me clean clothes and a razor, and a comb for my hair. The coroner is more likely to think me innocent if I do not look like a masterless man living wild in the woods.'

'I will ask her so,' I said, 'and advise her to bring them here to the back of the house and give them to Warin Hodgate. No need to trust to the charity of Lady Edith.'

'None indeed,' Sir Henry said.

After we had locked the cellar door and returned the key to Hodgate, Sir Henry and I stepped outside into a day becoming more overcast. I looked anxiously at the sky, torn between trying to discover whatever we could before the coroner's arrival on the morrow, and concern for Edmond's crop of oats. I hoped that there would be enough hands to finish the work today, for there was still the next picking of peas and beans to gather, though I had heard Susanna say that she would set the children to that today, under the supervision of Hilda. Yet, even more urgently than the harvest, the gathering in of evidence could not wait.

'Do you think it might be possible to find this man you spoke of?' I asked Sir Henry. 'Le Soten? While I am here at the manor, I should like to learn whether he may have anything to say which might touch on the murder of Gilbert Mordon. However,' I smiled ruefully, 'I am not sure that Lady Edith would welcome my presence in her house, or that her watchdog Baverstoke would even permit me to cross the threshold.'

'Aye,' he said, 'somehow he has had word that you are seeking to vindicate the huntsman, and he does not like it. Go you back into the orchard. I will seek out Le Soten if I can, and bring him to you there. If he is not to be found, I will come anyway, and tell you.'

I waited perhaps half an hour, wandering through the long grass and encountering a hedgepig trundling along with two infants no bigger than my thumb following behind. They would feast indiscriminately both on the fallen apples and on the slugs which were busy feasting in their turn, with no fear of attack from wasps. A marvellous example of God's creation, is the hedgepig. So small, so invincible! And every gardener's friend.

At last I saw Sir Henry approaching, accompanied by a short, slight man of about forty, clad as he had described, in clothes so dull that he seemed almost wraith-like, blending into the background wherever he might be. I realised now that I had seen him before, at the hunt breakfast, seated at the inferior end of the table. He was indeed a man who sought not to be noticed.

'Master Le Soten,' Sir Henry said gravely, 'may I present Nicholas Elyot, Master of Arts at the university of Oxford? Nicholas, may I present Master Reginald Le

Soten?'

We both bowed, and I hid my smile, that Sir Henry had not chosen to introduce me as a humble tradesman and bookseller.

'We are anxious, sir,' I said, 'as perhaps Sir Henry has told you, to establish the facts of Gilbert Mordon's death. We, with one other, my cousin Edmond Elyot, were the finders of the body, and must give evidence at the inquest. Everything points to the killer *not* being the huntsman Alan Wodville, who is held here on mere unsubstantiated accusation. However, to clear his name, it were best if the truth of the killing were established.'

He inclined his head, but said nothing.

'Le Soten,' Sir Henry said briskly, 'let us not ramble about the matter like grazing sheep half asleep in the meadow. Someone shot Mordon either for hatred or for gain. You make an odd addition to the party here at the manor. Like me, you are an outsider. I believe you may know something which may help us.'

Le Soten again inclined his head. 'That may be so, Sir Henry.'

'You are here, I suspect, on the king's business. May we know what it is?'

That was bold indeed of Sir Henry. The man had a look about him of one who dealt in secrets, and kept those secrets close to his chest. Why should he reveal them to us? I could see that he was debating with himself whether to trust us with some at least of those secrets.

'You are correct, Sir Henry,' he said at last, 'in assuming that I am here on the king's business. I did not come from London with the rest of the party, but from Winchester, where the king is at present. My arrival,' he gave a tight smile, 'came as something of a surprise to Master Mordon.'

'We know,' I said, to save time, 'that Mordon was not merely a pepperer and spice merchant. He was a moneylender, and had made loans to the king. It is said that this manor was a repayment of those loans.'

If he was surprised at the extent of my knowledge, he did not show it.

'It was,' he said. 'Mordon produced documents, deeds and descriptions of the property, claiming that the value of the manor would clear half the king's debt to him, including the accrued interest. The arrangements with the de Vere heir were made through an intermediary, Mordon's lawyer, Sir Thomas Baverstoke.'

'He is here now,' I said.

'Aye, he is.'

Le Soten paused and took a few steps deeper into the orchard. We strolled after him.

'However, quite by chance, it came to my attention that the manor is much more extensive than the king was led to believe, and its value considerably more than the debt against which it was set. The de Vere heir had never visited the property, and learned only recently that he had been cheated of its true value. His complaint came to my ears.'

Interesting, I thought. Did this really happen by chance? Or was Le Soten sent by the king to investigate the case? No matter. However the knowledge was obtained, it might have some bearing on Mordon's death.

'But,' I said slowly, 'if Mordon cheated the king, I cannot see how that might lead to his killing.' Greatly daring, I said, 'I cannot think that you shot him, sir.'

Again, he gave that tight smile. 'That is not my way. I came to assess the value of the manor myself. I have some experience in these matters. It was my intention, once Mordon was back in London, to have him summoned before the king, to answer for his conduct.'

He paused again, reaching up and plucking an unripe apple from a tree, then tossing it from hand to hand.

'There is, moreover, another issue here. Mordon has no children of his body, neither legitimate nor illegitimate. It would seem that he may be infertile. According to his will, properly drawn up on the occasion of his second marriage, to the Lady Edith, all his estate is left to her and their children, should there be any issue of the marriage. The most valuable part of Mordon's estate is, of course, this manor, although the spice business is considerable, and there remain the unpaid debts owed to him, including the king's outstanding debt.'

Sir Henry nodded. 'This is quite normal practice on a marriage, in naming as the heir or heirs, the widow and future children. Unless there is some close male relative to inherit . . . I believe the man Dunstable is kin, but distant.'

Le Soten nodded. 'You are correct, Sir Henry. However, shortly before leaving London for Oxfordshire, Mordon had a new will drawn up, which cuts out the Lady Edith entirely, leaving the estate neither to her nor to Dunstable, but to a nephew of his first wife. It has not yet been signed.'

'But why?' I said, startled. 'I noticed that matters were stiff and distant between Mordon and his wife, yet this seems monstrous. I cannot say I care for the lady, but to leave her with nothing but her dower–'

'And that small indeed,' Le Soten said, 'for her family, though ancient, has fallen on hard times in recent years. The lady would be left near penniless.'

'It seems the act of a madman,' Sir Henry said angrily. 'And of a man without honour. What could be the reason?'

'Reason enough,' Le Soten said. 'The lady is with child, and it is not Mordon's.'

Both Sir Henry and I were so taken aback by this, that no one spoke for some moments. I had noticed no signs of pregnancy about the lady, though if it was still early days, there might be nothing yet to be seen.

'How can you know this?' I asked bluntly. The man might be some sort of intelligencer for the king, but how could he have gained such intimate knowledge?

He favoured me with another of his narrow smiles.

'One of the ladies of her bedchamber is also in the king's service. The king has desired that a close watch be kept upon this household. The man Mordon could no more father a child than a eunuch at the sultan's court. The father of the expected child is Dunstable, who is much in favour with the lady. Somehow Mordon discovered the truth and took steps to disinherit both the lady and her bastard.'

'You say that this second will is not yet signed,' Sir Henry said, 'but the lawyer Baverstoke is here. Surely Mordon would have made haste to sign it.'

'Baverstoke is more her lawyer rather than his. Mordon made use of another lawyer in London to draw up the new will. The man was due to ride down here this coming week for the signing.'

'So the Lady Edith had good reason to prevent.'

'Aye. But as for myself, Mordon was more use to me alive than dead. Whoever inherits, it complicates the case all the more. The king could have taken Mordon to law for fraud. With Mordon dead and the property in the hands of his heir, by the terms of either the first will or the second, the lawyers will make a feast of fees before any judgement can be reached on Mordon's fraudulent dealing with the king.'

'The more closely we look at this killing,' I said, 'the more people are found who would benefit from it, either from hatred of what the man had done or meant to do.' I gave a shaky laugh. 'I am glad Sir Henry can speak for me, or I should begin to suspect myself. At least we know that Alan Wodville could *not* have fired the arrow that killed Mordon, and that you wanted him *alive* to face the king at law. Almost every other person present at the hunt must fall under suspicion, unless he was in sight of others for all the relevant time.'

'Or was unarmed,' Sir Henry said. 'There were men like Master Brinkylsworth who were present at the meal, but did not hunt, or the blacksmith, Bertred, who carried naught but the tools of his trade.'

'There still remains a great number of those both amongst the mounted hunters and the villagers on foot who might have shot the arrow. If we did but know what marked it out as distinctive!'

Le Soten looked at me enquiringly. 'What is this you say?'

It seemed that the king's man, like the huntsman, was unaware that the fatal arrow had been removed. I explained what we had seen when we discovered Mordon's body.

'There seems no reason for the killer to remove the arrow,' I said, 'unless it could point the way to his guilt.'

'Curious,' he said. 'I wonder–'

Then he shrugged. 'I will perhaps speak to you again before the inquest, Sir Henry.'

With that, he bowed to us both and began to walk back toward the house, tossing the unripe apple at a squirrel perched on a low branch. His aim was excellent, and the squirrel bounded up the tree in alarm. If Le Soten had wanted Mordon dead, despite his protestations, I judged that his marksmanship would have made a neat job of it. We followed more slowly.

'That was a parcel of news,' Sir Henry said.

'Indeed.' I nodded my agreement. 'Nothing we could have expected. So Mordon even dared to cheat the king! What arrogance! And the Lady Edith . . . but we have naught but his word for this.' I was unsure whether I could believe all the king's man had told us. He might have told us truth, or he might have woven a pretty tale with some purpose of his own, for, after all, why should he confide in us? He knew Sir Henry, but me he did not know.

Ahead of us, I saw Lawyer Baverstoke come round the side of the house and give a start at seeing Le Soten. Then he looked up, over the shoulder of the king's man. His face darkened with anger.

'I will not compromise you further, Sir Henry,' I said, realising that the anger was aimed at me. 'I shall slip away discreetly and go about my business of speaking to the villagers.'

He nodded, and I made a quiet exit through the trees which lay between the formal gardens of the manor house and the lane. As I walked toward the village, I could hear snatches of voices from the demesne fields, where the manor's villeins were continuing with the harvest. They had accomplished less than we had done on Edmond's farm, for I did not suppose they had much goodwill toward Mordon or his widow. I heard no singing or whistling amongst them, as though they went sullenly about their tasks.

Because so many of the villagers were away at field work, I was able only to speak to such as were free men but were not occupied today on their own land. Most of those at the harvest did not return for a midday meal at home, but made the best of the dry weather by carrying bread and cheese with them into the fields, although their children sometimes were sent with jugs of ale during the day. Harvesting is thirsty work.

After I had returned to the farm, I managed to give a hand myself to the last of our oat harvest. Considering the beating it had taken from the storm, the crop was better than expected. Alysoun and Rafe proudly showed me the baskets of peas and beans they had gathered with Hilda.

'The peas are to be laid out to dry,' Alysoun told me, as one instructing the ignorant, 'but Cousin Hilda says we shall salt the beans and layer them in a crock tomorrow, for there are already enough of the large beans already dried. These are the softer beans, so they are to be salted pods and all, and make good eating in the winter. The dried beans have to be soaked overnight, and then cooked a long time in a pottage.'

'Do you tell me!' I said, opening my eyes wide.

She looked at me sternly, jutting her lower lip.

'You *knew*!'

'Well,' I said mildly, 'I grew up here. I too have picked and salted beans.'

'See how many I have picked,' Rafe said, holding out his baskets, one in each hand. Some of the pods were a little torn, but he had done well for a little lad of four years.

'I do not think the harvest could have been completed

without your help,' I said.

'There is one more picking to be had,' Alysoun said, not quite relinquishing her pedagogical role. 'Then the haulms will be cut off level with the ground, to make bedding for the beasts, but the roots are left in the ground, to feed it.'

'Quite right,' I said.

'I wonder who discovered that.' She was thoughtful. 'Was it very long ago?'

'I do not know, my pet. I think some farmer – perhaps a lazy fellow – did not bother to dig up the roots and all when the crop was finished, then his idleness was rewarded when his land produced a better crop the following year than his neighbour's, who was a good, hard-working man.'

'You made that up!' she said, half cross, half laughing.

'I did, but I expect it went something like that.' Soon she would know all my secret inventions. She had a sharp mind, and an enquiring one.

After supper that evening I walked down again to the village, and Edmond came with me. My long years away from the farm meant I was no longer as well known to everyone in the village as he was, who had stayed here all his life long. Questioned by us, most of the villagers who had attended the hunt were prepared to admit that Alan Wodville had been in sight of themselves or their friends – or at least they were prepared to do so once we had pointed out the moral danger of lying while under oath.

It had occurred to me to take the opportunity – while we visited the cottages – to examine the arrows of those who had taken part in the hunt, although I agreed with Sir Henry's conviction that the angle of the fatal shot meant that it must have come from someone on horseback. The village hunters were mystified at my request to see their arrows, but showed them readily enough. There was nothing remarkable about any of them except the variation in their quality. Like my boyhood quills, they were mostly fletched with chicken feathers.

Earlier, when I had returned to the farm at midday, I had passed on Alan's message to Beth, and now, when we reached her end of the village, we found her just returned from the manor.

'Were you able to see him?' I asked.

'Aye.' She smiled quite genuinely. 'Master Hodgate took me to the cellar where he is held, and very ill clad he looked! But he will shave tomorrow morning before the coroner arrives, and don his clean clothes before he is summoned to the inquest. He is not too uncomfortably held,' she added bravely.

'You may thank Sir Henry for that,' I said. 'He has kept a stern eye on Lady Edith and her friends, and warned them of the danger of overstepping their rights.'

I felt that our visit to the village had not accomplished a great deal, but we were at least certain of substantial numbers to swear to Alan Wodville's innocence.

'Tomorrow,' I said to Edmond, as we walked back to the farm, 'I fear we will be much occupied with the inquest, that is if the coroner proceeds at once to work. We cannot know when he will arrive, or when he will call the inquest. I suppose we must simply wait upon his will.'

'At least all the grain is now cut,' he said. 'I shall turn the cattle to graze on the stubble tomorrow. Hilda tells me the young ones did well today. It needs another few days before the rest of the beans and peas will be ready for picking.'

'Then perhaps we should give the children a holiday while we await our summons to the inquest.' I smiled. 'I promised them a fishing trip. Where is it best to take them nowadays?'

He slanted a sideways look at me. 'While you were away at the manor this morning, James and Thomas went to investigate our mill stream and how Mordon diverted or blocked it.' He laughed. 'No better time than now to set matters straight again.'

'And?'

'And they had no difficulty restoring the flow down our leat. James saw trout in the stream and in our mill pond as it was filling. Glad to swim home to their own breeding grounds!'

'Then let us take the children there. On our own land.'

Before the children were sent off to their beds, I announced the fishing trip.

'Is it very difficult, Master Elyot? Catching fish?' Stephen looked worried.

'Nothing could be simpler,' I said. 'A flexible thin branch, about the width of my finger. Willow will suit very well, and there are plenty growing near the mill pond. A length of twine tied to it. And a juicy grub or worm or insect fixed to a hook at the other end of the twine. Your fish comes swimming up, bites the worm, is caught by the hook – and you have him!'

James laughed. 'I wish they might always be so obliging! But we have some rods left over from when we last fished. Thomas, you stored away the hooks, did you not?'

'I know where I put them,' Thomas said.

'That is settled then,' I said. 'Anyone who wants to come fishing must away to bed now and rise early, for once the sun is well up your fish is not so ready to come to the bait.'

As I had hoped, this sent all the children hurrying away without further ado.

It was a good morning for fishing, the sun not too bright, the air still a little damp with the dew fall. We made a considerable party, not only the children. As well as Alysoun, Stephen, and Rafe, the two students decided to come, and Edmond's two boys. At the last minute, Jordain and Philip joined us. Hilda felt such a pastime beneath her womanly dignity, and the two small girls, who had seemed eager at first, soon lost their enthusiasm when they saw the bucket of wriggling bait Thomas had dug up from around Susanna's cabbages.

Alysoun wavered at first.

'Must we put those things on the hooks?' she wrinkled her nose. 'And then the poor fish will stab his mouth on *that*!'

She pointed an accusing finger at the sharp barb at the end of the fishing hook, one of those Bertred Godsmith supplied to the farm.

'You need not fish if you do not want to, my pet,' I said. I knew she would ache with sympathy for any living creature, even a fish, though that did not prevent her eating it, when it was placed in front of her on the table.

'Do not worry, cousin,' Thomas said. 'They are only fish. They will not feel it as you and I would. And we throw the little ones back.'

I am not sure how much she was reassured by this, but when we had found a good spot where the restored stream ran into the mill pond, she watched closely as James, Thomas, and the two students baited their hooks. James had found some smaller rods for Rafe and Stephen who, boy like, had no qualms about the feelings of either worms or fish, and were soon trailing their bait in the water and watching keenly for any sign of fish. Philip sat on the bank, leaning back against the bole of willow, with his hands clasped behind his head. He had chosen not to fish, but watched his son's earnest efforts with a smile.

There had not been enough rods already made for all of us, so Jordain and I set to and cut ourselves whippy lengths of willow, and tied on twine and hooks. Before we were even ready to cast our hooks into the stream, Stephen had a bite.

'Do not hurry,' Thomas warned, 'or he will slip away from you. Bring him gently to the edge of the water, then flip him out on to the bank.'

Stephen, pale with excitement, did as he was told, and landed the trout at his feet.

'I caught a fish!' he cried. 'I truly caught a fish!'

'Aye,' Thomas said, 'and he is big enough to eat.'

Stephen's success seemed to change Alysoun's mind, for now she demanded a rod, but would not bait the hook herself. It was a good while before any more fish showed an interest in our lines, then Giles, Jordain, and Rafe all caught fish so small they had to be thrown back.

'But why?' Rafe demanded. 'I want to keep my fish.'

'We cannot keep the little ones,' James explained. 'Not worth eating, more bone than fish. Besides, if we kept all the little ones, none would ever grow into the fine big fish like Stephen's. It would be like slaughtering a week old lamb, instead of letting him grow into a fine haunch of mutton. Keep trying. Perhaps next time you will catch a big fish.'

Rafe sadly watched his fish thrown back, but pointed excitedly as it swam away, seemingly none the worse for its brief visit to dry land.

I caught nothing, but was happy to sit on the grassy back and put out of my mind, for as long as I might, any thoughts of the coming inquest.

We must have been at our sport about two hours, and a few more trout of reasonable size were lying in the shade under the nearest willow. Fortunately Alysoun had caught one, so she need not be jealous of Stephen any longer, and Rafe was gripping his rod as the twine stretched tight out into the stream, tugged by a large fish, when I saw Sir Henry hurrying toward us from the direction of the farm. I lifted my hook from the water – the bait was gone – and laid my rod on the grass before getting to my feet and going to meet him.

'Is the coroner come?' I said. 'Are we sent for already to the inquest? I had not thought it would be this early.'

Sir Henry was red in the face, and somewhat breathless. He shook his head.

'Nay, the man is not here yet. It is something else. Something serious.'

I took him by the elbow and led him out of earshot of

the children. Jordain threw us one curious glance, but must have decided that it was wiser to make no stir about Sir Henry's evident agitation.

'What is it?' I lowered my voice, even though we were now some distance from the group on the bank.

'It is the king's man,' he said. 'Reginald Le Soten. He has just been found in the orchard, where we spoke to him yesterday. He had been strangled.'

Chapter Ten

For a moment or two, Sir Henry's words seemed to make no sense. Le Soten strangled? He had seemed to me like a man well able to take care of himself. My next thought was that Alan Wodville could not be held to blame for this killing. Of all men, secured as he was in a locked cellar, he was certainly innocent.

'Had Le Soten been long dead?' I asked.

''Tis thought it must have occurred sometime during the night. He was seen for the last time at supper. His bed had not been slept in.'

'I suppose,' I said slowly, 'there might be any number of people at the manor who might fear him. We know what he told us of Mordon's affairs, but who can say what secrets he might possess about others in that party?'

'Very true.' Sir Henry grimaced. 'And to tell you the truth, Nicholas, I am very far from comfortable living in that household. Who knows but it may be my throat next? I shall be glad to make my way home.'

'I do not suppose the coroner has arrived yet? Now there will be two inquests to hold. At least we shall have no role in the second.'

'Unless we are questioned as having had converse with the man. Remember, we were seen with him by Lawyer Baverstoke.'

'But that was much earlier in the day.'

He shrugged. 'Mayhap. But we are outsiders to that household. You may be sure they will close up their ranks against anyone not of their party. Although . . .' he paused.

'I will not say there may not be certain hostilities between them. I sensed a good deal of unease amongst them, even before this new death was discovered.'

'I wonder which of the Lady Edith's waiting women is in the king's service. She might know who could have killed Le Soten. Or at least suspect who might have cause to want his death. Did he ever mention her name to you?'

He shook his head.

Before we could say more, Philip had risen from his seat beneath the willow and joined us.

'Trouble?' he said. 'Is the coroner come?'

'One of his servants arrived just as I left the manor,' Sir Henry said. 'His master would not be more than an hour behind. His horse had cast a shoe and he was obliged to stop at a blacksmith's. But, aye, there is trouble.'

Briefly he recounted to Philip what Le Soten had told us the previous day, and how he had been found dead this morning.

'I suppose someone might have wished to stop Le Soten's mouth,' Philip said, 'from what you say he told you.'

'Perhaps in a moment of panic,' I said, 'but what would be the use? Surely he would have already told the king all he knew about the fraud. Perhaps even about the two wills, since it might have a bearing on the pursuit of the fraud at law. The king has but to send another man to look into the matters Le Soten was investigating.'

'If it *was* exposure of the fraud his killer feared.' Sir Henry rubbed his chin thoughtfully. 'There is also the matter of the second will and who would inherit.'

'If this later will is still unsigned,' Philip pointed out, 'then it is not valid. Nothing done against Le Soten could change that. Although the killing of Mordon could well have been intended to stop the signing.'

'To the advantage of the Lady Edith,' I said.

'Or possibly Dunstable, if he is the father of the child.'

'I cannot see the Lady Edith strangling Le Soten,' I

said.

'Unlikely,' Sir Henry said. 'Strangling is not a woman's crime. Poison, perhaps, but no woman would have the strength to strangle a man like Le Soten. He was slight of build, but I would guess he was strong.'

'Baverstoke did not like that Le Soten had been speaking with us,' I said. 'I wonder–'

They both looked at me enquiringly.

'It might mean that you and I are in some danger. If it is thought he confided in us. I think, Sir Henry, you were better not to remain at the manor. For such time as you must remain here, why do you not come to the farm? It will not be such lodging as you are accustomed to, but it might be safer.'

He smiled grimly. 'I did not serve in the French wars without learning a few soldier's tricks of my own, Nicholas. I shall be safe enough for the day or two remaining. I had rather stay there and keep my eyes open, but I shall not relax my guard. And now, I think we should make our way to the manor, for I would prefer to be there when the coroner arrives. The sooner the inquest is held, the sooner we are all free to leave.'

The fish had not been biting for some time, so it was not difficult to gather up our gear and the sizeable trout which had been caught, together with one good sized bream. On the way back to the farm, we spoke cheerfully of nothing but the morning's sport, and left the children, contented enough, with Margaret and the other women, while those of us who would be needed at the inquest set off for the manor.

The coroner, William Facherel, had the look about him of a man who dined on beef twice a day. A big man, in every direction, he would have made two of Le Soten. Apart from his rich clothes, he looked more like a swineherd than a gentleman, though his small eyes, sunk deep in a fleshy face, had a certain alert cunning about them.

He had reached the manor before us, and when we

entered the Great Hall, where the inquest was to take place, he was deep in conversation with the Lady Edith, Dunstable, and Baverstoke. I saw him nod and smile complacently. I did not care for the appearance of conspiracy about that group. However, I knew that the lady's accusation against Alan must founder on the evidence we could produce. And if the murder of Le Soten was connected with that of Mordon – as surely it must be – then that must strengthen the case for Alan's innocence. As yet, however, I could not see how the two deaths were related. Moreover, the methods of killing were very different. On the one hand, an arrow shot by stealth into a man's back by a horseman, on the other, strangling, face to face with the victim. At least . . . had it been face to face? It is possible to strangle a man from behind, using an assassin's cord, what the French call a *garrotte*.

As soon as all the hunters and the party at the manor were gathered in the hall, one of Facherel's officers called the inquest on Gilbert Mordon to order, and those nominated as jurors were sworn in. They included ten from the manor, two of whom were, like Sir Henry, visiting lords from Oxfordshire, and ten from the yeomanry of the neighbouring villages. We three finders of Mordon's body, together with the jurors, were conducted with the coroner to view the corpse, laid in an open coffin in the manor chapel. Already the stench of death filled the place, making us gag, and it was clear to see why Facherel had decided not to hold the inquest *super visum corporis*, in the sight of the body.

Edmond, Sir Henry, and I all affirmed that this was the body we had found in Wychwood, in the late afternoon of the previous Friday. The jurors agreed that the man appeared to have been shot from behind, after Sir Henry gave his opinion that the fatal wound had been inflicted by an arrow, which was subsequently withdrawn. Master Facherel accepted this assessment of the wound. With considerable relief, we made our way back to the Great Hall.

The coroner turned to Lawyer Baverstoke. 'You may now give orders for the coffin to be sealed. The funeral can take place this afternoon.'

There was an audible sigh of relief throughout the room.

'We come now,' the coroner said, 'to the accusation against the huntsman Alan Wodville, that he did maliciously and intentionally slay Gilbert Mordon, his lord, thus committing the crime of petty treason.'

I heard a gasp of dismay from amongst the villagers standing at the back of the hall, behind the benches provided for their betters. For a man to murder his lord, or a wife to murder her lord and husband, counts in law as the crime of petty treason, and as such incurs the full horrors of execution for high treason.

'Yet Mordon was no longer Alan's lord,' Edmond murmured in my ear, 'for he had dismissed him.'

'A nice point in law,' Philip whispered from his other side. 'Since Alan was still fulfilling his duties as huntsman until the end of the hunt, it could be argued that Mordon was still his lord until Alan left the hunt at the end of the day.'

'It does not arise,' I said fiercely, scarcely choosing to lower my voice. 'Dozens here will affirm that he was never out of sight.'

Before this could happen, however, the coroner told his officer to bring forth Alan Wodville from his cell. Alan walked in between two servants and stood stiffly before Facherel. He had done his best to neaten his appearance and looked, I thought, what he was, an honest and upright man, without guile. He showed no sign of fear, though he must have been feeling it. The coroner then called on the Lady Edith to repeat her accusation, with such evidence as she could produce. She rose from the bench, where she was sitting at the front of the company, and stalked forward to face the coroner.

'As all who were present at the hunt breakfast will affirm,' she said, glancing round with cold eyes and a lip curled in disdain, 'this churl huntsman had a violent quarrel with my lord before the whole group, shortly before we departed in pursuit of the quarry. My husband had already dismissed him from his position as manor huntsman. He had every reason to hate my lord and seek vengeance against him. Moreover, he is known as the most skilled archer in the neighbourhood. He would have had no difficulty in putting an arrow through my lord, and would have taken pleasure in it.'

The coroner smiled and nodded at her.

'This seems a most likely solution to the murder. Clearly the man stands justly accused. What say the jurors?'

I hardly realised what was happening, everything was moving too swiftly. All the correct procedures of an inquest were being swept aside and the jurors were being asked – nay, prompted – to declare Alan guilty on the word of one malicious woman, without any evidence, and without any other testimony being brought forward. That close conference between the coroner and the Lady Edith before the inquest took on an unmistakable meaning.

'Wait!' I said. I stood up, ignoring all the correct procedures in a court of inquest. 'There are many here who will testify that Master Wodville was never out of their sight during the entire time of the hunt, and so could never have shot the deceased.'

'Sit down, fellow!' Facherel bellowed, his face growing bright red with fury. 'You will not speak unless called upon, or I shall have you for contempt!'

As I remained standing, he shouted again, 'Sit down!'

He signalled to two of his servants, who seized me by the arms and forced me down, remaining beside me, continuing to grip me painfully. An angry murmur began to rise from the villagers at the back of the hall, and from the group of dog handlers standing near one of the windows, all of them waiting to give evidence that Alan was innocent.

Before the coroner could again demand a verdict

from the jurors, Sir Henry rose to his feet. Clearly Facherel knew who and what he was, and dared not speak to him in the same manner as to me.

'Master Facherel,' Sir Henry said, politely but firmly, 'Master Elyot speaks quite correctly. We have found many witnesses who will swear on oath that Master Wodville could not have shot the deceased. Let us make a beginning with Aelfric, the senior dog handler for the manor, who had the huntsman always in sight.'

'Call Aelfric,' Facherel said, with obvious reluctance.

Aelfric came forward, sweating and twisting his cap in his hands, to swear the oath on the Bible held out to him. To do him credit, he declared, clearly and unequivocally, that he had been with the huntsman throughout the chase, until all had made their way home, at a time long past that at which Mordon had been killed. After Aelfric, and taking courage from him, one by one the dog handlers, hunt assistants, and village hunters came forward and swore that Alan Wodville could not have killed Gilbert Mordon. As their numbers swelled, Alan's rigid stance relaxed, and I saw his eyes fill with tears that so many came to his defence, in defiance of the coroner's brutal and illegitimate tactics and the fury of Lady Edith, who was most certainly counting up the heads of those she would dismiss from the manor's service.

When at last the jurors were again asked to give their verdict, they conferred scarce five minutes before declaring that the huntsman had no case to answer and that Gilbert Mordon had been killed by some person or persons unknown. Even before the coroner could close the inquest, and in defiance of all due ceremony, the Lady Edith stalked from the room, closely followed by Dunstable and Baverstoke. Facherel had no alternative but to declare an open verdict.

Outside, in the wide courtyard before the manor, Sir Henry, Edmond, and I stood speechless, as Jordain and Philip joined us.

'Jesu's wounds!' Sir Henry said, mopping his brow,

'that came very close to a hanging verdict without a scrap of evidence.'

Philip made a face. 'In my opinion, an arrangement had been made in advance. Money, I suspect, had changed hands. Or been promised.'

'Here is Alan,' I said.

He came, looking somewhat dazed. 'Is it over?'

'As far as you are concerned, it is over,' I said. 'But you spoke truly when you said that the shadow will remain until the real killer can be found. So, nay, it is not altogether over.'

'And there is yet another inquest to be held this day,' Jordain said. 'The inquest on the killing of the king's man. Will it be at once?'

Sir Henry shook his head. 'The coroner is to be entertained to dinner first, then the inquest on Le Soten will be held. Though there is very little can be said on that murder. No accusations have been made, and as far as I know there is no hint as to who might have killed him.'

'Then, I suppose,' I said, 'after that, they will hold Gilbert Mordon's funeral, and not before time.'

There was, of course, no dinner for us, nor, with our minds so filled with all these affairs, had we thought to bring food with us, so we kicked our heels, hungry, until the coroner's officer summoned all to the inquest into the death of Reginald Le Soten. With reluctance, Sir Henry attended the dinner at the manor, in the hope that he might learn something, but when he rejoined us, he shook his head.

'You will be called to give evidence,' the coroner's officer said, nodding toward Sir Henry and me, 'as you were seen to be in converse with the deceased on the last day of his life.'

I had not expected this, since our meeting with Le Soten had taken place in the morning and many others must have spoken to him later in the day, as he was known still to have been alive at supper time. However, one cannot avoid a summons to give evidence at an inquest, so Sir

Henry and I followed the officer to the Great Hall, while Philip, Edmond, and Jordain slipped into the crowd at the back. Alan, however, could not wait to shake the manor dust from his shoes, and set off at a brisk pace to the village, to bring the good news to Beth of the dismissal of the case against him.

Once again we were required to view the body, although Le Soten had not been laid reverently in the chapel, like Mordon. Instead, we accompanied the coroner to one of the outbuildings behind the manor, where his officer unlocked the door and stood aside for us to enter.

Le Soten had been laid out on a rough trestle table. Unlike Mordon, who had clearly been dead some days, Le Soten might have been asleep. He still wore the same nondescript clothes he had worn yesterday in the orchard, his hands lay relaxed at his sides, his eyes closed. Only the thin red line biting deep into his neck showed the outrage done to him. My guess had been correct. His murderer had not confronted him face to face and strangled him with his bare hands. Such an attack Le Soten would probably have been able to withstand. It had been a stealthy attack, from the rear, the murderer's cord cast over his head, throttling him before he could escape. In that, at least, it resembled the murder of Mordon, a coward's attack from behind.

We grouped ourselves around the table, looking down at the mortal remains of a man who had walked amongst us only hours before.

'Is this the man who has been staying at the manor this past week and more?' The coroner turned to Baverstoke.

'It is.'

'Can you name him?'

'He called himself Reginald Le Soten, but I have heard that he sometimes used other names.'

This provoked a stir amongst us, and I heard Sir Henry draw in his breath.

'Can any of you here present tell more about this man?'

'Aye,' Sir Henry said gravely. 'I have met him before. At court. He was in the personal employ of the king.'

At that I saw Facherel suddenly disconcerted. It seemed no one had warned him what manner of man he would be dealing with.

'You are sure?'

'I am sure.' Sir Henry directed a glare at Baverstoke. 'And to the best of my knowledge, Le Soten is his true name. It is slander to suggest any such deception as this man has implied.'

Baverstoke looked uneasy, but said nothing.

'You were seen in conference with him yesterday morning, in the orchard,' Facherel said, having recovered at least a veneer of composure. 'Together with this fellow.' He jerked his head toward me.

'Mind your tongue, sir!' Sir Henry allowed anger to enter his voice. 'This gentleman is Master Nicholas Elyot, Master of Arts in the university of Oxford. I will thank you to show him due respect. There has been too much arrogance already in the conducting of these affairs.'

I had never seen Sir Henry, usually the most affable of men, put down a man in office quite so decisively. The coroner was certainly taken aback, although he did not reply, but led us in silence back to the house.

As the proceedings of the inquest continued, very little information emerged about Le Soten's movements and actions for the remainder of his last day. He had spoken to few people, and then merely in passing. Or so, at least, they said. Finally the coroner turned to us.

'It seems, therefore, that the only conversation of any length held by the deceased yesterday was with you, Sir Henry, and with . . . Master Elyot.'

He got my name out with some difficulty.

'You will now recount the substance of that conversation.'

I left it up to Sir Henry to respond.

'Master Elyot and I have been concerned to ascertain

who was the true killer of Gilbert Mordon, since we had established that it could not have been the huntsman. In order that no suspicion should be cast over any innocent man, we had been making enquiries in the hope of establishing the truth. Master Le Soten was an outsider, barely known to Master Mordon. We hoped that he might throw some light on events here at the manor, being able to observe matters here with a clear eye. I knew him for a man trusted by the king, and thought he might be able to aid us.'

'And did he so?'

'He was certainly able to explain his purpose here, and reveal a number of matters concerning Mordon and his dealings with the king. However, we were told all this in confidence, and I do not feel I can reveal it at present. Perhaps if matters come to trial, that will be the place to speak of it. After permission has been given by His Grace.'

I came near to giving an audible sigh of relief. If Sir Henry had revealed what Le Soten had told us of Mordon's fraud, of the second will, of Lady Edith's bastard, and of the king's servant amongst her waiting women, then any chance of catching the culprit before he fled would have been lost.

It was evident that Facherel was unwilling to allow Sir Henry to maintain the secrecy of Le Soten's confidences, but although the coroner blustered and threatened, he could not intimidate him. I was grateful I had not to stand up to the man alone, for I was sure he would have used more violent means against me, quite possibly bodily violence. It was a fierce contest of wills between the two men, but no doubt Sir Henry had encountered more formidable enemies on the battlefield.

In the end, there appeared to be nothing which could point the finger at any man for the murder of Le Soten, and so the new jury again could make no decision except that the king's man had been murdered by strangulation, by some person unknown. Facherel looked mightily discontented with his day's work, but it must be left to the sheriff's court to take the matter further, or it might be referred to one of the king's justices in eyre. I was unclear as to the legal procedures.

Edmond, Philip, Jordain, and I did not stay for the funeral of Gilbert Mordon, aware that our presence would be nothing but an annoyance to the household at the manor.

'I feel obliged to attend,' Sir Henry said, 'and I should like to make my way home tomorrow.'

He had walked halfway down the lane toward the village with us, well out of earshot of the assembled company at the manor.

'What will become of Le Soten's body?' Jordain asked. 'Do they mean to bury him here?'

'Nay, word has already been sent to the court. No one here seems to know whether he has any family. It is likely his coffin will be despatched back to London, or to Winchester, if the king is still there.'

'If I were the king's servant who is waiting woman to the Lady Edith,' I said, 'then I should be watching every shadow with nerves a-stretch. Should she be discovered, her life may not be worth much.'

'She has two choices,' Jordain said, 'so it seems to me. Either she must remain very quiet and discreet, showing no emotion or fear at the murder of Le Soten, or else she must take to her heels and flee the manor before another day passes.'

'Not easy for a woman alone,' I said, 'but since we do not know who she may be, there is no way we can offer help.'

We walked on in sober silence as Sir Henry turned back to the house.

'As matters stand,' I said at last, in frustration, 'these two murders may remain unsolved. I had no love for Mordon, but his death should not pass unregarded. Could we but know what was so distinctive about that arrow! If we could find it, or even if we could make some guess as to what it was like, surely that must point the way directly to the murderer.'

'It seems that the murder of Le Soten was the worse

crime,' Jordain said slowly. 'To rob any man of life is a monstrous evil, but Mordon had wronged many, while Le Soten seems to have been a good man, trusted by the king, and acting on his behalf.'

'It might be easier to find that killer,' I said thoughtfully, 'for it must have been someone who knew how to use the *garrotte*, and who could approach Le Soten undetected from behind. A strong man, skilled in killing, and soft footed.'

We were almost at the end of the lane, where it joined the village street, and the deep shadows of evening lay across our way from a thick hazel copse at the corner. This coppice was another source of dispute between the village and the manor. By long tradition, the coppice wood belonged to the villagers, but because the coppice stood upon the boundary of the manor lands, Mordon had claimed that it was his by right. At the rustling of the bushes, we all stopped, alarmed. There had been a clear conspiracy to misdirect the inquest on Mordon, but might there be danger against us even now? Especially against Edmond and me, as finders of Mordon's body and witnesses to the exact nature of the fatal injury?

The figure which stepped forth into the slanting bars of the low sun, however, was not that of an armed assassin, but a woman. Silhouetted against the sun, she could not be made out clearly, but as we drew nearer, she took shape as a modest woman of middle years, her gown of excellent quality but a demure dove grey, her hands clasped before her, and a tight-drawn wimple framing a face tense with worry. There was a bundle at her feet.

'Master Elyot.' She dropped me a curtsey. Her voice was melodious and cultured. She knew me, it seemed, although I could not recall having seen her before.

'Mistress, you wished to speak to me?' I bowed and waited.

She glanced aside at my companions.

'You may trust the discretion of these gentlemen,' I said, beginning to guess who she might be.

'Reginald Le Soten told me I could trust to you and to Sir Henry Talbot,' she said, 'and I know that Sir Henry remains at the manor, so I have come to you.'

'I believe you must be the lady he spoke of,' I said, 'who also serves the king?'

She inclined her head. 'I am Alice Walsea,' she said, 'and was placed in the Mordon household to gain what knowledge I could of the master's dealings with the king.' She gave a tight smile which reminded me so much of Le Soten that I wondered whether they might be related. 'In the course of my time there I have uncovered other secrets which may have a bearing on the occurrences of the last few days.'

'Have you any knowledge of who might have killed Le Soten?' I asked.

'Knowledge, no. Suspicions, yes. The accusation against the huntsman was always a false trail, intended to divert attention from the household, where the real guilt must lie, but I cannot provide you with any evidence. I have come, instead, to plead for your help.'

'Anything I or my friends can do for you,' I said, 'we shall do gladly.'

'Late last night, I was seen speaking to Le Soten in the orchard. We have been careful to conceal our knowledge of each other, but this time we were seen.'

'By whom?'

'The lawyer. I bade him good e'en and returned to the house. I also passed Master Dunstable on the way. I believe I was the last to see Le Soten alive and that it was one of them who killed him.'

'Should you not have said so at the inquest?' Philip said.

She shrugged. 'I have more care for my own neck than that. My task is to observe and report, not to speak out. But I was seen. After I heard of the second murder this morning, I knew my own life was in danger. I come, therefore, to ask for shelter, until I may return to the court and report to the king.'

'Certainly, mistress,' Edmond said, 'you must return to my home with us. There you will be safe.'

He offered her his arm, and she took it gratefully. She lifted the small bundle from the ground near her feet. It seemed she had fled with very few possessions, yet despite that look of strain she was very composed.

Together, the five of us made our way slowly back to the farm, almost in silence. If Mistress Walsea wished to tell us more, she would do so in her own time.

Susanna accepted the arrival of yet another guest in her crowded household with an appearance of equanimity, though I am sure she was turning over in her mind how the lady might be accommodated. For it was clear that Mistress Walsea, for all her position as a waiting woman to the Lady Edith, was herself of good birth. While Margaret and Beatrice bustled about, preparing a supper for us all, Susanna beckoned Hilda to follow her upstairs, where they could be heard walking about overhead, rearranging the bedchambers.

The children were given their meal first, before being sent away – protesting somewhat – to bed. Clearly both Alysoun and Stephen were alive with curiosity about the new visitor, so elegant but so silent. Even when the adults sat down to supper, Mistress Walsea said little. She seemed, however, to become easier as time passed and no knock came at the door. Whether anyone at the manor might guess whither she had fled, I could not tell. They might suppose she had set off for Burford, as the nearest town, but so late in the day, and without a horse, they could not have thought it likely. Perhaps men from the manor had already been sent in pursuit along the road to Burford, hoping to overtake a woman on foot. Or perhaps she had not yet even been missed. Like Le Soten, she possessed the ability to blend quietly into the background.

When we had eaten and drawn round the small summer fire, I took a stool next to Mistress Walsea.

'You need tell me nothing you do not wish, mistress,'

I began, hoping that she might make matters clearer, 'but you have said you believe either Dunstable or Baverstoke killed Le Soten. Do you have any notion who killed Gilbert Mordon?'

She shook her head. 'I attended the hunt breakfast with Lady Edith's other waiting women, but I remained there with all those who did not hunt and saw nothing.'

As she spoke, I had that sense again that she reminded me of Le Soten.

'Forgive me if I speak out of turn,' I said, 'and do not answer if you think so, but are you related to Reginald Le Soten?'

She smiled sadly. 'He was my cousin. When I was left a widow, with little means, he found me a position in the king's service, like his.' She sighed. 'He was a good man, you know. Honest and loyal.' Her eyes grew angry. 'It was not true, what they whispered about him at the manor.'

'What was that?'

'They said he was the king's assassin. When I was tending to Lady Edith's gowns, I heard her speaking with Lawyer Baverstoke in the next chamber. He said that if they could not persuade the coroner that the huntsman shot Master Mordon, then they should turn the blame on my cousin, for he was the king's assassin, sent here to dispose of Mordon for cheating the king over the value of Leighton Manor. It was no such thing. The king wanted the man taken to court and publicly shamed. Reginald was a lawyer before he became an intelligencer for the king. He knew that if the case came to court, Mordon would be found guilty. The value of the manor speaks for itself, and the king holds the fraudulent documents Mordon produced. Of course Baverstoke was party to the fraud, so it was no surprise that he would have liked to pin Mordon's murder on Reginald.'

'A plan which clearly went awry when Le Soten himself was killed,' I said.

'That is true.'

'How long have you been in the Lady Edith's service?'

'Near enough a year.'

'And what do you make of the lady? She seems . . . very angry.'

She smiled bitterly. 'I did not care for her, but she has good cause to be angry.' She paused and drew breath. 'You yourself witnessed how Mordon attempted to rape that little serving maid, scarcely out of sight of his wife. She was far from the first of his victims. He had an appetite that could not be satisfied, and he humiliated Lady Edith from the time of their marriage, as I have been told by her other waiting women. Worse, he beat and abused her, and she a lady far above him in rank. Her family brought lustre to his mean, money-lending life. More than that. Her family, although of ancient nobility, has fallen into straitened means, yet she was well dowered in land and coin, the most they could afford. He stripped her of all. Selling her lands and seizing her gold.'

'But her dower would be protected in law,' I pointed out.

'Nay, for he had practised so cleverly that his schemes avoided any claims she might make. The man was a brute, but a cunning one. Abused, humiliated, impoverished – she led a most miserable life. As I say, I did not like her, but I could feel some pity for her, and I could understand why she held herself so proud and arrogant.'

She smiled. 'Though I did not care for it when she used me with that selfsame arrogance and pride.'

'And so she took a lover,' I said.

She shrugged. 'Little wonder. John Dunstable is a personable young man, near her own age, and though of lower rank than she he is better born than his kinsman Mordon. He has taken good care to please her. I believe there is true affection between them, not merely lust.'

This woman was certainly frank and unsparing in her speech. I hoped my sister was far enough away not to hear our words, for I feared she might take against Mistress

Walsea for her unwomanly outspokenness. As for myself, I found I admired her courage and sharp intelligence.

'Now the lady is with child, their affair must come to light,' I said.

'Oh, Mordon had guessed it, I think, a month or so ago. They have not been as cautious as they might. Whether he was quite sure that she was with child, I do not know, but he was able to see which way the wind blew, and knew from years of bedding many women that he could not get a child himself. It is little wonder he decided to make a new will.'

'By all you have told me,' I said slowly, 'and from what Le Soten told Sir Henry and me yesterday, those who would benefit most from Mordon's death are the Lady Edith and Dunstable. They had far greater reason for murder than the huntsman, or any of the villagers who held a grudge against him for his petty tyrannies, even the man Matt Grantham, whom he threatened to reduce to villeinage.'

'I know nothing of that.'

'It would never have succeeded. I think even Matt understood that, despite his anger. He *was* present at the hunt, and he can use a bow as well as any man, but Sir Henry is certain the shot came from someone on horseback. Like the other villagers, Matt was afoot.'

I pondered, locking my hands about my knees and staring into the dying embers of the fire. I realised that almost everyone else had slipped away to bed while we were talking. Susanna dozed with her sewing fallen into her lap, waiting to see her guest to bed, and Jordain was listening quietly to what was being said.

'Aye,' I said slowly, 'the greatest benefit would fall to the Lady Edith and Dunstable, yet there is no evidence against them more than any other who took part in the hunt. Perhaps the killer will never be found. Forgive me, mistress, I have kept you from your bed, and you must be tired after such a day. What do you plan to do next?'

'If your cousin will be kind enough,' she said, 'I

should like to borrow a horse and a man to escort me to Burford. I can return the horse from there and find a carter or some other means to travel south to Winchester, where I may report to His Grace.'

'I am sure he will lend you both, and gladly,' I said.

The following morning I did not rise as early as I had intended. I found only the women and children in the kitchen, the men having already gone to the threshing, all except Thomas, who was sent to herd the cattle from the meadow on to the field of wheat stubble to feed. Already the rain storm had brought forth the first shy blades of new grass to provide grazing, as well as the remains of the wheat stalks. Mistress Walsea had her bundle packed, ready to travel.

'You plan to leave at once?' I asked.

'As soon as the horses are ready. Your cousin's eldest son will go with me to Burford, then bring back my horse on a leading rein. If I cannot find a carter to take me south today, I will surely find one tomorrow morning.'

'It is best you were away from Leighton Manor before they come looking for you,' I said.

'Aye, and it is best I reach His Grace with the news of Reginald's murder. He will want a reckoning.'

'And for Mordon's murder?'

'That will not touch him so close, though it will set astray his intention of exposing the man's fraud.'

At that moment James came in to say that the horses were saddled and ready. It was no surprise to me that Mistress Walsea chose to ride a horse astride herself, rather than go pillion behind James. They would make better time.

Her thanks and farewells were soon spoken to Susanna, and I went with her out to the yard, where the horses were tethered.

'If there is any news about either murder,' I said, 'I will send you word. You will remain at Winchester?'

'As long as the king is there. I heard that the sheriff

had been sent for, before I left the manor. Perhaps he will be able to find out the killers and bring them to justice.'

I shook my head. 'He will have little enough to go on, and he does not have the cleanest of reputations, Master John de Alveton. He has been fined for corruption before this.'

'Send me word, whatever befalls.' She smiled at me. 'God go with you, Master Elyot.'

'And with you, mistress.'

As they rode off in a cloud of dust, which danced silver-gilt in the morning light, I went back into the kitchen to salvage something to break my fast, amongst the busy work of salting beans that was in progress there. Alysoun had begun by helping but soon grew tired of it and ran off. When she returned, she held something out to me.

'See what I found! Aren't they pretty? Could I make them into quills, or are they too short?'

I swallowed the last of my bread and washed it down with ale before I took what she handed me. It was a bunch of three feathers, iridescent in blues and greens, but trimmed and cut short.

'Nay, my pet, there is not enough of the shaft left to make a quill, even for your small hands.'

I laid them out on the corner of the table I had managed to secure for myself, away from the kitchen work.

'I've never seen such pretty feathers,' she said.

'They come from a peacock. Curious, for there are no peacocks hereabouts, not even at the manor. Some noblemen like to keep them, strutting about on their estates. I have sometimes see them, when I have ridden out to my rich customers in the country.'

'Do they sing as beautifully as they look?'

I laughed. 'Nay! They have the most terrible cries. They scream like a soul in torment. I would never keep them, despite their beauty. The cocks have huge tails, like a queen's fan, strolling about in their pride before the hens. It is those tails the nobles like.' I turned the feathers over. 'Wherever did you find these?'

'Oh they were not lying about in the grass. I will show you.'

She ran off again, and returned holding up a smooth stick before her like a king's sceptre. 'They were stuck on this, but I only wanted the feathers.'

Even as I took it from her, I had a sudden flash, a premonition of the truth. It was an arrow, now lacking its flight feathers.

'Where did you find this?' I asked quietly, so as not to alarm her. 'And when?'

'It was the day of the hunt. We stayed in that clearing where we had our meal, you remember? It was boring after a while, for we didn't see anything of the hunt, and we couldn't come home until you came back. I walked along the stream for a way, and this came floating along. I fetched it out.' She looked at me anxiously. 'I didn't do wrong, did I? Someone had thrown it away, they didn't want it any more, and the feathers were so pretty.'

'Nay, you didn't do wrong.'

I turned the denuded arrow over in my hands, then carried it to the open door to examine it more closely in the better light. The thing had been in the stream, but not, perhaps, for long. In the grooves where the iron head was bound to the shaft, there were still traces of a brown stain. Blood. I was certain of it.

'May I borrow this?' I said. 'And the feathers too? You shall have them back. Or else I will get you a whole peacock's feather in their place.'

She looked for a moment doubtful, then she nodded.

I stowed both shaft and feathers carefully in my scrip, then ran as fast as I could to the barn. It took but a few minutes to put on Rufus's bridle, but I did not bother with a saddle. If my luck held, I would not be going far. Rufus showed no surprise when I mounted, and set off down the farm lane at an easy canter.

Once we reached the village street, which led to the Burford road, I crouched down and urged Rufus to a gallop. James and Mistress Walsea had not been long gone. They would travel briskly, but would not drive their horses hard. It was no great distance to Burford.

I overtook them in about five miles. Hearing the sound of galloping hooves behind them, they looked over their shoulders in alarm, but, at the sight of me, they relaxed and reined in.

'What's amiss, Cousin Nicholas?' James said.

'Not amiss,' I said. 'Something has been found, and I need Mistress Walsea's knowledge of the manor's household.'

I reined in Rufus beside her and drew both arrow shaft and peacock feathers out of my scrip.

'Now, mistress, I know you must have had little dealing with the hunting gear, but perhaps you can tell me who was the owner of this arrow.'

She leaned across from her saddle and touched the feathers with her finger tip.

'Certainly these I have seen, for they were not kept with the other gear. These arrows were made especially for the Lady Edith.'

Chapter Eleven

I rode back to Leighton-under-Wychwood at no more than a walking pace. If Rufus was puzzled at the abrupt change from our outward gallop to this demure return, he accepted it, as always, placidly. As I made my way back toward the village, I reviewed what I knew or guessed about the killings at the manor. It had begun to seem, from quite soon after the discovery of Mordon's murder, that the person who would benefit most from his death was the Lady Edith. From the moment I had first seen them together I had noticed the coldness between husband and wife, and her evident preference for the young and comely Dunstable. Mordon's assault and attempted rape of Susanna's young servant girl in front of so many witnesses had been humiliating for Lady Edith. Looking back on it now, I wondered whether Mordon had been urged on as much by a desire to hurt Lady Edith as to yield to his notorious lust.

Reginald Le Soten's revelations about the second will and the lady's pregnancy, followed by Alice Walsea's account of Mordon's physical abuse of his wife and the alienation of her property, made her guilt all the more likely. Lady Edith's instant and loudly proclaimed accusations against the huntsman were now revealed as a crude attempt to divert attention from herself and lay the blame for the murder on a convenient scapegoat. No wonder that Lawyer Baverstoke and her other friends had regarded me with such hostility, when they realised I was bent on proving Alan could never have had the opportunity to fire the fatal arrow. And later, whether or not a bribe had been offered to the coroner to ensure a guilty verdict on the huntsman, the earnest conference between Lady Edith, Dunstable, Baverstoke, and Facherel, immediately before the inquest, was certainly open to that interpretation, as was the coroner's hasty demand that the jurors return a verdict before any evidence of Alan's innocence could be produced. However, it was unlikely that corruption could be proved against any of them, as long as they were all locked in a mutual self-serving silence.

The outlying cottages of the village had come into sight, but I was not yet clear what my next action should be. I now had in my possession the parts of an arrow that Mistress Walsea had identified as belonging to the Lady Edith. If she recognised them, then surely many other members of the manor household would also do so, even if some would be unwilling to admit it. I could not absolutely prove that this was the arrow which had killed Mordon, however much the evidence seemed to point that way. The traces of some reddish-brown substance in the grooves and binding where the arrow head met the shaft certainly appeared to be blood. The arrow cannot have been long in the waters of the stream when Alysoun retrieved it, although the grooves were so deep that even longer immersion might not have washed all away. If this was the murder weapon, there would originally have been a great deal of blood on both the arrow head and much of the shaft, possibly together with fragments of flesh and cloth, but these had vanished in the stream.

Whoever had fired the arrow had taken the first opportunity to dispose of it. I had been assuming from the outset that it had been burned in one of the manor fireplaces, but that would have meant the murderer carrying the arrow for the rest of the hunt, in amongst others in the quiver, where the blood might have stained more arrows and even the quiver itself, pointing the finger clearly at the identity of the killer. Instead, the killer had thrown the arrow into the stream, where it might, with luck, be lost. If it had been found much later, it would have been washed clean and could be explained as an unlucky shot which had gone astray, missing its target. It argued a cool and decisive mind behind the action, especially as the murderer had seized an unforeseen opportunity to kill Mordon when it offered. None of us could have known in advance that he would lead half the hunt into that confused ride through the dense woodland.

I tried to recall the course of the stream from the days when I had roamed Wychwood as a boy. I knew that it flowed through the trees not far from where we had found Mordon's body. After the point where the arrow must have been thrown in, the stream made a slow loop around an area of slightly higher ground, before curving back and running straight for a short distance, then passing alongside the clearing where we had eaten the hunt breakfast. Following this long hot summer, the level of the stream would have been low until a few days ago, when the recent storm had filled the watercourses, though that particular stream had never been very large. It emerged eventually from the wood and joined the larger and more vigorous stream which drove both the manor mill and the smaller mill on my cousin's lands.

Had Alysoun not seen the arrow, it would probably have eventually reached the manor mill, our mill stream having been blocked at the time. There it was likely to have been smashed on the weir or by the turning of the great waterwheel. Of course, none of the present inhabitants of the manor, apart from the few old servants still kept on there, would be familiar with the course of the stream. Throwing the arrow into it had merely been a swift and clever move to divert attention from its owner, and such an action was consistent with taking care to tear the arrow out of the wound. The arrow was, as we had suspected from the start, sufficiently distinctive to reveal its owner at once.

The arrow had belonged to the Lady Edith. Did that also mean that she had fired it? If someone else had done so, and wished to divert the blame to her, he would have left the arrow in the wound. If someone else had done so, but at her bidding, then, like the lady herself, he would have been anxious to dispose of it as swiftly as he might.

Was it possible that the Lady Edith had fired the arrow herself? I had seen her set out from the manor fully equipped for the hunt, with both bow and a full quiver of arrows, but had paid no particular attention to either, so I could not say whether the arrows she carried that day were fletched with peacock feathers. All the hunting gear had been laid aside while we partook of the meal, so it was possible someone might have removed one of her arrows then, but if it had been done by stealth, that suggested someone who would have left the arrow in the wound. That possibility should be ignored.

My arguments were going round and round in my head, leading nowhere.

I wished I knew how skilful Lady Edith might be with a bow. I should have asked Mistress Walsea. Unless it was a lucky accident, that shot had been a clean one, with force behind it, straight into a lung. Mordon would almost certainly have toppled from his horse, still alive but dying, and lain face down in the leaf litter, as his lungs filled with blood and he gasped his last breath. Had the killer stood over him, watching him die? Had the arrow been torn away while he still lived? To be tossed away with brutal forethought, into the nearby stream.

I shuddered. I had not allowed myself to think about the killing too vividly before now. From what I had heard and seen of the man Mordon, I had nothing but dislike for how he had lived, yet I could not but pity how he had died.

A passing cloud blotted out the sun, a silent echo of my own unpleasant musing, as I rode up the lane to the farm. Before all else, I removed Rufus's bridle and rubbed him down, though our slow progress back to the farm had cooled him and dried the sweat of the earlier gallop. From the threshing barn I could hear the swish and thump of the flails and the short bursts of somewhat breathless conversation. When I entered, the men looked up, but did not cease their labour. A good deal of the straw had been bundled, tied, and stacked to one side of the barn, and Hilda was sweeping the mixed grain and chaff into a heap, ready for winnowing, as soon as there was a good winnowing wind.

Something about me must have betrayed that I came heavy with news, for Edmond laid down his flail and walked over to the open door, followed by Jordain.

'What is afoot, Nicholas?' Edmond said.

Instead of answering at once, I drew both peacock feathers and arrow from my scrip and held them out.

'Alysoun retrieved these from the stream, near the clearing where we took our meal,' I said. 'Mistress Walsea has identified the arrow as belonging to the Lady Edith. I believe it bears traces of blood.'

Jordain took the shaft from my hand and turned it about in the sunlight that flooded through the door, examining the point where the iron head was attached to the wood. He nodded.

'I believe you have the right of it.' He ran his thumbnail along one of the grooves and examined the fragments of reddish-brown material left clinging to it. 'In truth, it looks like blood. So this may be the arrow that slew Gilbert Mordon.' He glanced at the three feathers I gripped between thumb and forefinger. 'Why have you removed the flights?'

'Not I. It was these peacock feathers which drew Alysoun's attention. She asked me if she could make them into quills, but of course they have been cut too short. Had it not been for this arrogant flourish of wealth, the arrow would have floated away unregarded. Indeed, there would have been no need to remove it from Mordon's body. Now thereby hangs a moral tale.' I gave a wry smile. ''Tis no wonder the killer was anxious to rid himself of so distinctive a weapon.'

'He?' Edmond said. 'Or she?'

I shrugged. 'What do you think? Could a woman

have fired that shot? With enough force and accuracy to kill a man? To kill her own husband?'

Jordain was examining the arrow head more closely than I had done. 'This is exceptionally sharp, Nicholas. With such wicked barbs. No wonder it tore the wound so badly, as you and Sir Henry have described it.'

'The problem,' I said, 'is what to do now.'

'While you were away chasing after the lady,' Edmond said, 'Sir Henry sent a message by his serving man. The coroner had summoned Sheriff de Alveton, so it seems, before ever the inquest was held, so certain was he that the huntsman must go to trial. Now that the huntsman has been proved innocent, Facherel finds himself in something of a quandary, for the sheriff is due to arrive this afternoon. Too late, now, to put him off.'

'He cannot hold a trial if there is no prisoner to be tried,' Jordain said, handing the shaft back to me.

I looked down at the damning objects in my hands.

'If I take these to him,' I said slowly, 'it is clear evidence that Gilbert Mordon was shot with one of Lady Edith's arrows, but not who drew the bow.'

'*If* the sheriff believes you.' Jordain shook his head. 'Since Lady Edith is a woman of rank and position, it may be convenient *not* to believe you, to dismiss this arrow as proving nothing.'

While we had been speaking, Philip had joined us. 'We should not forget the other death,' he said. 'Reginald Le Soten. Surely Lady Edith cannot be held guilty of that. No woman could have strangled him in that manner.'

On that, we were all agreed.

I stowed away the parts of the arrow in my scrip. 'I think this afternoon I will ride over to the manor and show these to Sir Henry. I will also tell him all that Mistress Walsea has told me. It may be better that he should take the arrow to the sheriff. It will not be so readily dismissed, coming from a man of his birth. As for Le Soten, his murder *must* be linked to that of Mordon. He would have reported all that he knew to the king. Not only about

Mordon's fraud in securing the manor, but the existence of the second, unsigned will. That second will casts even more suspicion on the Lady Edith.'

'However,' Philip said, 'even if the arrow belonged to the Lady Edith, you say quite rightly that it cannot be proved that she fired it. It might have been that fellow Dunstable.'

'If so, it was with her knowledge.' I was sure of that. 'But if Dunstable shot Mordon, would he not have used one of his own arrows? His arrows, we must assume, are *not* in any way distinctive. Why should he use one belonging to the lady? From all we can judge, they did not ride to the hunt planning the murder beforehand, though both must have wanted Mordon's death, before that will could be signed. When chance offered, one of them shot him. At that fatal moment, would Lady Edith have handed an arrow to Dunstable and said, "Shoot him with my arrow, if you love me!" Nay, I think not.'

From their silence, I saw that they agreed with me, however distasteful the thought of a woman, a lady gently born, killing her husband in cold blood.

'It still leaves no answer to the question of who killed Le Soten,' Philip said.

A soft breeze stirred the fragments of chaff about our feet, lifting the golden dust raised by the threshing until it danced about us, shimmering in the sunlight. It seemed a gross insult to the day and the age-old tasks of the farming year to be standing here and talking of violent and cruel death.

'There are two men who are always seen in close company with the Lady Edith,' I said slowly. 'John Dunstable, her lover and distant kin of Mordon, and Lawyer Baverstoke – Sir Thomas Baverstoke, as we should remember. From what Le Soten told Sir Henry and me, Baverstoke used to be the man of law for both husband and wife, since he acted for Mordon in the exchange of Leighton Manor for some of the king's debt. However, Mordon used a different lawyer to draw up the new will, and, according to Le Soten, Baverstoke is more the wife's lawyer than the husband's.'

'Either man might have strangled Le Soten,' Philip said. 'Dunstable is the younger man, but Baverstoke the more formidable.'

'I wonder whether either has served in the king's French wars,' I mused. 'If Baverstoke holds knightly rank, it cannot be by virtue of being a landowner, else he would not serve others as their man of law. Such lawyers are often younger sons, are they not?'

'You are thinking,' Jordain said, 'that he might have been knighted on the battlefield.'

'It is possible. Perhaps, when he was younger, he fought in the king's army, then returned to a more peaceful life in practising the law. The man must be near fifty.'

'But still strong and vigorous,' Edmond said. 'He appears more likely to be a man of his hands than Dunstable. I have seen very little of the younger man, but he strikes me as someone fond of a comfortable life at another's expense, an idler, unlikely to take action unless driven to it. I would say also that he is less likely than the lady to have shot Mordon. Indeed, she is strong-willed and aggressive, as we have seen in her attempt to have Alan Wodville found guilty. Women *are* sometimes guilty of murder.'

Behind us, the rhythmic slap of the flails had gradually died away. We had been speaking quietly, so little of what we had said could have been heard while the threshing continued, but it was clear now that the labourers in the barn had paused in their work with their ears stretched. Edmond shook himself, shedding a scattering of husks from his clothes like a golden waterfall.

'All this speculation will not speed the threshing,' he said. 'Go and confer with Sir Henry this afternoon, Nicholas, and discuss all we have said with him. He may be able to cast some fresh light.'

Philip nodded his agreement. 'And I think you have the right of it, Nicholas. Best if it is Sir Henry who approaches the sheriff with the evidence of the arrow.'

'I shall be happy to pass everything over to him.'

I smiled. It would be a relief to shed any responsibility for matters which were no concern of mine. My only interest was in trying to find out the true killer of Gilbert Mordon, since that would lift any last shadow of suspicion from Alan Wodville. How matters arranged themselves afterwards was not my affair. I would return with my family to Oxford and take up my usual life once more. And perhaps – a voice whispered in my head – Emma would come back to Oxford soon.

After dinner I mounted Rufus and rode slowly over to the manor, my reluctance holding the horse back to a plodding walk. The children had begged for another fishing trip, and James, returned with the two horses from Burford, had agreed happily to take them, continuing his holiday from the tedious labour in the threshing barn.

'Mistress Walsea is safely bestowed, then?' I asked him.

He nodded. 'She stays at the Lamb Inn tonight, and she is in luck. There is a carter leaves for Oxford and Newbury on the morrow. From Newbury she will easily travel to Winchester.' He smiled. 'A formidable lady! Had there been no carter, I believe she would have hired a horse and ridden, alone and unescorted.'

So Mistress Walsea seemed safe from any pursuit from the manor, once her absence was noticed. She was indeed a formidable lady, well worth the king's trust.

I would gladly have gone fishing with the others. To tell the truth, I would even have spent the afternoon threshing in preference to going to the manor, but the sooner the evidence of the arrow was handed over to the sheriff, the better. Afterwards, I might regard myself free of the matter. Let others follow what evidence there was, whithersoever it might lead. That is, if the arrow and its ownership would even be recognised as evidence.

Although we normally walked the short distance to

the manor – not more than half a mile – I chose to ride, through some dim notion that I gained more dignity and status by arriving on horseback, rather than ploughing my way up the dusty lane like one of the manor's villeins. Nevertheless, I took the precaution of riding round to the stableyard without approaching the front of the house. Aelfric, with one of the kennel lads, was returning with a dozen of the lymers after exercising them, and called a groom to take Rufus.

'I shall not be long,' I told him. 'Give him a drink, but no need to unsaddle him.'

Mindful of the necessity for discretion, I entered the house through the back premises, and sent one of the scullions to find Sir Henry.

'Ask him, if he would please to meet me in the orchard,' I said, and left the house to make my way there. As before, the orchard offered itself as the best place to speak with some privacy, since most of the house faced the opposite way, and one could cast a watchful eye in all directions. I walked to the far end, where I noticed that the early ripening apples were beginning to drop to the ground, as well as the lesser windfalls. I knew every tree in this orchard from stealthy visits in boyhood. There was one tree which bore very early fruit – a small apple of an intense red, almost purple, the size and shape of a large plum. They were exceptionally sweet, though they were poor keepers. I stowed a few in the breast of my shirt for the children, feeling a faint boyish guilt, despite the fact that the orchard was now so ill cared for that a few missing apples would hardly be noticed. I bit into one myself, savouring the sweet remembered juice.

'Stealing apples, are you?' Sir Henry had come up softly through the long grass.

I grinned. 'Sir Yves always looked the other way. I am sure he knew we helped ourselves, but his own children were older, nearly adults when we came foraging. I expect he felt he could spare our small pickings.'

'He was a good man. One of many we lost in the

Pestilence.'

I did not answer, for some memories are too painful to speak of.

'Now what news have you for me?' he said. 'I have news of my own for you.'

'And what is that?'

I thought it best I should learn how matters stood at the manor before I embarked on my own account of all that I had learned in the time since I had seen him the previous day.

'The sheriff is come,' he said, 'a little earlier than expected. He has dined, and I persuaded him to allow me to answer his questions today, before the formal trial, so that I may hasten back home. My written testimony may be read at the trial. If ever the sheriff is able to hold a trial. I am eager to be on my way. I came for a day's hunting and have been here nearly a week.'

He found a seat on a grassy mound at the end of the orchard. It had once been a turf bench, planted with camomile and other low growing herbs, where ladies might sit and enjoy a pleasant time out of doors, while shaded from too intense sun by the trees. The seat was now overgrown and covered with weeds more than with fragrant herbs, but it was still comfortable, so I joined him.

'Sheriff de Alveton agreed,' he went on, 'so his clerk has written down everything that I could tell him. But that is not all that has happened. Every day a new alarm at Leighton Manor. One of Lady Edith's waiting women has disappeared! It seems she was not on duty yesterday evening, and she is a quiet, self-effacing woman, who keeps to herself, so she was not missed until today. As far as we can tell, she was last seen at the inquest. The general belief is that she had some part in Mordon's death, and has fled to escape justice.'

I realised suddenly that Sir Henry had left us yesterday before Mistress Walsea sought our help. He could not know that she had been with us and was now in Burford, on her way to Winchester. Nor would he know that she was Le Soten's cousin.

'Who is urging her guilt?' I asked, already certain of the answer.

'The Lady Edith, you may be sure. *Her* waiting woman, and an intimate of the family. And it seems that Mordon made one of his assaults on her a few months ago, although she was able to withstand him.'

That, I could well believe.

'Then why should she want to kill him?' I said. 'And it makes no sense. She had no opportunity, for she was not one of the hunters, carried no bow. She would have remained behind where we took our meal, like my sister and the other ladies.'

He shrugged. 'There is nothing to point the finger at her, save her disappearance before the arrival of the sheriff.'

'Would the name of the lady by any chance be Mistress Alice Walsea?'

He stared at me. 'How did you know?'

'Because she only fled as far as the end of the manor lane, and has been with my family ever since, until a short while ago. She is Le Soten's cousin, and the king's other intelligencer.'

He gave a low whistle, then listened intently as I recounted all that Mistress Walsea had told me about Mordon's treatment of his wife. I did not yet mention the arrow.

'So that is the way of it. Not another useful scapegoat after all. And the sheriff was about to send out a party of his soldiers to search for her and bring her back for trial. Once again we have a trial with no accused.'

'Perhaps not,' I said, taking the arrow shaft and the peacock feathers once more out of my scrip. 'I think I have found the weapon that killed Gilbert Mordon.'

I explained how Alysoun had fished the arrow out of the stream near the clearing where we had eaten, drawn to it by the beautiful feathers, which she had detached from the shaft. The traces of what appeared to be blood I pointed out to him, and recounted how I had ridden after Mistress Walsea when she was on her way to Burford.

'She has identified it as an arrow belonging to Lady Edith, without any hesitation. But of course we cannot know who fired it. Whoever it might have be, he – or she – was determined it should not be identified, so threw it in the stream.'

He took the shaft from me to examine more closely.

'Aye, I think we may say with certainty that this is blood. Not much, but I have seen many arrows which have killed men in battle, and examined them later, when the blood has dried. I would take my oath that this is blood.'

This was excellent confirmation of what both Jordain and I believed, for Sir Henry had far greater experience than we of violent death, as well as the injuries inflicted by arrows.

'I have been turning all these matters over in my mind, ever since Mistress Walsea identified the owner of the arrow,' I said, taking the shaft back and turning it so the reddish fragments were clear to see. 'There is no proof to show who the murderer of either man might be, but the arrow suggests that Lady Edith, or someone acting with her knowledge, shot Mordon. However, Le Soten must have been strangled by a strong man, who knew the use of an assassin's cord. Dunstable? Baverstoke?'

Sir Henry frowned. 'I can see nothing wrong with your reasoning, Nicholas, but it is no kind of proof.'

'That, I understand all too clearly,' I said ruefully. 'However, I should like to hand over these parts of the arrow to you, that you may take them to Sheriff de Alveton. He is more likely to heed you than me.'

'I am willing to do so, though he may not heed me either. He will not care for the finger being pointed at the Lady Edith.'

He took the shaft and the feathers from me and peered at them closely. 'The sheriff may agree that this is the shaft that killed Mordon, but claim that the feathers are no part of it.'

'As I have said, Alysoun removed them, but I will not have her brought before the sheriff. If you look closely, you will see small fragments of the blue vanes still attached to the shaft.'

He nodded. 'Well, I will do my best. I leave for home tomorrow morning. I will call at the farm on my way, and tell you how I have fared.'

I smiled with relief at having handed the matter over to someone who might hope to make some impression on de Alveton, though I agreed that, with his reputation for minor corruption and bribe taking, the sheriff would be unlikely to pursue a woman of Lady Edith's standing.

We both got to our feet, and I brushed the fragments of greenery off my clothes.

'One final thing, Sir Henry. Do you know anything of Sir Thomas Baverstoke's history? How he came by his knighthood?'

'I know very little about him, I fear. Third or fourth son of a family of northern nobility, I believe. So his was probably a knighthood on the field of battle, not a title inherited from his sire.'

'So he might know the use of the French *garrotte*?'

He looked at me shrewdly.

'Aye. Indeed he might.'

We had reached the stableyard and I was bidding Sir Henry farewell before fetching Rufus, when I turned at the sound of a heavy footstep on the cobbles of the yard. A man of florid complexion, with a fine head of grey hair and wearing a sumptuous gown, came striding toward us. Ignoring me, as clearly being someone of no importance, he addressed my companion.

'Ah, Sir Henry, I thank you for making your statement to my clerk, but there are one or two points I would like to discuss with you, while we have our leisure.'

Turning his back on me, he took Sir Henry by the arm to draw him away to the house, but Sir Henry stood firm.

'One moment, Sheriff de Alveton. May I present Nicholas Elyot, Master of Arts at the university of Oxford?'

The sheriff gave me a disparaging look. It was clear that an Oxford Master of Arts was of no more account to him than one of the manor's household servants. He gave me the briefest of nods in return for my bow, and sought to urge Sir Henry away again. Somewhat stung by his manner, I had kept my bow barely short of insulting. His was a name notorious for corruption in office. He did not merit subservient behaviour.

'Nay, Sheriff. Master Elyot is deep in this business,' Sir Henry said, 'as I am. He was one of the finders of the body with me, and he has now discovered most compelling evidence concerning that murder.'

Sir Henry now allowed himself to be urged slowly back toward the front of the house, but indicated with a slight nod of his head that I should accompany them. With considerable misgiving, I followed a pace or two behind them, while Sir Henry briefly explained the finding of the arrow, the evidence that it was owned by Lady Edith, and the small traces of blood to be found where the head joined the shaft.

By this point we were standing at the bottom of the steps leading up to the front door of the manor, and Sir Henry handed the arrow shaft to the sheriff, who – to do him credit – had listened carefully and now examined the shaft with close attention.

Before more could be said, the two men began to climb the steps. I hesitated at the bottom, but Sir Henry urged me on. This was precisely what I had hoped to avoid by handing the parts of the arrow over to him.

Inside, in the doorway to the Great Hall, they paused.

'So you must agree, Sheriff,' Sir Henry said, 'that a blood-stained arrow, removed from the body and thrown into the stream, easily identifiable by the peacock feathers used to fletch it, must point to the owner of that arrow either as the killer or in connivance with that killer.'

'Perhaps, perhaps,' de Alveton said with reluctance.

'However, we must take account of other matters. You cannot suggest that someone of Lady Edith's quality would kill her own husband, nor would she connive with another to do so.'

'I have already told you of Mordon's second will, disinheriting his wife.'

The sheriff waved a dismissive hand. 'Hearsay, Sir Henry. Merely something unsubstantiated, told to you by a person now dead. No such will can be shown to exist.'

I saw that Sir Henry was keeping a hold on his temper with some difficulty.

'The person in question was a confidential agent of the king. No doubt His Grace will be able to testify to his reliability.'

I thought de Alveton flinched a little at this. His past dealings with the king cannot have been comfortable.'

'Moreover,' Sir Henry said, 'I am sure it would be possible to trace the lawyer who drew up the will. He was due to ride down here for the signing. If news of Mordon's death has not reached him, he may still do so. If not, Lawyer Baverstoke may well know what other man of law Mordon might have consulted.'

As if summoned by their words, at that moment Sir Thomas Baverstoke emerged from the Great Hall. He moved very silently, I noticed, and I wondered whether he had been listening at the other side of that open door.

'Ah, Sir Thomas,' the sheriff said, 'we have need of you. Can you tell us anything of this reputed new will made by Gilbert Mordon? And do you know the lawyer who drew it up?'

I thought I caught a brief flicker of alarm in Baverstoke's eyes, before he lowered them in a semblance of modesty in the presence of the High Sheriff.

'A new will, sir? I am afraid I know nothing of this. But I will make enquiries. I am sure Lady Edith will know if such a thing exists. She has withdrawn to the solar.'

Bowing deeply, he drew back and turned to where a carved oak staircase led to the upper floor. I had seen his glance drop briefly on the arrow shaft, which the sheriff still held in his hand.

'He lied,' I breathed in Sir Henry's ear, while de Alveton's attention was briefly on the departing figure of the lawyer. 'I am sure of it. If he speaks to Lady Edith–'

I had no time to say anything further, but Sir Henry nodded.

'There is more, Sheriff,' Sir Henry said, 'which I have not yet had the chance to tell you. Master Elyot has conversed with the missing waiting woman, Mistress Walsea, who it seems was also in the king's employ, and has now set off to return to him.'

At this de Alveton's eyes widened. He looked at me for the first time, but did not speak.

'Master Elyot will be able to tell you what he has learned better than I can do.'

There was no escape from it. I would have to speak to the sheriff myself. Taking care to recall Mistress Walsea's words as closely as I could, I recounted all that she had told me the previous night – Mordon's physical cruelty to his wife and his alienation of her property. When I spoke of the affair with Dunstable and Lady Edith's pregnancy, I could see that de Alveton was growing very angry, not with Gilbert Mordon or Lady Edith, but with me. Who would choose to be the bearer of such unwelcome news? Clearly a man such as I had no business to be making these monstrous accusations against a lady of noble birth. This was a situation I had wanted to avoid, but since I found myself trapped in it, I recounted everything as carefully and truthfully as I might.

When I had finished, de Alveton paced back and forth, saying nothing. We were still standing just inside the front door, which had remained open, and Baverstoke had not yet come down the stairs again.

'Like everything else the two of you have brought to me,' de Alveton said at last, with a supercilious air, 'this is all hearsay, passed from one person to the next, without evidence. Did you witness any of this abuse you speak of,

Master Elyot? Have you seen this phantom second will? Have you even any real proof that broken arrow belonged to the Lady Edith? Or if it did, that it was not discarded days ago? The marks you claim are blood might be anything. Or indeed, they might be blood, animal blood, since the lady rides to hounds and has no doubt shot game before this.'

That was a possibility which had not occurred to me. True, it might be animal blood, but why had the arrow been in the stream which ran so close to the spot where Gilbert Mordon had been murdered?

I had opened my mouth, greatly daring, to refute de Alveton's arguments, when my attention was drawn to a distant noise from the stableyard. I clamped my jaw shut. I would leave the sheriff to his business, retrieve Rufus from the stables, and ride home. I had told all I knew. Sir Henry still had charge of the arrow shaft and feathers, which he could leave with the sheriff's clerk. Clear evidence, so we both believed, of Lady Edith's part in the killing of her husband. Probably I would be summoned to attend the trial, but now all I wanted was to ride back to my children. I wondered whether they had caught any fish.

Baverstoke was coming down the stairs with slow dignity. His face revealed nothing.

'My lord sheriff,' he said, with an obsequiousness that seemed false to me. 'The Lady Edith asks that you might step into the solar. She wishes to explain several matters to you.'

'Very well.' The sheriff drew away from us, toward the stairs. 'Will you direct me?'

'I am going to fetch my horse,' I said, starting toward the door.

'I will come with you as far as the stable,' Sir Henry said.

We walked together around the side of the house toward the rear.

'The sheriff is disinclined to believe us,' I said. 'Like the coroner he will ignore or twist any facts to suit himself, and ensure the trial proceeds the way he chooses.'

'I fear so.'

As we neared the stableyard, it seemed to be in some confusion. Grooms and kennel lads were rushing about, or huddled together, muttering. A cloud of dust drifted in the air, settling slowly, as though there had been recent and urgent activity. I remembered the noises I had heard a short while before.

'Will you fetch me my horse?' I said to the groom who had taken Rufus earlier.

'Aye, maister.' I thought he looked bewildered, yet excited.

'Has something happened?'

He nodded. 'Aye, that there has. Down the back they came, must have used the servants' stairs, and out through the kitchen. Both carrying bundles, but hardly dressed for a journey. Saddle our horses, they says.'

Sir Henry had come up behind me. 'Who said?'

'Why the mistress, sir.' The groom bowed deep. 'Lady Edith. And that cousin of the master's, Dunstable he's called. That's it. Master Dunstable, he is.'

'They called for their horses?' I found I was suddenly short of breath.

'Aye. Wanted them saddled at once, and saddlebags and all. Did not stop to load the saddlebags, though, just tied their bundles on top. Then they was off.'

'Off? Did they say where?'

'Nay, maister. They didn't take the road to the village neither. Headed the other way.'

I turned to Sir Henry.

'While we were talking to de Alveton, Baverstoke must have warned them. Lady Edith and Dunstable have fled.'

I did not stay to witness the sensation which would follow the flight of the most likely suspect for the murder, in the company of her lover. I had had my fill of Leighton Manor and its people. I rode Rufus briskly down to the village and up the lane to the farm, where I met the fishermen returning triumphant with a string of plump trout. I slid down from my horse and on impulse hugged all three children, my own and Stephen too. If I could manage it, I would continue to keep from them the knowledge of the tragic events occurring at the manor. Let them take away from their time in the country only happy memories.

'Your chest is very lumpy,' Alysoun said, patting the front of my cotte.

I laughed. I had forgotten the apples. 'Try these,' I said. 'Some of the sweetest apples you will ever taste.'

There were enough for them to have two each, leaving three to be sliced amongst the older members of the party. Edmond would remember them, and even Margaret had come scrumping with our brother John and Alan and me one year, before she was married off at fourteen.

Once Rufus was tended, I took my turn with a flail before supper, relieving Philip, who had raised painful blisters on his palms with the labour of the harvest.

'I have grown too soft amongst Merton's books,' he said, ruefully studying his hands. 'As a boy I could do a man's work at harvest and never suffer for it.'

'Susanna will have a salve for you,' Edmond said, with sympathy. 'Go you in now, we shall not be long.'

I was glad to return to the simple but worthwhile labour in the threshing barn after the dark world of murder and suspicion. Yet I could not shake it from my mind. The sheriff would surely have sent a party of his sergeants and soldiers in pursuit of the Lady Edith and Dunstable. They could not expect to get far before they were overtaken and brought back ignominiously to stand trial, for their flight cried out their guilt aloud. Had they remained and brazened out the accusations, it would have been difficult to prove anything against them for certain.

And what of Baverstoke? He must have taken the chance to warn them of the closing trap, having overheard the discussion outside the Great Hall. Telling the sheriff that Lady Edith wished to see him was merely a ruse to gain them a little more time. Had they been caught yet? And would Baverstoke also come to trial for aiding their flight?

Sir Henry had promised to call at the farm on his way home in the morning, so I must contain myself until then. When Susanna called us in to supper, I went readily with the others to wash at the well and sit down to a peaceful meal of onion soup and fresh trout, lightly cooked on a grid set over a small brazier and sprinkled with dill.

In the event, there was no need to wait until the following morning to hear what had happened at the manor. The children were abed, and the rest of us were thinking of following them, when the clatter of hooves in the yard reached our ears. I followed Edmond to the door to see who could have come to the farm in the falling dark.

It was Sir Henry, tired and grim faced.

He slid down from his horse, and his legs buckled. Suddenly he looked more than his fifty-two years. James ran to take his horse by the reins, while Edmond and I hurried out to greet him.

'Are they taken?' I asked. 'Dunstable and the Lady Edith?'

He straightened, pressing his fists into the small of his back, and shook his head.

'Got clean away.' He smiled grimly. 'I do not think the sheriff's men exerted themselves with any great zeal to overtake them. But there is more.'

'More?' I could not think what he meant.

'Sir Thomas Baverstoke is dead.'

Chapter Twelve

Sir Hemry passed a hand over his face. He looked suddenly worn thin, like an old silver penny which has been rubbed away by passing through many hands. I felt guilty that I had unloaded on to him all the evidence of the arrow and the revelations made by Mistress Walsea. As I boy I had always known him as my father's friend, although he was a few years younger. Still in my mind I leaned on him, yet I was the stronger man now and should not have burdened him. Moreover, living at the manor while all these events had been occurring would have taken a toll on any man.

'Come within, Sir Henry,' I said slipping my arm through his. 'Take a cup of spiced ale and tell us what you can when you have rested.'

He gave me a wry smile. 'Aye, lad, that would be welcome, for it will not be pleasant in the telling.'

As James led his horse away to the barn, we walked across to the house.

'Why do you not pass the night with us here?' Edmond said. 'There is no need for you to return to the manor.'

'I should be glad of that. My man can bring my belongings here from the manor before we leave on the morrow.'

Once we were withindoors, Susanna hurried to heat a pan of spiced ale, while Margaret drew a cushioned chair for Sir Henry close to the kitchen hearth and Beatrice made up the cooking fire, which had already been covered for the night. Despite that it was still late summer, we had all seen Sir Henry shiver, though I thought the chill came from within, rather than from without. Hilda and Thomas, I was glad to see, had already followed the younger children to bed. When James came in, he sat down quietly in a corner.

We were all glad of the spiced ale, I believe. Susanna offered food, but Sir Henry shook his head.

'I supped at the manor, Mistress Elyot. I have no need of food, but I will be happy to accept your husband's offer of a bed tonight.'

None of us wished to hurry him, but I found I was fretting to know the truth. Had Baverstoke, too, been murdered? If so, all our conclusions about the original murders must be at fault, for surely there could not be yet another killer at the manor.

Sir Henry sighed, stretched out his legs, and set down his cup on the hearthstone at his feet. Already his colour was looking better.

'I had best tell you everything, as it happened,' he said.

'It was some time after you left, Nicholas, that the sheriff sent out his men to pursue the Lady Edith and Dunstable. He claimed at first not to believe what the grooms told him about their flight, then seemed to find other reasons for delay. I am sure he had no wish to overtake them. The lady comes from a powerful family. It is understandable, if regrettable, that he should have some hesitation in risking their anger. Eventually the men set off, and not in the direction the grooms had said, but into the village.'

'When would that be?' I asked.

'About the time the family priest was saying Vespers in the chapel. We went to supper, with the search party not yet returned. Baverstoke was absent, but that was to be expected. The sheriff knew he must have warned Lady Edith of the evidence against her and so provoked her flight. Baverstoke would want to avoid de Alveton.'

He shook his head. 'I am not certain that anything had been openly said, but it was being whispered about the house that Sheriff de Alveton would put Baverstoke on trial, for having helped the choicest birds to fly the coop. Since he had done so, there was a clear suspicion that Baverstoke was implicated in the murders, if by nothing more than giving them warning. The sheriff must have something to justify his journey to Leighton, and I think both he and the coroner were thirsting for some form of revenge, having been made to look foolish more than once over this whole matter.'

'But surely there can have been no real evidence against Baverstoke,' Philip said, lawyer that he was to his fingertips. 'You have not said that anyone saw or heard him warn the Lady Edith.'

'So far as I know,' Sir Henry said, 'no one did. It was all supposition. Like so much else in this matter, there are clear signposts that any man may read, but no certain evidence, no witnesses to any of the crimes.'

He bent down and lifted his cup, draining the last of the ale. Beatrice rose quietly and refilled it, then moved about amongst us, pouring.

'As I have told Nicholas, I had already arranged to leave on the morrow. I had made a statement and answered Sheriff de Alveton's questions, all of it written down by his clerk, signed and sealed by me, to be used if anything came to trial. After we had supped, I set my man to pack our belongings, ready to leave early, and went myself to see that my horse had been properly attended to, and given a good feed of oats, before his journey the next day. The grooms and stable lads were still in a pother, ever since Lady Edith and Dunstable had come demanding their horses. None of them were about. There was still some late daylight then, though it was dim in the stable. I thought the horses seemed restless.'

He paused, and took another pull at his ale. 'I do not know what drew me to the back of the stable. There was a small breeze flowing in through the open doors. Perhaps something was set swinging. Perhaps it was the way my horse rolled his eyes in that direction. I made my way past the stalls, and there he was, at the far end of the stable. Hanging from a beam. Lawyer Baverstoke.'

There was a horrified gasp. It might have been any one of us. I felt the rise of nausea in my throat.

'Dead?' I said.

'Aye, dead. Not long dead, he was still warm. It needed no skill to see that it was too late to save him. I will spare the ladies.'

He bowed vaguely toward Margaret and the other women, who were sitting a little apart, but had heard everything. Beatrice had her hand clamped over her mouth. From the dark corner where James was sitting, there was a brief movement.

'Murder?' Jordain said. 'Or *felo de se*?'

'At first, of course, we could not know. It would be difficult to suppose the existence of even more killers amongst the company at the manor, but why should he kill himself?'

'Unless he feared trial before Sheriff de Alveton,' I said, 'and the consequences. Perhaps he chose the quicker way.'

Sir Henry nodded. 'So also I reasoned. Some of the stablemen were sent for and they cut him down, then carried him to lie in the manor chapel. It was when we were laying him out that I heard a rustling of paper from the breast of his shirt.' He looked thoughtful. 'It was the first time I had seen him without his lawyer's gown, for he wore nothing but shirt and hose. It diminishes a man.'

He sighed. 'I drew out the paper. On it he had written a confession for Sheriff de Alveton. It seems he has been in love with the Lady Edith for years, even before her marriage to Gilbert Mordon. As a younger son, he had nothing to offer her until he had made his own way in the law. He served her family first as one of their men of law, then came with her in her household when she married.'

For the first time, one of the women spoke.

'Did she return his feelings?' Margaret asked.

'He did not say.' Sir Henry smiled sadly. 'In everything he wrote, he sought to protect her. He claimed that he had shot Gilbert Mordon, during the hunt. He had used one of her arrows because he had brought none of his own, intending to use his hunting spear. Realising, afterwards, that it would implicate her, he threw it away. Later, he killed Le Soten, for fear that his discovery of the existence of the second will would throw more blame on the lady.'

'I believe he *did* kill Le Soten,' I said quietly.

'So also do I. Finally, he wrote that he had urged the Lady Edith to ride at once for London, lest rough country justice should set the blame on her. She would be safer in London. Of course, we do not know if that is true. Even if it is, she may have gone elsewhere. Both murders should be laid at his door, he said, and to avoid scandal and harm to the lady and her family, arising from a murder trial, he was taking steps to end his life, and with it the blame for the killings.'

'But of course,' I said, 'he did *not* kill Gilbert Mordon.'

'Nay, like you, I am sure he did not.'

'He must have loved her very much,' Beatrice said quietly, 'to take all the blame on himself.'

Jordain nodded. 'Not only has he taken the blame in this world. He has condemned his immortal soul to everlasting torment.'

For the first time, James spoke. 'Does this mean he cannot receive Christian burial?'

'It does,' I said, and shuddered. 'He will be buried in unconsecrated ground.'

We were all silent. How mysterious is every human creature. I had thought Baverstoke nothing but a pompous lawyer, strong in defence of his client, nothing more. Yet the man had acted with almost inconceivable courage, calling down upon himself the eternal fires of Hell. I bowed my head, clasping it between trembling hands.

It was difficult to understand how any man could have so loved that proud and bitter woman. Yet perhaps, before her family sold her unwilling into marriage with Gilbert Mordon, she might have been different. She was beautiful. Or she would be if she lost that hardness about the eyes and mouth. As a young girl her nature might have been equally fair. Marriage to Mordon would have been enough to twist many a woman's nature, had she no inner strength to resist the corrosive effects of such a life.

'And now what does the sheriff propose to do?' Edmond asked.

'Before I left the manor,' Sir Henry said, 'he spoke of holding a brief formal trial in which Baverstoke's confession would be read out and the jury instructed to find him guilty, with no need for any further evidence or enquiry.'

'So the real murderer of Gilbert Mordon will escape justice,' I said. 'Despite all the evidence which points to the Lady Edith.'

'If he would have been found guilty in any case of the murder of the king's man,' Margaret said quietly, 'perhaps he thought he could at least do this one final thing for the woman he loved.'

'She may escape justice in this world,' Jordain said. 'God sees all. He will decide.'

Sir Henry spent the night at the farm, Edmond and Susanna having given over the best bed to him, while they rested – in poor comfort, I suspect – on a chair and a settle in the kitchen. Not long past dawn Sir Henry's manservant arrived on his own mount, a sturdy pony, encumbered with two pairs of saddlebags. The mockery of a trial would be held later that day, and we were not summoned to attend, for which we were all heartily grateful.

'Baverstoke is to be buried without ceremony tomorrow,' Sir Henry said, as he was preparing to leave. 'In an unmarked grave, somewhere out along the road beyond the village.'

'Sad that there will be few or none to mourn him,' I said, holding his horse steady while he mounted. 'The villagers barely knew him, and I never saw him in company with any of the household at the manor, save for the two who have fled.'

'Nor I,' he said, gathering up his reins. 'At least Le Soten's body is coffined and shortly to be returned to the king's court, and to any family he may have.'

'At least there is his cousin, Mistress Walsea, who will truly mourn him. She should reach the court before his coffin arrives.'

Sir Henry and his servant rode away down the lane. The dust raised by their horses' hooves floated between the hedges, lingered in a soft cloud, then slowly sank and settled again. And the farm, after all the disturbance of recent days, subsided once more into the simple cycle of the agricultural year. A soft and steady breeze arose later that same day, allowing the women to begin winnowing the wheat, tossing it high from the winnowing baskets, so that the wind might blow the chaff away, then catching the grain as it fell back. Again and again, with an age-old rhythm of its own, the winnowing continued, leaving the arms aching but the grain clean and ready to be milled. After Mordon's encroachments, our mill would be grinding again.

The last of the peas and beans were gathered and the haulms cut for bedding and fodder. James and Thomas harnessed the new yoke of oxen to the plough and turned the soil over, feeding the roots back into the ground to enrich the field, which would next be planted with wheat. Edmond's small flock of sheep was brought down from the high pasture to graze on the stubble of the barley field. The shepherd had served my father as far back as I could remember. Godfrid was a man of indeterminate age, as tough and gnarled as a windswept oak, who said little to men, but cherished his sheep, and nourished each newborn lamb as tenderly as a woman.

We remained another week at the farm after Sir

Henry's departure. Aelfric brought word that all the London party had left as soon as the brief trial was over. The remaining servants were to stay until ownership of the manor could be ascertained. Mordon's original will was still valid, leaving his property to the Lady Edith, but the king's officials were looking into his original fraud. Besides, no trace had been found of either Lady Edith or Dunstable. The villeins continued their customary labour, though with little enthusiasm, and brought in the rest of the harvest from the demesne lands. Who would eventually benefit from it, no one could say.

Two days before we were to leave, Edmond had an announcement to make as we all sat, breaking our fast at leisure, with most of the harvest work done, apart from the remainder of the threshing, which would continue over the coming weeks.

'Susanna and I have decided,' he said, smiling across the table at his wife, 'that we should hold a greater harvest feast than usual. Thanks to your help, we have gathered in more than we could ever have hoped.'

'And besides,' Susanna said, 'it was always the custom of the manor in the past to hold a feast to celebrate the first hunt of the season. Since there is no longer a lord of the manor, and since it is unlikely that there will be any more hunts this season, we thought we would make the occasion a celebration of both harvest and hunt.'

'I have had a word with the manor steward,' Edmond said, 'and he will give us the haunch of the deer Alan shot at the hunt, and both cook and cellarer will help in the preparation of the feast.'

'And who is to be invited?' Margaret asked.

Susanna spread her hands wide. 'The whole village!'

'The whole village? Even those labourers who hired themselves to Mordon for higher wages, and left you stranded?'

'Especially them.' Susanna gave a wicked grin. 'I think next year they will come back humbly asking for work!'

The following day saw the whole farm turned over to preparations for the feast. We had always held a harvest supper in my parents' time, but this was to be a feast like no other. My mother arrived early in the day, her sleeves rolled to the elbow and her face flushed with the eagerness I remembered from my childhood. She was followed shortly by several of the village women, including Alan's wife Beth. At the manor, it seemed, the cook and scullions were busy roasting the venison on a great spit and dressing conies from the manor warren to be made into pies, while Warin Hodgate despatched several barrels of fine French wine by a careful cart to the farm, in time for them to settle quietly before the feast, for he said that Mordon had no more use for them, and the king would surely not begrudge his loyal subjects the means to drink to his health.

The men were banished from the kitchen, but once the regular day's farm work was done, we were occupied in setting up all the trestle tables we could lay our hands on, including those carried up from the village. By late afternoon, all was ready, and a steady stream of people began to arrive from the village, many of them – especially the truant labourers – bringing gifts of custards or cakes or meat pies to add to the feast. The invitation had been extended to the manor servants, so that I do not believe so great a gathering can have been held at Leighton since the marriage of Yves de Vere, before I was born.

'I have never seen so many people together,' Alysoun said, slipping her hand into mine, 'or so much food! Is it true we are going home tomorrow?'

'It is. Shall you be sad to leave?'

'Happy and sad. I love it here, but I miss Jonathan. And the hens.'

I laughed. 'You miss the hens? There are hens here.'

'Aye, but they are not as friendly as our hens.'

'That is because no one has time to make pets of them.'

She frowned. 'Do you think they miss us?'

'Our hens? Perhaps, but you will soon see them

again. And Jonathan too.'

Rafe had been listening and now took my other hand. 'You promised you would teach me to ride this summer, and you never did.'

I bit my lip guiltily. 'I am sorry, my little man, but there has been too much work at the harvest. Still, you did learn to fish.'

He grinned. 'Aye, I did. And I caught two fish, the day you didn't come with us. James said the little one had to be thrown back, but we ate the other one. Only, when they were cooked, I didn't know which one was mine.'

'I am sure I ate some of it, and it was very good. Perhaps I can teach you to ride in Oxford. The Mitre has no small ponies, but I think Master Harvey, out at King's Mill, has a pony that his children ride. Perhaps he would let you ride it.'

Once everyone had settled to eat, the feast was a mighty success. There was a little stiffness at first, between those labourers who had remained loyal to Edmond, and those who had defected to Mordon, but it eased as the ale and the French wine went round. The manor villeins and servants were celebrating their release from a hard master, reckoning that whoever the king placed in the manor, he could hardly be worse than the recent lord. The free villagers were relieved of Mordon's exacting tolls at the mill and his restrictions on their hunting of conies and other small game. Matt Grantham boasted loudly of how he would have bested Mordon, had the case of his supposed villeinage ever come to court. Alan and Beth simply looked content, with young Jane restored to them from Burford, even though Alan's position as huntsman was still unsure.

The feasting lasted well into the dark, after moonrise, when a blaze of stars in the unclouded skies dwarfed the candle lanterns hung in reckless abandon about the yard. Alysoun and Rafe had both fallen asleep, with their heads amongst the dishes, by the time Jordain and I gathered them up and carried them to their beds.

After I had tucked them in – Alysoun, of course, had

woken and claimed she was not sleepy – and returned to the yard, I found guests beginning to drift away. Despite the pleasures of the double feast, the morrow would be a working day for most. And for us, the journey home. I found my mother with Susanna, who was removing a pile of used trenchers from her hands.

'Leave all to us, Mother Bridget,' she said. 'There are hands enough here to do the clearing, without the need for yours.'

I was warmed by her words, for with all her children gone, I knew my mother would be glad of this substitute daughter. I put my arms around her and kissed her cheek, thinking that she seemed to grow a little smaller every time I saw her. The bones of her shoulders felt fragile beneath her best gown.

'You will come at Christmastide, Nicholas?' she said.

'If the weather permits. Or perhaps you might wish to come to us? You have not been to Oxford since you came to my marriage.'

She looked doubtful. 'It is a long journey.'

'I would come to fetch you, and we would make two days of it.'

'We shall see.' She smiled and squeezed my hand. 'I am glad to see the children so well and happy. And you, Nicholas, are you happy?'

'All is well with me, Mother. Very well.'

I smiled privately to myself, but it was never possible to hide my feelings from her. She gave me a knowing look, and I wondered what she and Margaret had been saying of me and my affairs behind my back.

James had said he would walk home with my mother, and I let them go, for I hate prolonged farewells.

One of the last to leave the farm was Sire Raymond.

'Will you walk a little way down the lane with me, Nicholas?' he said.

'Gladly. All the way, if you wish.'

'Nay, not so far.'

We set off companionably, our way lit by the full

moon which was now well risen and turned the workaday farm lane into a tunnel of silver light and blue-black shadows, as fine and delicate as an altar cloth worked in silver thread upon velvet.

The priest was never one to come at a subject roundabout.

'You are ill content about all these affairs at the manor, Nicholas,' he said, not making a question of it.

'Aye,' I said. I would not prevaricate with him. 'Three deaths. Two outright murders. One self murder. Now, I believe Lawyer Baverstoke told no lie when he said he murdered the king's man, Reginald Le Soten, a decent, honourable man, doing his duty. And I believe that what he said were his reasons were the truth. If it became public that Gilbert Mordon had made another will, disinheriting his wife, then all the more would suspicion fall on her for the first murder. Baverstoke had seen Le Soten talking to Sir Henry and me in the orchard, but he could not know – not then, at least – that Le Soten had already told us of the second will.'

I paused. 'I never thought so at the time, but now I realise that Le Soten wanted us to know about the fraudulent acquisition of the manor and the existence of that will because he was in some fear for his life. In the work he undertook for the king, he must often have been in danger. In a straightforward and honourable fight, he seemed to me a man who could hold his own, but he was treacherously taken from behind. A coward's way.'

In the shafts of moonlight through the trees, I saw a brief smile flit over Sire Raymond's face. 'You speak like a courtly knight. All murder is dishonourable, but I grant that confronting a man face to face is less so, for it gives the man a chance to fight for his life. But, all the same, I think it is not so much the injustice of Le Soten's murder that most troubles you.'

'The injustice of his murder, that does trouble me, but the murderer has made admission and paid the price with his own life. But you have the right of it. The other murder, the murder of a man both cruel and despicable, was not done by the hand of the man who confessed to it.'

'You are sure of that?'

'Beyond a doubt. Had Baverstoke come to trial for Le Soten's murder, he would have been found guilty and been hanged for it. But the other–' I shuddered. 'Father, the man knowingly condemned himself to everlasting torment in the fires of Hell for a murder he did not commit, while the true murderer – the murderess – has ridden away, free from justice.'

He laid his hand on my arm and brought me to a stop, for I had been striding more and more quickly in my agitation and distress.

'Son,' he said, 'the woman has escaped worldly justice through the actions of a man who loved her. It is for God to judge the rights and wrongs on all sides. It is not for us. Have you considered? The woman is with child. You would not want an innocent child condemned to death. And even if the mother had been condemned, but spared until after she gave birth, as the law permits, what then of the child? The bastard of a murderer?'

'I would not condemn the child,' I said. 'You know that I would not.'

'You see, Nicholas, God may have some purpose in all this. It is not unknown for the child of sinful parents to rise to heights of holiness. Even saints have come into the world thus. We cannot know, but it may be that God put it into the man Baverstoke's mind to take the blame because in His wisdom and intention, He has some purpose for the child.'

I heaved a sigh, but his words left me feeling cleansed, though very weary.

'You have the right of it, Father,' I said. 'And I find great comfort in that.'

'Do not come any further,' he said. 'Away to your bed. You have a long journey tomorrow.'

I nodded. 'Give me your blessing before you go, Father,' I said, and knelt before him on the mossy path.

He laid his cool hand on my head, and spoke a blessing over me, just as he had done when I was a boy. When I rose, he kissed my forehead, then walked away down the lane without looking back. I turned toward the farm again, my mind calm and filled with the silver moonlight. But there were tears on my cheeks.

The journey back to Oxford the next day was uneventful. The children slept in the cart most of the way, weary from the previous night's celebrations, until, a few miles past Witney, Alysoun woke and demanded to be taken before me on Rufus's back. Not to be outdone, Rafe complained that he too should return mounted, 'Not in a cart with the women,' he complained.

Jordain laughed, holding up the reins of the cart horse and pointing out that Rafe was not the only man in the cart.

'But you are *driving*,' Rafe said. 'I should not mind if I could drive.'

'Not yet a while,' Jordain said, 'for if the horse should take fright, you could not hold him.'

The cart horse had shown never a sign of nerves since he had been with us, but Jordain made a sound point.

Guy rode up close to the cart. 'Pass the lad up to me, Mistress Makepeace,' he said. 'I will take him on my horse.'

Once Rafe was settled proudly before the student's saddle, I saw that Stephen was looking up at him wistfully, but he said nothing. I turned and caught Philip's eye. He could not acknowledge Stephen openly in Oxford, but we were a mixed party. If Rafe could ride with Guy, might not Stephen ride with Philip?

It was a more difficult manoeuvre to lift Stephen on to the withers of Philip's horse, but it was managed at last, and so we rode the last miles down the Woodstock Road and St Giles, into Oxford by the North Gate, with the three children like conquering paladins, high above the heads of the shoppers in Northgate Street.

Already with the passing of summer the hours of

daylight were growing shorter, so that it was nearing dusk by the time we reached my shop on the High. When we had unloaded the cart, Giles would return it to the Mitre. Margaret offered to make a meal for all, but Beatrice shook her head.

'Best if we take Stephen home to his own bed,' she said quietly. 'He is growing tired, though he would rather bite his tongue than admit it. Philip can ride on ahead with him and light a fire, while I follow on foot. We have some of the food left which your cousin gave us.'

Indeed, we had fared well for food on our journey, Susanna having loaded us down with remnants from the previous evening's feast.

'You and the boys, at least, will eat with us,' Margaret said firmly to Jordain, having little faith in what the cook at Hart Hall might be able to provide. So our slightly diminished party ate a scratch meal in a kitchen which felt forlorn and chilly until I had the fire alight and Margaret had placed candles along the table to cheer us.

When Jordain and the two students had gone back to their hall, I walked Rufus up the street to the Mitre and paid over the remaining fee for his hire to a sleepy groom. I rubbed his head fondly, sorry to part with him. He had been my mount of choice for some time now, but I had never been so long in his company. He had served me well, whether on the long journey to Leighton and back, or galloping through Wychwood on that misbegotten hunt.

When I returned home, Margaret had already put the children to bed, and we soon followed. Even Rowan was almost too tired to climb the stairs and slip into the children's room, while I pretended not the notice.

A new dawn, and a return to normal life. As far as I could tell, Walter had not opened the shop while I had been gone, for everything was as I had left it, no books sold, no papers or inks moved. Roger had left a pot of green, such as he used for grass, poorly stoppered, so that it had dried up. I was annoyed, for it was unnecessary waste, though fortunately it is not a costly colour and there was not much left in the bottom of the pot.

Margaret bustled about, deploring the quantity of dust which had accumulated in our absence, shooing us out of her way, except for Rafe who was inexplicably doleful and followed her about. Alysoun could not make up her mind between spending her time with Jonathan, who might have found new friends while she was gone, and the hens, which had been fed by Mary Coomber, but would have had none of Alysoun's accustomed chatter to brighten their days.

I turned my attention to the shop, where dust had also fallen. It finds its way in from the street, however tightly the shutters are closed. It had been good to visit the farm and the village again, but this was where I now felt most at home. I ran my hands lovingly over my neat piles of parchment, and lifted a fat copy of Tully's *Orations* and sniffed its aroma appreciatively – leather, parchment, ink, and that indescribable perfume which, even with my eyes closed, I can identify as Book.

In the next day or two, I would make enquiries about procuring a pair of spectacles for Walter, despite his protests. Only after I had tidied, and borrowed a cloth from Margaret to dust the desks and shelves, did I allow myself to remove from my strongbox what I had been promising myself. I sat down behind my desk, and laid the parcel before me, untying the tape which held the pages together.

Emma Thorgold's unfinished book of hours lay before me.

Slowly I turned the pages over, studying each in turn. When I had first seen them, I had thought all the drawings were but outlines. Later, I discovered that she had painted in the colours on some. About a third were complete, the scribing finished, the illuminations drawn, coloured, and gilded. Then a few pages where some of the colours were laid on, but which still awaited completion. The final pages were lettered, but the drawings merely outlined. Even in their simplest form these drawings had immense vigour and life to them. When brightly coloured inks and gold foil are used in abundance, even clumsy drawings can appeal to the eye, but they are flat and disproportionate. When the first swift outlines leap from the page, like these, filled with life, then you know they are the work of a true artist. Ah, if she were not a woman, what a scrivener and illuminator she would be!

Yet I could not wish her any less a woman.

'Margaret,' I said, putting my head around the kitchen door, but not daring to enter, for she was on hands and knees, scrubbing the floor.

'Aye?' She did not bother to look up.

'I am off to Bookbinder's Island. Do not wait dinner for me. I am not sure how long I shall be.'

She answered with a nod, and I withdrew.

There were two blank sheets amongst Emma's pages. These I placed in the stiffened satchel I use for carrying the pages of books and set off at a brisk pace toward Carfax, then down Great Bailey to the bridge over one of the branches of the Thames which leads to Bookbinder's Bridge.

'Can you match this parchment?' I asked Dafydd Hewlyn without preamble, catching him as he tightened the cords holding a stretched skin to its frame.

He glanced down, without stopping what he was doing.

'Aye. Let me finish this.'

When he had tightened the skin to his satisfaction, I followed him into the room where he did the final finishing of the skins and kept stacks of the different sizes and grades of parchment on shelves. He fingered the sheet I gave him, then went unerringly to a pile on one of the lower shelves.

'How much do you want?'

It was not a large pile. 'I will take all that you have,' I said.

He raised his eyebrows, but he was not a man to turn down a sale.

I hurried back with my purchase and set the fresh parchment down beside Emma's pages. The original parchment had come from Hewlyn, I knew. It was fortunate that he still had some of the same stock.

'Do you want any dinner?' Margaret had come through into the shop. 'Why was it so urgent to replenish your supplies of parchment? Surely you have plenty?'

'I needed to be sure I could obtain a match,' I said, hardly listening. 'Dinner? Nay, I may take a bite later.'

She glanced down at the pages spread out on the desk.

'Mistress Farringdon has been here,' she said. 'You know that she works at the cheese making with Mary Coomber, over the way. She saw that we were back, and put her head in the door at midday. She says you loaned Juliana a book before we went away. She wants to return it, and borrow another. I said she might bring it round.'

'Fine,' I said, distracted, counting sheets to be sure there would be enough. 'Any time.'

Margaret went back into the house and I sat down at my desk. There would be enough sheets to complete the book of hours, with some to spare. I would need to replace the green ink Roger had spoiled and I did not keep more than a small amount of gold foil. I would need to buy more. Otherwise, I thought I had almost all the colours, even the costly lapis blue.

I had lowered the shutter which served as a counter below the window on to the street, although I did not expect any business today. Tomorrow I would send word to Walter and Roger that it was time they returned to work. There were a few weeks yet until the beginning of the Michaelmas Term, but some Fellows came up early, and the new young students would come looking for lodgings in one of the halls, or in those town lodging houses, likely Tackley's Inn, where I had first stayed as a boy. So when a shadow passed the window I did not look up from the list I was making of the few inks I would need.

There was a click of the latch as the shop door opened, and a girl's light footfall on the threshold.

'Juliana,' I said, 'you wanted to return the book I

loaned you? I must think what you would care to read next.'

She did not answer.

I looked up.

There, framed in the doorway, with the southern slant of the sun turning her into a silhouette, she was standing quite still, her face in shadow.

'Emma!'

I leapt to my feet, nearly overturning my inkwell and dropping my quill so that it smeared my list but mercifully missed the pages of the book.

I recollected myself. 'Or should I say, "my lady"?'

She stepped forward, so that the light falling through the window lit up her face.

'What nonsense you talk, Nicholas.'

'As Sir Anthony's heir–'

'I am who I am. I have not changed. Have you forgotten how we rode one horse, and I in my boy's attire?'

'How could I forget?'

And how could I forget her, clasped in my arms as we rode from her stepfather's pursuing hounds.

'So not Lady Emma?'

'Not Lady Emma.'

She came toward me, but her eyes were not on me, but on her illuminated pages spread out on my desk.

'You have been looking at my book of hours?'

'I have. And I have been to see David Hewlyn today, to buy the rest of that batch of parchment, before he sold it to someone else. Now it can be finished.'

She came closer, so that only the desk and the beautiful pages lay between us. She reached out and laid her palms protectively on the sheets.

'You will not let Roger complete it!' It was a cry of outrage, an order, not a question.

'Should I not?'

'I would tear them into tiny pieces myself, rather than let them fall into other hands.' Her voice was fierce.

Her hands still rested lightly on the pages, but she did

not pick them up.

'It is not easy to tear this fine quality of parchment into tiny pieces,' I said solemnly, 'but I suppose I could help you. Or I have a pair of scissors here.'

I reached into the drawer where I kept some of the tools of my trade. It was a fearsome pair of scissors, used for cutting leather when I mended a damaged binding.

She stared at the scissors in horror, then lifted her eyes to my face and began to laugh.

'Nicholas Elyot, you are quite wicked.'

'Will you think me wicked when I tell you of my plan?'

'What plan?' she said cautiously.

'What would you say to finishing the book? It was, after all, ordered by Lady Amilia. I should be sorry to disappoint one of my wealthiest customers.'

'Complete it? Myself? But as a woman I cannot work for you as a scrivener.'

I patted the front of my shirt, where her letter rustled faintly.

'I thought that was what you were suggesting in your letter.'

'But–'

I reached out and lifted her hands from the desk, holding them in both of mine. When we had first met, I had seen the ink stains on her fingers which matched those on mine. Both were faded now after some weeks of disuse, but ink marks the hand so deeply it never quite disappears. Her hands were cool in mine, but though they were slender, they were strong, and the evidence lay before us that they were skilled. I lifted her hands, one after the other to my lips. They were trembling.

'No one else need know that you are working for me as my scrivener.'

'Do you mean it? It is not a jest? Like the scissors?'

'I promise you, Emma, it is not a jest.'

'For this book only? Or will there be others?'

'I see no reason why there should not be others. Will

you accept?'

She began to glow, as if a candle had been lit behind her eyes. She looked from her illuminated pages to me.

'I accept,' she said.

I sighed, and smiled at her. But was the glow for me? Or for her art?

Historical Note

Until fairly modern times, agricultural work was very labour intensive, and never more so than at harvest time. In the medieval period, although all farms of any size would have had permanent agricultural servants, and the manors would have had a body of villeins owing so many days' work a week on the manor's demesne, as a form of rent for their holdings, at harvest time day labourers would need to be hired.

This group of labourers was made up of the poorest cottagers, and villeins who were anxious to augment their income. At one end of the social scale, even free men and women might take on the work when times were hard; at the other, homeless vagrants might earn a few honest coins.

Employment of these day labourers was an established part of the rural economy until the violent disruption of society by the widespread deaths caused by the virulent plague now known as the Black Death, but at the time generally referred to as the Great Pestilence. Suddenly landowners found themselves without the workers to plough, plant, and harvest. Landless labourers and villeins tied by customary service to their lords' lands discovered that the work of their hands had a monetary value. They began to demand higher pay. Owners of estates, desperate for workers, found they must offer it.

Faced with an unprecedented situation, and anxious about the effects on both the economy and social mobility, the government of the time passed, in 1351, the Statute of Labourers, fixing agricultural wages at the level which had existed before the Black Death. (It also required all able-bodied men and women under sixty to work, and forbade workers to move away from their homes in search of better conditions.) To pay more than the legal rate set by the Statute would incur punitive fines. In the short term, it may have had some effect. In the long term, it could not halt the tide of changing social conditions.

The disruption and misery which followed the Black Death also, ironically, offered opportunities. Restless villeins sought better conditions on manors other than those to which they were bound by customary service. The boldest of them fled to towns where – if they could find work and remain uncaptured for a year and a day – they would become free citizens.

It was not only the labouring classes whose numbers were decimated by the plague. Ecclesiastics, gentry, and nobility were cut down in comparable numbers. Where a manor was left unoccupied, it fell into the hands of an overlord, often the king, who might grant it as a reward or – in the case of our manor of Leighton – to cancel a debt. Edward III was constantly in need of money to finance his on-going French wars (which have come to be known to historians as the Hundred Years War).

Where a manor was adjacent to a royal forest, the lord could be granted the rights of the chase, the most noble quarry being the stag, although hares were also a popular if lesser quarry. Boar were hunted, but by the latter part of the fourteenth century they were becoming rarer in the more southerly parts of England, where wolves had all but disappeared. The lord of a manor usually also had rights of warren, that is, he could maintain an artificial warren for the snaring of rabbits, not an aristocratic form of sport, but profitable in both skins and meat.

The two forms of hunting deer described here did exist – *par force de chiens*, the most noble, on horseback, with dogs, and *bow and stably*, a less dangerous sport, where the hunters were on foot and at little risk. Over the years since the Norman Conquest, the rituals of the hunt, and especially the ceremonious 'unmaking' or 'unlacing' of the kill, had grown ever more complicated. All young noblemen were expected to know the exact details of these rituals, and the senior huntsman on a manor was every bit as skilled, entrusted with training his assistants (and probably those young nobles as well). He held a senior position in the manor household and was very highly paid, for the chase was the nobleman's chief sport and entertainment. Moreover, experience in the mounted hunt was felt to train young men in many of the skills they would need in battle.

The lavish hunt breakfast, as described here, was part of the day's enjoyment, and is illustrated in contemporary manuscripts. Its much diminished descendent is to be found in the modern stirrup cup. I have written about medieval hunting here: http://bit.ly/2lkP3rv where more details of all that it involved can be found.

Women quite often took part in *bow and stably* hunts, which became more popular toward the latter part of the Middle Ages and into Tudor times. They were also keen on hawking, a less strenuous but nevertheless skilled sport. However, a few bold women rode to the chase *par force de chiens*, as Lady Edith does. They must surely have ridden astride, for to ride side-saddle in the dangerous conditions of a wild gallop through woodland would have been to invite disaster.

The Author

Ann Swinfen spent her childhood partly in England and partly on the east coast of America. She was educated at Somerville College, Oxford, where she read Classics and Mathematics and married a fellow undergraduate, the historian David Swinfen. While bringing up their five children and studying for a postgraduate MSc in Mathematics and a BA and PhD in English Literature, she had a variety of jobs, including university lecturer, translator, freelance journalist and software designer. She served for nine years on the governing council of the Open University and for five years worked as a manager and editor in the technical author division of an international computer company, but gave up her full-time job to concentrate on her writing, while continuing part-time university teaching in English Literature. In 1995 she founded Dundee Book Events, a voluntary organisation promoting books and authors to the general public.

She is the author of the highly acclaimed series, *The Chronicles of Christoval Alvarez*. Set in the late sixteenth century, it features a young Marrano physician recruited as a code-breaker and spy in Walsingham's secret service. In order, the books are: **The Secret World of Christoval Alvarez**, **The Enterprise of England**, **The Portuguese Affair**, **Bartholomew Fair**, **Suffer the Little Children**, **Voyage to Muscovy**, **The Play's the Thing,** and **That Time May Cease**.

Her *Fenland Series* takes place in East Anglia during the seventeenth century. In the first book, **Flood**, both men and women fight desperately to save their land from greedy and unscrupulous speculators. The second, **Betrayal**, continues the story of the dangerous search for legal redress and security for the embattled villagers, at a time when few could be trusted.

Her latest series, *Oxford Medieval Mysteries*, is set in the fourteenth century and features bookseller Nicholas Elyot, a young widower with two small children, and his university friend Jordain Brinkylsworth, who are faced with crime in the troubled world following the Black Death. In order, the books are: **The Bookseller's Tale**, **The Novice's Tale**, and **The**

Huntsman's Tale. Both series are being recorded as unabridged audiobooks.

She has also written two standalone historical novels. *The Testament of Mariam*, set in the first century, recounts, from an unusual perspective, one of the most famous and yet ambiguous stories in human history, while exploring life under a foreign occupying force, in lands still torn by conflict to this day. *This Rough Ocean* is based on the real-life experiences of the Swinfen family during the 1640s, at the time of the English Civil War, when John Swynfen was imprisoned for opposing the killing of the king, and his wife Anne had to fight for the survival of her children and dependents.

Ann Swinfen now lives on the northeast coast of Scotland, with her husband, formerly vice-principal of the University of Dundee, a rescue cat called Maxi, and a cocker spaniel called Suki.

www.annswinfen.com

Printed in Great Britain
by Amazon

81427071R00150